PRAISE FOR PET PEEVES

A Haskell Blevins Mystery

"OH, JOY, HERE IS A WICKEDLY DELIGHTFUL FIRST NOVEL from a woman who should be chained to her word processor until she promises to give us many, many more. . . . A new novelist of this promise is very welcome in a world that keeps losing its John D. MacDonalds."

—*Washington Times*

"McCafferty's characters are amusing and her story is fast-moving and entertaining. She also gives her tale a twist at the end that will fool most readers. . . . THIS DOWN-HOME-STYLE WHODUNIT IS A LOT OF FUN."

—*West Coast Review of Books*

"Taylor McCafferty has a fair eye for small-town eccentricities and country kitsch."

—*The Louisville Courier-Journal* (KY)

"Soft-boiled in style, light-handed in its use of humor, and well structured as a mystery. Recommended."

—*Mystery News*

"*Pet Peeves* is a promising effort from a first-time mystery novelist. Taylor McCafferty establishes pace and setting early on, and she makes the most of her off-the-wall locale."

—*Rave Reviews*

"HASKELL BLEVINS IS DOWNRIGHT HILAR-IOUS. . . . GREAT FUN."

—*The Toronto Sun*

Books by Taylor McCafferty

Pet Peeves
Ruffled Feathers

Published by POCKET BOOKS

To Brackan County
Public Library —

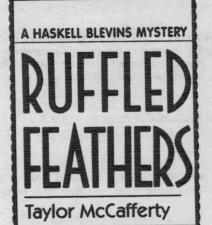

A HASKELL BLEVINS MYSTERY

RUFFLED FEATHERS

Taylor McCafferty

Taylor McCafferty (signature)

POCKET BOOKS

New York   London   Toronto   Sydney   Tokyo   Singapore

11-21-92

This book is a work of fiction. Names, characters, places and inci-
dents are either products of the author's imagination or are used
fictitiously. Any resemblance to actual events or locales or per-
sons, living or dead, is entirely coincidental.

An *Original* Publication of POCKET BOOKS

POCKET BOOKS, a division of Simon & Schuster Inc.
1230 Avenue of the Americas, New York, NY 10020

ISBN: 0-671-72803-2

First Pocket Books printing May 1992

10 9 8 7 6 5 4 3 2 1

POCKET and colophon are registered trademarks of
Simon & Schuster Inc.

Cover art by John Zielinski

Printed in the U.S.A.

To Marjorie and Allen Taylor,
my mother and father,
who have smoothed my own
ruffled feathers many times.

My heartfelt thanks to Dean and Norma Sims, of Sims Poultry in Mayfield, Kentucky, for helping me with my fowl play. I hope they will forgive my grossly exaggerating—for the sake of humor—the odor around Vandeventer Poultry.

I also want to thank my twin sister, Beverly Herald, for serving as my first reader; my husband, John McCafferty, for serving as my second reader; and my brother, Gene Taylor and his wife, Judy, for all their encouraging words.

RUFFLED
FEATHERS

CHAPTER
1

Never assume. That's one of the first things you learn as a detective. It's also, I reckon, one of the first things you forget. Of course, the eight years I spent working homicide in Louisville helped me a lot in that forgetting. During those years I found out over and over again that in the vast majority of cases, the guy you suspected from the very beginning—the guy who said, "Well, sure, we had our little arguments, but that don't mean I killed her"—he's the one who did it. Ninety-nine times out of a hundred.

I was doing some heavy assuming that April morning when I saw Jacob Vandeventer heading up the stairs to my office. My assumptions were all wrong, of course, but I took one look at him and there wasn't a doubt in my mind as to why Jacob Vandeventer had come all the way into Pigeon Fork to see me. Hadn't I just talked to his daughter-in-law, Lizbeth, the night before?

Lizbeth had apparently phoned me at home that Tuesday night to do her amazing impression of Kate, the female lead in *The Taming of the Shrew*. If the Pigeon Fork High School ever does that particular Shakespearean play, they ought to call in Lizbeth Vandeventer as a consultant. "Is this Haskell Blevins?" she'd said. "The detective?"

Like a fool, for a moment there I'd thought I might have myself an honest-to-God client on the line. Something, I might as well admit, I haven't seen a lot of ever since I opened up my office here in Pigeon Fork, Kentucky.

Being as how Pigeon Fork only has a population of 1,511—and that's just on the days everybody shows up—I don't know why I should've expected things to be any different. I reckon, though, when I hung out my shingle some eleven months ago, I'd been counting on a considerable number of them 1,511 folks to be up to no good. So far, they'd all pretty much let me down.

At the time Lizbeth called, I'd left work early on account of there being so little to do, and I was right in the middle of cooking me up some pork chops for dinner. I answered in my best professional voice, though. "Yes, ma'am, this is Haskell Blevins. What can I do for you?"

Talk about asking for trouble. "I'll tell you what you can do," Lizbeth said. "You can get yourself over here and clean up the mess your dog made!" She was so mad, her voice was shaking.

In the face of such unbridled fury, I tried to remain calm. "*My* dog? Are you sure?"

That was all I got out before the Shrew started in again. "Of course I'm sure! I saw him with my own eyes this afternoon, right about three o'clock, tearing my garden to shreds!"

I started feeling relieved. At three that afternoon, I'd still been at work. There was no way my dog Rip could've been in anybody's garden then. "There must be some mistake—"

"I'll say there's been a mistake, and *you* made it! Letting your stupid dog run loose! Well, maybe you don't realize who you're talking to," the Shrew on the phone said. "*This* is Lizbeth Vandeventer." She said it the way I imagine Queen Elizabeth might identify herself on the phone. With heavy emphasis on the word *this*. Only I think the queen would use a lot nicer tone.

Lizbeth's tone was a little hard to take. Her tone might make you think she'd been born with a silver spoon in her mouth. True, Lizbeth's income bracket *was* a little higher than mine these days, but when she'd been born, her mouth had been just as empty as mine. We'd even gone to the same high school. Of course, that *had* been more than fifteen years ago. I'm pretty sure, though, that even back then Lizbeth was already using that tone with me.

Lizbeth had been two grades behind me, blond, tall, willowy, *and* a cheerleader—which meant that, as far as she was concerned, I didn't exist. I wasn't on the football team, I didn't drive a sports car, and before I got my growth spurt in the eleventh grade, Lizbeth was taller than me. I also had red hair and freckles. Believe it or not, there were those who actually said that I bore a distinct resemblance to Howdy Doody. Come to think of it, there are still those who say this today. I've always hoped that these folks are just being cruel, but back in high school, I counted myself lucky that Lizbeth didn't run screaming when we happened to be in the same room.

Back then, Lizbeth's name had been Betty Jean Prunty. I'd heard, of course, that she'd changed it. For a while there, Betty Jean changing her name had been the talk of the town. Of course, around these parts, it doesn't take much to get tongues wagging. A heavy dew could probably set them off.

The way I heard it, Betty Jean had changed her name right about the time she married R. L. Vandeventer, the only son of Jacob, one of the richest men in Crayton County. A lot of folks said that Betty Jean was putting on airs, but—to give her the benefit of the doubt— maybe she figured that as long as she was going to all the trouble of changing her last name, she might as well change the first, too.

I tried to put the proper amount of respect into my voice. It was hard, considering how bad I wanted to call her Betty Jean. "Why, Lizbeth, how nice to hear from—"

Lizbeth said a word under her breath I'm real sure

Queen Elizabeth would not use over the phone. "You'll
think it's nice to hear from my *lawyer* if you don't get
over here and clean up this mess! I want every one of
my tulips replaced, mind you, *replaced!* And not with
anything you can get at the Kmart, neither. I ordered
those tulips direct from Holland—five hundred dollars'
worth!"

Five hundred dollars? Lizbeth had blown five hundred
dollars on a bunch of flowers, and she expected *me* to
do the same? This conversation was taking an ugly turn.
"Lizbeth," I said, "I'm trying to tell you, it couldn't
have been my dog—" If she'd let me finish, I'd have
explained how come it was absolutely impossible that
Rip could've done the dirty deed.

Half German shepherd, half big black dog, Rip was
standing right next to me at that very moment, his
brown eyes as innocent as a newborn baby's. Of course,
how innocent he looked was not why I was convinced
he hadn't trampled Lizbeth's tulips. Rip had also looked
particularly innocent the night I caught him chewing my
brand-new Italian boots into pulp.

Lizbeth seemed determined, however, never to let me
finish a sentence. "Oh, it was your dog all right. No
doubt about it. I've asked around, and everybody said
the only big black dog that lives near my house belongs
to Haskell Blevins."

Lizbeth was using the word *near* real loosely. Rip and
I don't exactly live *near* the Vandeventers. True, their
land adjoins mine, but while I own 5 acres, the Vandeventers own 1,200. If the Vandeventers' land were a
pickle, my land would be a bump.

To get from my house to the Vandeventer house—
actually, the word *mansion* would describe it better—
would take a good twenty minutes of running at top
speed through the woods. That's how long it would take
me. Rip, I'm sure, would take longer, on account of his
never having done anything at top speed in his life.

As I said, I would've liked to have pointed out all this
to Lizbeth, but she seemed intent on never giving me
the chance. "Your stupid dog has made my beautiful,

gorgeous, wonderful flower garden into a shambles! A *shambles*, do you hear?"

I heard. "Look, Lizbeth, my dog couldn't possibly have torn up your—ah, garden." I decided to leave off that part about beautiful, gorgeous, and wonderful. All that seemed a bit much. Next, Lizbeth would be comparing *her* garden to those hanging ones in Babylon. "It had to be someone else's dog. Or maybe a stray. *My* dog never gets off my porch," I went on. "At least, not while I'm at work."

Lizbeth made a noise in the back of her throat. I thought for a second that it was static on the line. "Did you ever think that maybe he broke his chain or something?"

"Oh, I don't keep him tied up—"

Lizbeth made another one of those noises. It managed to convey disbelief and outrage in one ugly sound. "Are you trying to tell me your dog is so well trained that he never leaves—"

This time I thought, what the hell, I'll interrupt *her* for a change. "Oh, no," I said. "Rip's not well trained. Not at all. Rip is crazy."

Rip had decided to take a load off his feet by then and had lain down at my feet, a bored look on his face. At the mention of his name, however, Rip lifted his head, cocked it to one side, and stared at me. His brown eyes looked reproachful.

Sometimes I think that dog knows exactly what I'm saying. I took a couple of steps away from him and lowered my voice a little. "He's a nut. Really. Rip's always been afraid to go downstairs. Ever since he was a puppy. And my house has this big deck around it, so—"

Wouldn't you know, Lizbeth interrupted me. What a surprise. "Nonsense! I never heard of such a thing!"

Was her point that if she'd never heard of it, **it** didn't exist? I remembered what a real brain Lizbeth had been back in high school. There was a strong possibility she'd never heard of Czechoslovakia. Or, say, Wisconsin.

"Look, Lizbeth," I said, "I'm telling you the truth."

A truth which I could've told her was a major inconvenience, and something I should've thought of before I moved me and this dog out to where we live now.

Rip and I live in an A-frame in the middle of the woods, about seven miles from downtown Pigeon Fork. The entire house is surrounded by a large deck, so you have to go down quite a few steps to get to my front yard. Rip has never gone down any of those steps on his own accord. Believe you me, I know. I'm the one who has to carry him down those particular steps twice a day—once in the morning and once in the evening—so that Rip can do his business on my lawn, instead of my deck.

Back when Rip was a puppy, it was sort of cute, having to carry him up and down steps. Of course, back then we were still living in a first-floor apartment in Louisville. There was only a couple of steps to go down to get to the yard. I was still working homicide then, and it was kinda nice coming home to a frisky little puppy. So what if he had a few mental problems?

Of course, back then I was also still living with Claudine—I call her Claudzilla—the woman who was shortly to do me the honor of becoming my ex-wife. Compared to Claudzilla's mental problems, Rip's looked like a piece of cake.

These days, however, Rip is no longer a puppy, and lying around on my porch all day has not kept him slim and trim. That dog's got to weigh all of sixty pounds. Picking him up is worse than hoisting a feed sack. I've actually tried coaxing that fool dog downstairs with pieces of steak, but Rip refuses to budge.

Over the phone I tried to give Lizbeth the *Reader's Digest* condensed version of all this, but Lizbeth evidently thought I was talking fiction. As soon as I paused for breath, she snorted. "I've never heard of anything so preposterous in all my life!"

"Lizbeth, you can check it out with my vet. Rip has got himself a bad case of stairs-o-phobia." According to the veterinarian, poor Rip is psychologically scarred.

Lizbeth wasn't buying any of it. "Stairs-o-phobia, my eye! You must think I'm stupid."

She had me there.

"Well," Lizbeth went on, "you've got another thing coming, if you think I'm letting you off this easy. If you don't replace my tulips, I'm calling up Alton Gabbard— I guess you've heard of *him*—"

Inwardly, I groaned. Alton Gabbard was Pigeon Fork's version of F. Lee Bailey. Word was, he'd never lost a case.

Lizbeth had worked herself up so much she was practically stammering. "And—and I'll call up Vergil Minrath, too! I guess *he'll* have something to say about all this!"

I suppressed another groan. Vergil was the town sheriff, and while he was something of a family friend, if Lizbeth bothered Vergil with something like this, Vergil was real likely to blame *me* rather than Lizbeth Vandeventer. Particularly since the Vandeventers had contributed quite a bit to Vergil's reelection campaign the last go-round.

Lizbeth hadn't even paused for breath. "And I'll call up the Crayton County dog catcher, too. We'll see if you still want to tell *him* some stupid, stinking story about stairs-o-phobia!"

That last part must've been a real tongue twister, but I had to hand it to her. Even as angry as she was, Lizbeth didn't falter once. I took a deep breath. "Now look, Lizbeth," I said. I thought I sounded real soothing. "There's no need to drag all these other folks into this. Surely, we can work this out between ourselves."

Lizbeth didn't sound soothed. "Are you going to replace my tulips?"

"I don't think so," I said, "but surely we don't have to resort to—"

"As far as I'm concerned, we might have to resort to shotguns!" Lizbeth snapped. *"That's* what we might have to resort to! Now, you better order me some new tulips and clean this mess up, or—or *else!"* With that, she slammed the phone down.

I believe we can put Lizbeth Vandeventer down as being *for* canine capital punishment.

I hung up the phone and looked at Rip, lying at my feet. Other than the Italian Boot Caper, he's been a pretty good old dog. It's not like I named him Rip because that's what he does all the time—rip things up. In fact, I named him Rip because I'd had two other dogs before him. Both of them had died before they were a year old. For a while there, I was having some real bad luck with dogs. I got them all their shots, took them for all their checkups, and still they up and died. When I got this third pup, I was so discouraged, I just wrote R.I.P. on his doghouse.

Now, six years later, I'm pretty sure Rip is going to live. He is, that is, if I can keep Lizbeth away from him.

That's why the next morning I was already on the road, headed into my office, by 7:30. Dogwoods were blooming in the distant hills, and there was the sweet smell of spring in the air, but to tell you the truth, I hardly noticed. I was too intent on what all I had to do. If Lizbeth was going to be siccing all those folks on Rip, I needed to find his dog license and his rabies vaccination papers right away. So's Rip didn't get himself hauled off to the county pound.

I would've liked to have been able to just show Rip's collar with all its brightly colored metal tags to Vergil and the dog catcher and F. Lee Bailey, but Rip had lost his collar months ago on one of the rare occasions he took off the second I carried him off the deck.

Rip's been doing this every so often here lately. Can you believe it? The dog who works up a sweat wagging his tail. I figure old Rip's going through some kind of mid-life crisis. They say a dog ages seven years for every human year, so that makes Rip about forty-two this year—right about time for him to be seriously questioning his life-style.

I figure Rip's soul-searching has led him to realize recently what a real dull dog's life he's been leading—lying around all day, being a porch potato. So now,

every once in a while after I carry him off the deck, Rip
rouses himself to run down the road a piece, barking at
anything that moves and, in general, looking for
adventure.

Rip's never gone more than about ten minutes, so he
doesn't go far. Certainly not as far as the Vandeventer
place. The farthest for sure I've known him to go is
down to the Renfrows. The Renfrows, my nearest neighbors, are a family of back-to-nature types who live in a
log cabin, raise their own chickens and ducks, and have
a huge garden complete with compost heap. Even
though they're a mile down the road, I know Rip has
made it to their house because occasionally he brings
back some of their compost, and slings it all over my
side lawn. Doing what he can, no doubt, to improve the
ecology of the neighborhood.

Hurrying into my office to get a head start on looking
for Rip's papers didn't do me much good. To begin with,
once you get into Pigeon Fork's city limits, there's no
such thing as hurrying. The speed limit is twenty-five
miles an hour. I've decided they made the speed limit
this low so's the town folks can get a real good look at
you as you creep by. That way they can spot any strang-
ers in town real quick.

Driving into town in my Ford pickup, I turned the
heads of Zeke Arndell, who at that hour of the morning
was already out unfurling the green-striped awning in
front of his furniture store, and Pop Matheny, who was
out polishing the old-fashioned striped barber pole in
front of his shop. Both men gave me a perfunctory wave
as I went by. Driving slow, but still feeling like I was
hurrying on the inside, I nevertheless took the time to
wave back at both Zeke and Pop. If you don't return
their waves, folks around these parts start thinking
you're uppity. They especially lean toward this way of
thinking if you happen to have moved away to the Big
City some years ago and have only recently moved
back.

I fairly ran up the stairs to my office, but it only took
me about fifteen minutes after I hit the door to make

one of them logical deductions we private detectives are famous for. Having looked in about ten different places, I deduced this: Melba Hawley doesn't do filing any better than she answers the phone.

Melba Hawley is the secretary I share with my brother Elmo. This should've been a real convenient arrangement, being as how my office is over Elmo's drugstore. I've got it rigged so that my telephone rings down in the drugstore, too, so that Melba doesn't even have to leave her desk to get my phone. All she has to do is punch a button and pick up the second line. Melba is also supposed to come up here every once in a while and do a little filing. For which I actually pay part of her salary.

Like I said, it should've worked out real well. Except that Melba answers my phone about as often as she answers Elmo's. Whenever the mood strikes her. Apparently, that's the rule she goes by when it comes to filing, too. Judging from the condition of my files, the mood had not struck anytime lately. There was stuff filed in the wrong file and some stuff crammed into the back of the cabinet. Hidden, you might say.

Finding out about all this was something of a revelation. I mean, long before that April morning I'd been painfully aware that Melba was a little lax answering my phone, but up until then, I'd been under the impression that Melba was actually doing my filing. Obviously, I was wrong. I couldn't even *find* a file for Rip's official papers. I looked for folders marked "Dog," "Rip," "License," and "Vet." There were no such files.

After looking through my files a couple more times, and using up every curse word I knew, I decided to give Melba a call. Actually, as it turned out, what I really did was dial the drugstore downstairs to listen to the phone ring. It was past eight-thirty by then—past when Melba was supposed to be on the job—and yet the phone rang again and again.

It was on the fifth ring when I heard the footsteps outside on my stairs. Hanging up the phone, I went to the window, thinking that this was no doubt why Melba wasn't picking up Elmo's phone. She was on her way up here.

That was the first in a long line of wrong assumptions.

One look out the window, and I was back to muttering curses. It was—as I said before—Jacob Vandeventer climbing slowly up my stairs. I braced myself. Having heard about Rip's tulip transgressions from Lizbeth, Jacob had obviously come around to add a few more threats to those Lizbeth had snarled at me the night before.

Thin, muscular, and deeply tanned, Jacob still had to be at least sixty-five. He didn't look it, though. Oh, his hair had thinned some, of course, but it was just as glossy black as it had been when I was going to high school with Lizbeth and both Jacob's kids. When Jacob left a room, rumors of Grecian Formula invariably followed him.

Jacob may have looked young, but he climbed those stairs to my office like the age he was. Jacob was frowning, but that didn't mean anything. Jacob Vandeventer always frowned. In fact, the rare times I've ever seen Jacob smile, his eyebrows were still frowning. Old Jacob's got the kind of eyebrows you can't help but notice, too. They're like big bird's nests. Bird's nests built by birds who were none too picky about their building.

When Jacob got to my door, he didn't even pause. Just walked right on in, without knocking. This wasn't any more of a surprise than his frown. Jacob started ignoring doors right about the time Vandeventer Poultry landed the Chick Delish account. That's got to be at least ten years ago. Ever since then, the Vandeventer family's been supplying broilers to Chick Delish franchises all over the country, and Jacob's been walking around like he owns everything in town. I reckon in Jacob's mind being the richest man in Pigeon Fork has its privileges.

Jacob immediately sank into the big overstuffed chair next to my desk. He was wearing what he apparently thought country gentlemen wear these days. Brown corduroy slacks, white shirt with the cuffs neatly buttoned, and a red polka-dot bow tie. From where I sat, the polka dots looked distinctly faded.

I stared at that tie, wondering for a second if maybe there was a tie shortage. Then I started wondering if I was looking at the first and only tie Jacob had ever owned. I'd heard about Jacob's legendary stinginess. Word was, he'd make Silas Marner look like a spendthrift.

Jacob was breathing hard when he came in my door, but you could tell he was trying to conceal it. He swallowed once or twice before he finally said, "You Haskell?" Jacob's voice is a low rumble, so it always sounds as if a thunderstorm is going on in his throat.

I nodded, preparing myself for the worst. "That's right, I'm Haskell Blevins."

The old man's temper was as legendary as his stinginess. In fact, I reckon you'd call Jacob Vandeventer the town temper. I've seen him in action a couple of times myself, once at Lassiter's Restaurant when his soup was served cold, once at the Crayton Federal Bank when there was an error on his bank statement. Both times, I'd thought old Jacob might ought to register his tongue as a lethal weapon.

Jacob's small gray eyes were traveling around my office. Finally, he looked back at me and lifted one bird's nest. "You give a lot for this place?"

I believe his point was that if I gave anything at all, it was too much. Melba Hawley calls my office the Bermuda Rectangle. She says it looks as if some mysterious force has dragged all the papers and wrappers and other debris from within a twenty-five-mile radius and deposited it on my desk and floor. She's exaggerating. She really is. Besides, after what I'd just seen that she'd done to my files, Melba had a lot of room to talk.

I looked Jacob right in the eye. Truth was, my brother Elmo let me have office space up here for free, as long as during slow times I helped out downstairs in the drugstore, mopping up and running the soda fountain. So far, Elmo was making out like a bandit on the deal, being as how it was slow in Pigeon Fork most every day of the week. I wasn't about to tell Jacob that, though. If he thought I had some time on my hands, he might think I should be using it to dig in Lizbeth's garden. "This place costs me a small fortune," I said, "but I think it's worth it." I gave him a smile.

Jacob just stared at me. Deadpan. Like maybe he couldn't decide if I was serious or not. Finally, he cleared his throat and rumbled, "I reckon you know who *I* am." His tone didn't quite match Lizbeth's, but it was close.

I nodded.

"I was a friend of your dad's, you know."

Matter of fact, I did know. My father's been gone a little over nine years now, but I remembered him talking about Jacob. *Friend* is not exactly what my dad called Jacob Vandeventer. *Asshole,* I believe, was the term Dad most frequently used in connection with the man. I smiled again and nodded. "My dad spoke of you often," I said.

Jacob tipped his head toward me. As if to say, well, of course he did.

I said nothing, growing more and more puzzled by the minute. By now, I would usually have asked what it was that had brought him to my office, but I was—as I said—already pretty sure of that. I sure didn't want to bring up the subject of Rip and, no doubt, invite attack. Jacob did seem to be taking his time about jumping down my throat.

The old man had now stretched out full-length in the chair and was looking at the floor. In Jacob's line of vision was yesterday's *Pigeon Fork Gazette* and a copy of the latest *Popular Mechanics* magazine, both of which had fallen off my desk. I was expecting Jacob to say something unkind about my housekeeping habits, but instead he drawled, "You come pretty highly recommended."

I knew immediately, then, why he wouldn't meet my eyes. If Jacob Vandeventer had to stoop to give somebody a compliment, it was, no doubt, an embarrassment for him. I tried not to look surprised. When somebody says something nice about you, you don't exactly want to look shocked. "Oh?" I said.

Jacob nodded. "Eunice Krebbs has been a-saying for months now that if I ever needed a detective, I should come to you. That you're one smart cookie."

My last big case had been investigating the murders of Eunice Krebbs's grandmother and her grandmother's cat and parakeet. Believe it or not. It was a case that hadn't even come close to putting me on the detecting map, like I'd thought at first it might. Still, I'd ended up with a real friend in Eunice.

I smiled. "That was right nice of her to say."

Jacob raised his gray eyes to mine. He stared at me a while, his bird's nests twitching a little like maybe he was sizing me up, and then, his mind apparently made up, Jacob reached into the front pocket of his shirt and slowly pulled out a crumpled envelope. "I got this in the morning mail today," he said, and handed it to me.

I had no idea what was in that envelope, or I would've moved faster. As it was, I opened the envelope, took out the note inside, slowly unfolded it, and started reading.

I hadn't read two words before my mouth went dry:

GET $100,000 IN SMALL BILLS OR YOU'LL NEVER SEE PRISCILLA ALIVE AGAIN. NO COPS. WAIT FOR MY INSTRUCTIONS.

The message had been made by tearing words out of a newspaper and gluing them down on a sheet of white bond paper.

Good Lord. I knew Priscilla. Priss and I had graduated from Pigeon Fork High the same year. Back then the Vandeventers hadn't yet struck poultry pay dirt, so she and her brother had seemed like average folks. Priss was just your average thin, lanky girl. With a boyish haircut and a trigger temper. I remembered once seeing her deck some guy for calling her "Skinny."

Temper apparently ran in the family.

In the past few months, since I'd been back, I'd even

seen Priss on the street a couple of times. We hadn't actually spoken or anything. She'd seemed different somehow, hurrying by in a tailored suit—more remote, more unapproachable. Like they say, money changes everything.

Jacob was looking at me, his bird's nests all aquiver. I almost started to ask him why in the world he hadn't hurried up here. In cases like this, time is everything. I swallowed all that, though. No use jumping on a bereaved parent. Although, I must say, Jacob didn't look all that bereaved. He didn't even look particularly angry, which was odd for him. I cleared my throat once before I asked, "How long has Priscilla been gone?"

Jacob shrugged. "Oh, Priss ain't gone. She was a-standing right next to me when I opened the letter."

I stared at him. Then I believe I responded the way any other private detective in a similar situation would have.

"Huh?" I said.

CHAPTER
2

I couldn't help it. I kept on staring at Jacob like some fool. "Are you telling me Priss has *not* been kidnapped?"

Jacob looked at me as if he was starting to wonder how smart a cookie I really was. No matter what Eunice had told him.

It's a look I get quite a bit from clients. I think it's on account of them never really getting over the fact that I don't look anything like Peter Gunn. Peter's the one they come up here looking for. Instead they end up with me, an ordinary-looking guy with red hair and too many freckles. Believe me, I can identify with their disappointment. "I *said*, Priss was a-standing right next to me," Jacob said.

I looked back at the note, ignoring the irritation now in Jacob's voice. "Do you think you could've gotten this note by mistake? That maybe some other Priscilla has been—" My voice trailed off, because even as I said this, I realized that in all probability this was not the case. In a town the size of Pigeon Fork, how many missing Priscillas could there be? Besides, the envelope was plainly addressed to Jacob Vandeventer, Vandeventer Poultry, Route 2, Box 167, Pigeon Fork, Kentucky 40199. I stared at the writing. It had been done in blue ballpoint pen, the words written in all capitals. As if someone wanted to make damn sure his handwriting wasn't recognized.

All those capitals looked like maybe some elementary school kid had written them. This brought up yet another possibility. Maybe this whole thing was just a prank. Maybe some school kid thought it would be a hoot to send a note like this to the richest man in town.

The postmark told me that the note had been mailed yesterday from Pigeon Fork. Hardly a surprise. No doubt, whoever was behind this had to be somebody familiar with Jacob and his family—someone right here in town.

Which made me think of something else. I took a deep breath before I asked my next question. "Is everybody where they're supposed to be? There's no chance that the kidnappers could've mistaken someone else for your daughter, is there?"

Jacob had to know what I was getting at. It was common knowledge around town that about a year ago Jacob had divorced Wife No. 1, Ruby, the mother of his two children, in order to tie the knot with Wife No. 2, Willadette Sweeney, an ex-waitress at Lassiter's Restaurant. According to my secretary Melba, who—as best as I can tell—heads up Gossip Central in Pigeon Fork, Willadette is only five years older than Jacob's only daughter, Priscilla. It appears to me, then, that a mistake could've been made.

This had apparently already occurred to Jacob. He didn't look any too happy about my bringing the subject up, though. His bird's nests jammed themselves together, and his small gray eyes suddenly looked like little burning rocks. "Nope," he said. "I called around right after I got the note, and *everybody's* where they're supposed to be." He put a little extra emphasis on the word *everybody*, so I would get what he meant without him having to spell it out for me.

I decided to move on. Jacob was clenching his fists, looking like he might be working himself into a snit.

Having to duke it out with a guy in his sixties didn't seem like such a great idea. My luck, Jacob would beat me to a pulp, and I'd never live it down. "Do you think there might've been some other kind of mistake?" I asked. "Maybe there was more than one kidnapper, and there was a breakdown in communications. Maybe the note got sent a little too early." This seemed pretty farfetched, but stranger things have happened. I reckon there's as much chance for error in the kidnapping line as in any other kind of work. Besides, it was the best I could do on short notice. At least, it gave Jacob something else to think about besides socking me in the jaw.

Jacob almost—but not quite, of course—stopped scowling as he thought it over. Rubbing his chin, he said, "I reckon." That's Pigeon Forkese for "Why, yes, now that I think of it, that *is* a distinct possibility."

I hurried on, as something else occurred to me. "You know, the kidnappers might still be planning to carry through with this. Just because nobody's missing yet doesn't mean they've given up. Priss shouldn't be left alone."

Jacob drew back his thin shoulders as if I were accusing him of something. "I left strict orders that Priscilla was not to leave the office or go anywhere on her own." His tone had turned belligerent. "I ain't stupid, you know. I know it could still happen."

I stared at him. No matter what I said, Jacob didn't seem to be taking it any too well. Either he was in one foul mood all the time, or I had a real knack for rubbing him the wrong way. At a loss for words, I chose to do what I always do in situations like this. I said nothing.

Jacob filled up the silence right away. "Before I came over here, I went by the sheriff's office. Vergil was real interested in this here note until I told him Priss wasn't missing. Can you believe that?"

Actually, I could.

Jacob got up and walked over to the window. That particular window looks directly out on the red brick Crayton County Courthouse, with its domed clock tower and its arched windows and its white park benches out front. You also get a pretty good view of the Crayton Federal Bank next door. The bank has fat granite columns and long narrow windows always closed against the sun, and it looks as if it's been picked up out of the nineteenth century and dropped down in the twentieth. There are no drive-in windows or teller machines to spoil the illusion, either. Crayton Federal Bank no doubt figures that if you want your money, you damn well better park your car and come inside and get it.

This time of day, the morning sun slants sharply across both buildings, sending long blue shadows stretching across their old-fashioned facades. I've had folks visiting from out of town look out on that view and comment on how charming downtown Pigeon Fork is.

Jacob, however, didn't look charmed. He looked agitated more than anything else, swinging his arms as if he were winding himself up. I watched him, wondering if it were possible for a man in his sixties to have PMS. "You know what that no-account sheriff told me?" Jacob said. "He said he couldn't do a damn thing until a crime was committed! Can you believe that?"

Again, I couldn't think of a thing to say. That did seem to be the way the law worked.

A vein had started to bulge on Jacob's forehead. Ugly and purple, it pulsated right between his bird's nests.

"Now, Mr. Vandeventer," I said, in the same soothing tone that had totally failed to soothe Lizbeth last night, "there's no reason to get yourself all upset. There's every reason, in fact, to think that all this is just a prank."

Jacob turned and stared at me. It looked like somebody had poured lighter fluid on his little rock-eyes. "A prank! Well, if somebody out there thinks it's funny to play pranks on *me,* I want to know who it is! Do you hear? I want to KNOW." Jacob's vein was really going to town now. "That's where *you* come in. I want you to find out who's behind this! I won't have folks a-snickering behind my back. I won't have it!"

In that case, Jacob probably didn't want to hear what Melba and her gossipy friends had to say about his mar-

rying somebody thirty years younger. "Mr. Vandeventer," I said, still in that soothing tone, "it's not going
to be easy to find out who's behind this. Unless something actually happens. Which, I'm sure, you don't
want—"

Jacob interrupted me. You might've thought that he
wasn't all that interested in what I had to say. "I won't
have folks saying I don't look after my own, neither.
And I ain't about to throw away a hundred thousand
dollars on something as stupid as this. Why, folks would
think I was a damn fool!"

I stared at him. That was definitely one way to look
at it.

Jacob was definitely geared up now, strutting around
my office, waving his thin arms around. "I want you to
find out who's behind this. And I want you to be Priscilla's bodyguard. I don't want you a-letting her out of
your sight. I'm a-counting on *you* to make sure nothing
happens to her. Unnerstand?"

I understood, all right. Jacob seemed a tad more
concerned about his reputation—and the possibility of
losing his money—than he was about losing his only
daughter. It made me feel kind of sad for Priss. I gave
Jacob an insincere smile. "Well, sure, I'd be—"

Jacob interrupted me again. I was beginning to suspect that maybe this was where Lizbeth had picked up
the habit. "Yeah, yeah," he rumbled, holding up a
gnarled hand. "How much is this a-going to cost me?"

A blunt question deserves, I think, a blunt answer.
"Thirty dollars an hour, or two hundred dollars a day."

Jacob did what a lot of folks around here do when I
tell them my fee. He laughed. His bird's nests were still
all jammed together in one monumental frown, but his
mouth was laughing out loud.

It's real disconcerting to have a client laugh right in
your face. Especially when you know that, as far as
rates go, you could've been having a sale. I've actually
considered changing my sign to "Haskell Blevins, *Dis-
count* Detective."

"Now, look," Jacob finally got out, wiping his eyes,

"you and I both know that thirty dollars an hour is ridiculous. And two hundred dollars a day ain't nothing but highway robbery. This is Pigeon Fork, Haskell. It ain't New York."

I stared at him. Oh. Well. That explains why I haven't been able to find the Statue of Liberty anywhere around here. Gosh, thanks, Jacob. That clears up a lot.

I took a deep breath before I answered. "My rates aren't out of line. In Louisville, private investigators get forty dollars an hour or more. And at least three hundred dollars a day. Plus expenses."

Jacob smirked. "Does this look like Louisville to you, boy?"

Being called "boy" at the age of thirty-three is real irritating. I decided, though, to let that one pass. If you got all riled up at every irritating thing Jacob said, you'd be riled up all the time.

"Tell you what I'll do," he said. "I'll give you a hundred dollars for a day's worth of work. Take it or leave it."

Now it was time for me to laugh. Except I didn't exactly feel like it. I mean, this man—who, let us not forget, was the richest man in the county—was dickering about the cost of protecting his own *daughter*. It made you feel a little creepy.

But not creepy enough.

"A hundred dollars? Are you kidding? I'll tell you what *I'll* do," I said. "I'll leave it."

I know. I know. There's some that would say I was just as bad as Jacob, haggling like this when a person's life could be at stake. But at the time, mind you, I was still under the impression that all this was going to turn out to be, without a doubt, nothing more than a prank. And doing a little haggling over investigating a prank didn't seem in all that bad taste.

Besides, Jacob started it.

Jacob walked over to the window again, real deliberate-like. "You got any more cases you're working on right now?"

Jacob's point was well taken. A hundred dollars a day *is* quite a bit more than zero dollars a day.

Still, I wasn't about to let this old goat get mine. "Matter of fact, I'm real busy," I said. "I'd have to put some of my caseload on hold if I take your case on."

Lying must not be my strong suit. Jacob snickered. "Hm-mm," he said. "I reckon." Which, this time, was Pigeon Forkese for "Right. And if I believe that, I'm sure you've got a bridge to sell me." Jacob stared at me for a couple of seconds, his rock-eyes glittering away. "OK," he finally said. "Make it a hundred fifty. That's my final offer."

I hated myself, but, what the hell, my head started nodding before I could stop it.

Jacob snickered again. This time with a decidedly triumphant ring. He returned from the window, sat himself back down in my overstuffed chair, and whipped out his checkbook.

I couldn't believe it. Jacob Vandeventer, paying up front? Was I witnessing a miracle? From what I'd heard around town, all of Jacob's transactions were ninety days same as cash.

"I'm a-giving this to you now," he said, "on account of I don't want to be a-getting any bill from you in the mail with your regular fee on it. I want my account marked paid in full right from the start, unnerstand?"

So that was it. Jacob was making sure I didn't up my price on him. What a truly trusting human being.

Jacob continued to write, his gnarled hand moving slowly across the page. "I'm a-making this out for three days' work. That's four hundred fifty dollars." He said the words with a kind of reverence in his voice. "I figure, if you're as good a detective as Eunice Krebbs says you are, you ought to have this thing sewed up by then."

I tried to look appropriately grateful for his confidence.

Jacob's rock-eyes were sharp now. "Of course, if'n you solve this before three days—like maybe in the next hour or two—I'll expect a refund."

Right. Sure. Of course. I gave Jacob a wide smile. Jacob could definitely take that one to the bank.

As soon as he handed me the check, Jacob stood up, looking at his watch. "OK," he said. "It's eight fifty-seven, let's get a-going. I got you for the next seventy-two hours and we need to get out to Vandeventer Poultry so's you can get to work." Apparently determined to get full value for his dollar, Jacob was actually tapping his foot.

"I need to let my secretary know where I'll be," I said, reaching for the phone.

Jacob frowned. "On *my* time? You're a-going to make personal calls on *my* time?"

I gave him a level stare and kept right on dialing Elmo's Drugstore downstairs. There was every chance my dad had been right about this guy.

Melba answered Elmo's phone on the first ring. This was probably a bigger miracle than Jacob paying up front. "Yeah?" she said.

What professionalism.

I couldn't help wondering if that was how Melba was answering *my* phone these days. Jacob was already glaring at me, though—looking first over at me and then back at his watch—so I decided that a conversation on phone etiquette might not be a good idea right that minute. Talking faster, I told Melba where I'd be for the rest of the afternoon, and then added, "—and, by the way, I need you to come up here and find Rip's license and vaccination papers, OK?"

There was a short silence during which I realized that the vein was showing in Jacob's head again. He moved over by the door, his eyes glued to his watch.

"Uh, I don't know if I'll have time," Melba said. "I'm pretty busy."

This, I knew, was an absolute falsehood. Melba has never been pretty busy in her life. Unless you counted being pretty busy looking out the window.

If the vein in Jacob's forehead had been a little less prominent, that phone call probably would've taken a little longer. As it was, I gritted my teeth and said, "Get up here and find Rip's papers. OK, Melba?"

"Well, you don't have to be nasty about it," she said. Her tone sounded injured. As if she couldn't understand why in the world I always sounded so annoyed.

I took a deep breath and reminded myself that Melba *is* the sole support of five kids, being as how her husband Otis saw fit to have himself a heart attack about two years ago. Some might call that good planning on Otis's part, but I keep trying to remember that poor Melba *is* a bereaved widow lady who I really shouldn't want to strangle. "Thanks for your help, Melba," I said through clenched teeth. "I really appreciate you helping me out."

"Well, now, that's better," Melba said. I could just see her giving her brown beehive hairdo a quick patting down the way she does when she feels like she's won one.

I hung up the phone and turned back to Jacob.

Jacob was glaring at me. "That took fifty-one seconds. I'm expecting you to make that up to me."

I stared at him. Fifty-one seconds? He wanted me to pay him back for fifty-one seconds?

Jacob went on. "You can give me a refund for the time, or you can work it off. Either one."

I decided I better not say a word to that. Just in case my mouth started saying a whole lot of things I might regret later.

Speaking of things I might regret later, I put on my shoulder holster just before we left. Now that I'm no longer a cop, I don't like carrying a gun unless I absolutely have to. It would seem real dumb, though, to be acting as a bodyguard without one. If it turned out all this wasn't a prank—and somebody really did try to kidnap Priss—how else was I going to stop it? I didn't think holding up an empty hand and yelling "Stop!" would do it.

Jacob and I started down the stairs. Once on the street, I made another one of them deductions we private detectives are famous for. Jacob didn't have his car

24

with him. This was a pretty easy deduction to make since there were no cars at all parked out in front of Elmo's Drugstore. Or across the street in front of the courthouse.

Jacob noticed my look. "Nope, I didn't bring my car into town," he said. His tone said unkind things about my intelligence. "I hitched me a ride with one of my neighbors. I knew you'd be a-going back with me, so what would be the use in both of us driving? It'd be a waste of gas."

I decided this was another one of those times when I should keep my mouth shut. I led the way around back of the drugstore to where I'd parked my truck.

Jacob got in with an air of satisfaction. "You know, you'd be real surprised how much you can save on gas if'n you're careful."

Careful is not the word I would've used to describe Jacob.

We drove on out to Vandeventer Poultry. It wasn't an awful long drive, only about thirty minutes, but driving with Jacob right beside me—telling me every two miles how much I could save on gas if I geared down every time I came to a curve—made the drive seem a lot longer.

I hate backseat drivers. Particularly when I don't have a back seat.

I was real glad to see the Vandeventer Poultry sign come into a view. With bright red letters against an even brighter yellow background, it's a sign you can't miss. Every time I see it, the yellow of that sign always reminds me, appropriately enough, of egg yolk. Suspended on a chain between two posts about the size of telephone poles, the wooden sign is almost as big as a billboard. Jacob has apparently decided that his sign should accurately reflect just how big an operation he has these days.

When I was a kid, Vandeventer Poultry used to be just a small frame farmhouse and a barn and a few chicken coops out back. Back then, folks around Pigeon Fork speculated how long the little family operation would last. They wondered how the Vandeventers would ever be able to compete with the big poultry farms. That was, of course, before Jacob landed the Chick Delish account. Now Vandeventer Poultry *is* one of the big poultry farms.

These days the little farmhouse, the barn, and even the chicken coops are long gone. Instead, the first thing you see when you turn in to the driveway is a long, low, concrete block building with two blacktopped parking lots, one in front and one on the right. Painted white, the concrete block building is about as plain a building as I ever did see. In fact, if its white shingled roof had been flat instead of peaked, the Vandeventer Poultry office building would've looked exactly like a concrete shoe box with openings cut in the side for windows and doors. Jacob Vandeventer had apparently decided that spending his profits on a frivolous thing like office construction was as wanton a waste as driving his own car into Pigeon Fork when he could hitch a ride with a neighbor.

The building, of course, was hardly a surprise. Folks in Pigeon Fork had been talking about the Vandeventer Poultry office building ever since the day it was finished. I'd bet money that every one of the 1,511 folks in Pigeon Fork had driven out here at least once, just to see it for themselves. Concrete evidence of Jacob Vandeventer's penny-pinching.

As you drove into the parking lot, you could also see what had replaced the small chicken coops of yesteryear. In back of the office building, several huge broiler houses, all about the size of a good-sized pole barn, stood side by side, as a wide gravel driveway wound around and between them. With silver aluminum roofs glinting in the morning sun and tan walls broken up at regular intervals by vents and small rectangular windows, the houses looked a lot like barracks—chicken barracks for the vast Vandeventer Poultry army.

Beside me, Jacob must've decided I was interested in knowing exactly how vast his poultry army was. As we pulled up in front of his concrete shoe box, Jacob nodded toward the broiler houses and said, "Got me thirty thousand broilers in each of them houses. Seven houses in all," he said. Jacob's tone was that of a small boy, bragging. "When the chickens are full growed, it'll take eight tractor trailer trucks to haul them away from just one of my houses."

I tried to look stunned by the news. "Really," I said.

Jacob nodded again, managing to look as if he were strutting even though he was still sitting in my truck. "Really," he said.

We got on out, and right away I started looking stunned without any effort at all. Even though the broiler houses were some distance in back of the office building, the wind must've been blowing just right. The odor that attacked my nose was a mixture of chicken feed, wood shavings—used to litter the floor of poultry houses—and one other thing. The chalky ammonia smell of chicken shit.

It's an odor that, once smelled, you don't ever quite forget. Over my lifetime, I've known quite a few folks who kept chickens, but I had to hand it to Jacob. He surpassed them all in the smell department.

I glanced toward Jacob, but apparently Eau de Chicken Shit was an odor that the old man had smelled so many times, he no longer noticed it. Or maybe, since he associated it with making lots of money, he kind of liked it.

I headed toward the door of Vandeventer Poultry, concentrating on not taking deep breaths. In the distance, up on the hill, I could see the white Vandeventer mansion. All the way up there, they must've been out of smelling range. It was a good thing, because you'd think a thing like Eau de Chicken Shit might affect your property values. And if old Jacob had been a tad miserly on his office building, apparently he'd gone to town on his personal residence. It looked as if maybe the White House had been moved here, piece by piece, column for column.

Jacob noticed me glancing over at his White House. He stopped and puffed out his chest like—yes, I'll say it—a rooster. "That there's one of the most beautiful homes you'll ever want to see," he said.

Modesty, apparently, was not Jacob's strong suit.

The old man puffed out his chest a little more. "It houses the entire Vandeventer clan," Jacob said. "R.L. and Lizbeth in one wing, me and the wife in t'other. The *entire* clan." Jacob paused here, scowling. " 'Cept for Priss, of course. She up and decided to get her own place a few years back." Jacob said this last part real low as if confessing a private shame.

I stared at him. Let me see. Priss was my age—thirty-three. The way I saw it, her deciding to move out on her own didn't exactly qualify her as a wild woman. I didn't particularly want to discuss it, however, out here, with my nose coming up for the third time for air. I took a couple of steps toward the building, hoping Jacob would follow me.

Jacob didn't budge. Instead, he snorted contemptuously. "The place is so big, we had to put in two phone lines—one in R.L.'s wing and one in mine. So there's all the room in the world, but Prissy Britches had to up and leave. It was tomfoolery, that's all. Tomfoolery!" He looked over at me as if he expected me to argue with him.

I could've told him that if his daughter had any idea he called her Prissy Britches, it probably didn't help his case any, but I wasn't going to bring that up, either. I was getting ready to haul Jacob bodily inside.

Thank goodness, it turned out not to be necessary. Jacob seemed to have run out of complaints about Priss, and to my relief, he actually headed inside. It was a good thing. I was actually feeling light-headed, breathing so shallow.

Once inside, with the door swinging shut behind us, the odor outside was immediately replaced by another strong odor—Eau de Room Deodorant. A cloying flowery scent. Ordinarily, I would've hated it. This time I took several deep, cleansing breaths, feeling grateful.

The interior of the Vandeventer Poultry shoe box continued Jacob's penny-pinching theme. The receptionist's desk in the middle of the lobby was metal, not wood, and the green carpeting on the floor was that thin industrial-grade stuff that looks a lot like indoor/outdoor. I only took a quick glance around, though. Almost immediately, my attention was focused on the slim figure standing in front of the receptionist's desk, arms folded against her chest.

You would've thought that Priss would've been more than a little relieved to have herself a bodyguard, what with folks writing notes about her being kidnapped and all.

Like I said before, never assume.

Apparently, Priss had watched Jacob and me pull up and had immediately come running out of her office. No doubt intent on making me feel welcome.

"What the hell is *he* doing here?" she asked.

I just stared at her. Wearing flat shoes and little, if any, makeup, Priss didn't look a lot older than she'd looked in high school. The lines at the corners of her mouth were a little deeper, but I could've been looking at the girl I'd known back then. One thing had changed, though. Priss was no longer thin and lanky. In fact, she was downright curvy, even if she was trying real hard to hide it in that navy blue tailored suit. I looked at her, remembering how back in high school I'd once thought about asking her out. That was, of course, before she decked that guy who called her "Skinny."

"This is Haskell Blevins," Jacob said, walking right past Priss without even slowing down.

"Howdy, Priss," I said. "It's good to see you again." I thought I sounded real friendly.

Priss didn't even glance my way. Her eyes were on her father. "I know who he is. I also know *what* he is. What's he doing here?" Priss said.

Priss was obviously directing her question at Jacob. I looked over at him, but Jacob just kept on walking, past the blond receptionist in the lobby, down a long hallway toward a heavy mahogany door with a brass plate that said "Jacob Vandeventer, President." He nodded curtly at the secretary stationed outside his door and went on into his office.

Since Jacob didn't seem to be answering Priss, I thought maybe it was only good manners that I should. I smiled in her direction and said, "Your father's hired me to look into this kidnapping thing."

Priss gave me a sharp glance and quickened her pace. She was almost running by the time she reached her father's office.

So much for good manners.

I followed Priss and Jacob both, scooting past the secretary outside Jacob's office. She was an older woman with silver hair and large, round, purple earrings—it looked as if her ears had been attacked by a couple of big grapes. She gave me an uncertain smile as I ran by her.

"Look," Priss was saying to Jacob when I came in, "I thought we discussed this. I thought we decided this wasn't necessary." Priss had her father's gray eyes. Only where his were small and round, hers were very large and fringed in long, thick lashes. Right now, though, Priss's eyes looked pretty much the same as Jacob's did when he was angry. Like round glowing coals.

Remembering her temper, I took a couple of steps away from her. Getting hit by a woman would probably be even more humiliating than being beat up by Jacob.

Jacob was now sitting behind his desk in a swivel chair upholstered in black leather. I couldn't help staring for a second at the ornately carved, massive oak desk, the burgundy plush carpeting, and the mahogany paneling on the walls. Apparently, in Jacob's office penny-pinching had come to an abrupt halt.

Jacob picked up a couple of sheets of paper from the top of his desk, looked them over, and put them back down, all the while Priss looked like lava was about to start flowing out of the top of her head. Finally, Jacob looked back up at Priss and said, "Haskell's a-going to do a little investygating for us. He'll be keeping an eye on things for the next few days."

It was Mt. St. Helen's all over again. "Things? You mean *me*, don't you? Well, I won't have it! I won't be treated like some helpless, fluffy-headed female!"

Fluffy-headed she definitely was not. In fact, it looked as if maybe Priss had put a bowl on her head and trimmed around it. Her dark brown hair was almost as short as mine.

Jacob cleared his throat. "I'm giving Haskell free rein, and—" Here Jacob gave Priss a level-eyed look. "—and I expect you to give him all the help he needs." The old man picked up a bronze statue off the corner of his desk, and as he talked, he pointed it at Priss for emphasis.

Jacob's gesture probably would've had more impact if the statue he held had not been that of a chicken.

The chicken statue looked to be about a foot tall, and, from where I stood, it looked as if it had a half-smile on its bronze beak. Sort of like the Mona Lisa of the poultry world.

Jacob noticed my eyes on the statue. "You know what this is?" he said. "It's the Vandeventer Brown—the hybrid breed I developed." He looked at the statue fondly. "The chicken that made it all happen."

"You don't say," I said. I tried to look impressed.

Jacob's eyes looked like they were actually getting misty. "I worked for years—*years*, mind you—to develop this new strain. A strain that would be meatier and more economical to raise than the Rhode Island Reds I used to have. And I did it. I finally did it."

I tried to look even more impressed. But to tell you the truth, how excited can you get about a chicken?

Apparently, quite a bit, judging from the rapt expression on Jacob's face.

Priss, on the other hand, seemed to be somewhat lacking in enthusiasm. In fact, she still looked as if she were erupting. All of this was, no doubt, a tale Priss had heard many times before. Moreover, I reckon, she'd noticed right off that Jacob seemed to have rather abruptly changed the subject on her. Priss gave an exasperated sigh and said, "Then I don't have a say in *this?*" She jerked an accusing thumb toward me.

Jacob pulled his eyes away from his beloved chicken and focused once again on Priss. "Of course you have a say." He glanced down at the statue again. "But I have the *final* say. And I *say,* I'm a-hiring Haskell here. I want to get to the bottom of this. I won't have folks a-thinking I don't look after my own."

Jacob's eyes were still on the chicken. You might've thought he was talking to it rather than Priss.

"You have the final say," Priss repeated. "Just like always." Her voice was bitter.

Jacob looked affronted. "I'm doing this for you. *Everything* I'm doing, child, is for your own good."

Priss apparently didn't like being called "child" any better than I liked being called "boy." She turned on her heel and stomped out of the room.

Her leaving so quick took me completely by surprise. So that, for a second, I just stood there. With Jacob looking pointedly at me. As if to say, "All right, earn your keep!"

So, a couple of seconds late, I ran out of Jacob's office.

The woman with the grapes on her ears looked startled as I shot past her. I gave her what I hoped was a reassuring smile as I loped on down the hall after the woman I wasn't to let out of my sight. Priss had on a pretty good head of steam, so it took me about a minute to catch up. When I did, I saw that Priss was so angry, her mouth was white.

Once again, I was at a loss as to what to say. I'm not real good in situations like this. "I lack interpersonal skills" is, I believe, how my ex-wife Claudzilla put it.

Scrambling around in my brain for something to say, I finally came up with, "Look, I'll try to stay out of your way, but surely you've got to realize that—" I'd been about to tell Priss how she really did need somebody watching out for her for a while, that she really could be in danger, but she interrupted.

"Really, Haskell. Did you have to practically fawn all

over him? He developed a chicken, for God's sake. Not the Salk vaccine. A *chicken!*''

Now, that stung. ''I don't believe I was fawning—''

''Oh, you were fawning, all right. It made me want to throw up. I mean, REALLY.''

I stared at her. Maybe I *should* let her out of my sight. Like, immediately.

Priss wasn't finished. ''Furthermore, you know that dumb statue he loves so much?'' she said. ''My *mother* gave it to him. She had it made special for him for Christmas.'' Her jaw tightened. ''A month later, that old bastard left her. For that tramp of a waitress!''

Now what was I supposed to say to that? How nice it was that Jacob had liked his Christmas present? Or, maybe, yes, you're right, Jacob did appear to be an old bastard? Somehow, that seemed a tad on the disloyal side, talking about a client like that.

Priss didn't seem to need a response, anyway. Striding down the hall, clenching her small fists, she hissed between her teeth, ''I could kill him. I could just wring his neck!''

It was just what you might expect the daughter of a chicken farmer to say when she was mad. And yet Priss looked real serious. Like maybe she meant every word she said.

I was suddenly even more at a loss for words.

CHAPTER

3

By the time Priss got to her office, which was just off the lobby we'd come through a few minutes ago, she looked like she'd calmed down a little. At least her mouth wasn't quite so white. She was still moving at a pretty brisk pace, though.

I might as well admit it. I'm not exactly in the best of shape. I used to be, back when I was in Louisville, back when I was still a cop. The possibility of somebody shooting your ass if you're a step slow is a real powerful motivator. Back then I worked out in the gym three or four days a week. And I ran two miles a day on an indoor track.

Here in Pigeon Fork, I reckon I just don't have the same kind of motivation. I also don't have a gym or an indoor track any more, and the idea of running down the gravel road I live on doesn't exactly appeal to me. Somehow, I don't think I'd particularly enjoy running with rocks in my shoes. Or with my neighbors coming out on their porches, wondering what's chasing me.

Priss, on the other hand, looked like she might actually be one of them jogger types. She sure had the legs for it. Muscular, well developed. Of course, she might've gotten all the exercise she needed just storming down the halls every day. I was breathing pretty hard by the time we went past the receptionist's desk in the lobby, but I was feeling kind of proud that I'd managed to keep Priss just a step ahead of me.

The woman behind the desk looked up from her typing, saw us go past, and ducked her blond head down again. Reddening. I couldn't tell if the woman was real shy, or if she was embarrassed for us. A grown man and woman playing chase in the halls.

When I started to follow Priss into her office, Priss's mouth paled up again. "Oh, for crying out loud," she said, glaring at me. "You're *not* going to be following me around every single minute, are you? I mean, is this really necessary?"

Now what do you say to something like that? *No, of course not. Everybody knows that bodyguards do their best work when they're not anywhere near the person they're supposed to be bodyguarding.* I gave Priss a level stare, went over to the gray metal chair next to her desk, and sat down. Still staring at her.

I was also still breathing kind of hard, so it was a good thing that I'd decided there was really nothing to say. Being as how I wasn't at all sure I could've gotten any words out anyway.

Priss gave her short dark hair an angry toss. "I can't believe my privacy is being invaded like this!" Obviously not at all short of breath, she was talking to the room at large, throwing her arms out in a gesture that reminded me of her father. It made you wonder if a bad mood could be a genetic trait. "And all because of some stupid note! I can't believe it!"

Believe it. That's what I was tempted to tell her, but I knew better. After being married to Claudzilla for four years, I've had a lot of practice dealing with an irate woman. I've learned that the thing you most don't want to do in situations like this is to say anything—anything at all—that might possibly make them any more irate. Particularly if there's anything breakable within easy reach.

I could see a cut glass paperweight holding down a

stack of papers on the corner of Priss's desk. It wasn't ten inches from Priss's right hand. It also looked right hefty, like maybe it could leave a pretty good dent in the side of your head. I looked at that paperweight, looked back over at Priss, and clamped my mouth shut.

Don't get me wrong. It's not that I'm afraid of women or anything. It's just that I have a healthy respect for their throwing arms. I have no doubt that Claudzilla could've made it big in the major leagues.

To be honest, I didn't see what Priss's problem was. So what if she had to have a little company for a few days? Big deal. If I didn't know better, I could take this personally.

"Now, I don't want you to take this personally, Haskell—" Priss was saying. I just looked at her. "—but there's really no reason for you to be dogging my every step. I'm perfectly safe. And I think you know it."

I decided it was safe to talk. Priss had moved to the other side of the desk. It would've taken a pretty good leap to get to the paperweight from there. I had also, incidentally, gotten my breath back. "To tell you the truth," I said, "I don't know any such thing. You shouldn't take chances with something like this. If this note *is* the real thing—"

"But it isn't! It's a damn prank!"

I glanced over at the paperweight. Still out of reach. "You don't know that for sure, do you?" I said.

"Of course I know it," Priss snapped. "Why, the very idea of there being some big kidnapping plot here in Pigeon Fork is ridiculous!"

I just looked at her. Apparently, Priss felt that kidnapping was something that only happens in big cities. No doubt, it should be listed right up there with smog and traffic jams as one of the ills of urban life. I considered for a split second asking Priss how she'd arrived at such a conclusion, but then I remembered asking Claudzilla something real similar once.

I took another reassuring glance at the paperweight. It had to be a good three feet away. "Well," I said,

"I'm going to investigate this note as if it *were* the real thing, Priss. Because it would be stupid not to."

Priss's gray eyes flashed. "Are you calling me stupid?"

Lord. This woman was as touchy as her father. I held up my hand. "No, of course not," I said. I might call her bad-tempered, rude, and downright exasperating. But stupid? Never.

"Can we get on with this?" I went on. "I do need to ask you a few questions." I said this last part real calm and easy. Like maybe I was talking to a pit bull. That hadn't eaten in a while. Priss rolled her eyes, but she kept quiet. For a change. "Have you noticed anybody suspicious hanging around lately? Anybody you don't recognize, anybody that could be watching you?"

Priss made a skeptical little noise in the back of her throat. It was sort of like the ones Lizbeth had made over the phone last night. Lizbeth, though, was better at it. "Certainly not," Priss said. "I'm telling you, all this has *got* to be a prank." Her voice was getting real crisp.

"Has anything happened lately that might make somebody angry? That might make somebody think that your father owed them?"

Priss blinked at that one. For a split second I thought she wasn't going to answer at all, but then she gave an odd kind of laugh. It was one of those laughs that don't sound like the laugher is at all amused. *"My* father? Doing something that might make somebody mad at him?" Priss said, moving toward me. "Surely you're joking."

Priss may not have been good at making skeptical noises, but sarcasm she had down pat. "Look, Haskell, I've got work to do," she went on, glancing toward her desk pointedly. "I don't have time to answer any more of your idiotic questions."

Since Priss's desk was covered with folders and files and whatnot, I didn't doubt that she probably did have some work to get done. I did doubt, however, that my questions were idiotic.

I opened my mouth to say so, but Priss cut me off.

"I don't think we need to be Siamese twins or any-thing," she said. "You can wait for me outside my door. I'll be perfectly safe in here. Unless, of course, your mysterious kidnappers can walk through walls." She took a deliberate look around the room, then looked straight at me, raising an eyebrow.

I got her point. Actually, you would've had to be blind not to get it. Priss's office didn't have any windows. Not a single one. In fact, her office was hardly the office you'd expect the daughter of the owner of the company to have. In here, once again, penny-pinching had reared its ugly head. Priss's office was small, uncarpeted, and it seemed to have gray metal as an overall decorating scheme. Gray metal desk, gray metal chairs, gray metal nameplate that said "Priscilla Vandeventer, Administra-tive Assistant." In gray metal type. And, as if that wasn't enough, the office walls were painted light gray, the floor covered with dark gray linoleum. Priss's office, let's face it, had all the warmth of a crypt.

Not unlike Priss herself.

"You can take that chair with you," Priss said.

What a generous soul. At least I wouldn't have to squat Indian-style outside her door. Gosh thanks, Priss.

There really didn't seem to be anything else to do but pick up the chair I was sitting in and walk outside with it. I tried to do it with dignity, though. I lifted my chin, squared my shoulders, and hoisted the chair. My digni-fied exit was somewhat spoiled by the way I misjudged the width of the door frame. I ended up giving it a nasty crack with the side of the chair as I went out.

I didn't look around. Priss's irritated intake of breath was all I needed to hear to pretty much decide how Priss felt about my putting a big scratch in her door frame. I also decided, without looking around, that Priss had apparently gotten up and followed me to the door. I knew this because as soon as I cleared the door, it slammed in back of me.

I can't say Priss was endearing herself to me. In fact, I was beginning to think that she was probably right. Not only would kidnappers not want her, but probably most of the civilized world wouldn't be any too happy to have her around.

As soon as I sat down in that metal chair outside Priss's door, I was immediately reminded of high school. It was just like sitting outside the principal's office, knowing all the while that when the door opened next, it was not going to be pleasant.

I glanced around. Across the way, also opening into the reception area, was another office door identical to Priss's. The door was closed, but I could clearly see the brass nameplate on the front. "R. L. Vandeventer," it read, "Vice President."

R.L.'s real name is Roscoe Leroy—a name he inherited from one of his great-great-grandfathers, as I recall. I'd bet, though, that R.L. hasn't been called that since elementary school. It was one of the lessons all us kids learned back then. Reading, writing, 'rithmetic—and if you call R.L. "Roscoe Leroy," he's going to break your face.

I stared at that nameplate. Hadn't Priss's nameplate said "Administrative Assistant"? It looked like R.L., Priss's brother, had made it a little higher in the poultry pecking order. I could only imagine how delighted Priss must've been about this. I also couldn't help feeling surprised. The R.L. I remembered from high school hadn't exactly been corporate material.

What R.L. had been was a jock. Period. He was on the football team, the basketball team, and every other team that required that you get hit a lot around the head and shoulders—and enjoy it.

I've always thought that the stereotype about jocks wasn't exactly fair. That it wasn't right to assume that a jock is always ninety percent brawn and ten percent brain. R.L., though, was one of the guys that kept the stereotype going. Although he was a year older than me and Priss, he graduated a year behind us. On account of his general academic excellence. The only time I can remember that R.L. distinguished himself in the classroom was the day he stuck the most spitballs to the ceiling.

I glanced over at the blond receptionist, sitting behind the green metal desk in the middle of the lobby. Even though I couldn't have been three feet away from her—and I was sitting facing her—she didn't once look my way. It was as if I were suddenly invisible. This really reminded me of high school. You always knew you were in big trouble when the school secretary wouldn't look at you.

The blond receptionist went right on typing, her eyes never leaving the page. I did notice, though, that as I watched her, her cheeks were getting pinker and pinker. With an oval face and straight hair that hung to her shoulders, she wasn't bad looking. She was a tad on the pale side, though. Pale blond hair, pale blue eyes, pale pink lips. Even her dress was pale green. She looked like maybe she'd stood outside in the sun too long, and she'd faded.

When she paused in her typing, I smiled and said real quick before she could get started up again, "The name's Haskell Blevins. What's yours?"

The woman actually jumped. "Jolene Lacefield," she said. Only she said it real low to her typewriter, not me.

You could get a complex around here. I mean, I realize that there are some women in the world who, oddly enough, don't find the Howdy Doody type all that attractive, but the women at Vandeventer Poultry seemed to be going out of their way to step all over my ego.

I put on my best friendly, disarming voice. "Well, I'm real glad to meet you. I'm here doing a little investigating work for Jacob Vandeventer, you know." Since Priss's door had been open right up until she kicked me out of her office, Jolene had to have heard every word Priss and I had said. If she hadn't known before then, Jolene surely knew now the exact nature of the investigating work I was doing.

Jolene gave me one quick glance and then looked back down at her typewriter again.

It was like talking to some little wild animal. Any minute now I expected her to get up and run into the underbrush. Or maybe the bathroom.

I talked a little faster. "You haven't noticed anybody hanging around here the last couple of days, have you?"

Jolene shook her head no, her eyes still on her typewriter. Whatever she was typing must've been fascinating.

I couldn't help but wonder how good a receptionist this woman could be. You'd think that if a visitor actually came in and said hello to her, she might jump under her desk. And hide there, quivering. You'd think that a cowering receptionist wouldn't be real good for public relations.

"Have you noticed anybody suspicious at all? Inside or out?

Jolene shook her head. Eyes, of course, still on her typewriter.

"Have there been any strange phone calls lately?"

This time Jolene actually spoke. She still didn't look at me, of course, but a sound actually came out of her mouth. "No," she said, shaking her head again.

We were obviously starting to get real chummy.

"Has anything unusual happened around here recently? Anything out of the ordinary?"

This time Jolene's pale eyes flickered to my face. She quickly looked away, shaking her head. "No," she said, "nothing."

It was the look that made me doubt what she was saying. That quick, anxious look. "Are you sure?" I asked. "It would help me a lot in my investigation if I knew everything that's been going on around here. No matter how unimportant it might seem."

Jolene's eyes met mine. "I *said*, nothing's been going on." Her voice was as soft as a spring breeze, and yet there seemed to be an edge to it now. As if, in that spring breeze, there was a hint of winter.

I stared at her. *Had* something happened lately? Or was I seeing things in this shy woman's face that weren't there? Maybe Jolene had an edge to her voice because she was shy, and she didn't like being questioned.

I didn't have time to think about it, though, because at

41

that moment the front door opened, and R.L., wearing a three-piece gray pin-striped suit, came strolling in.

Tall, muscular, with thick black hair and a smile that could advertise toothpaste, R.L. is what all the womenfolk in Pigeon Fork call "movie-star handsome." If I hadn't noticed this on my own, I'd know it because Melba has told me. Time and time again. It's something, in fact, she tells me every time R.L. walks anywhere near Elmo's Drugstore. Melba also usually does a little swoon.

Of course, in Melba's case, that doesn't mean a whole lot. Ever since her husband Otis died, Melba has been pretty much swooning every time any man walks by, movie-star handsome or not.

The movie star, I reckon, that R.L. resembles most is Sylvester Stallone. I reckon R.L. must work out some, because his arms and shoulders have always looked as if he's attached them to a bicycle pump. I've never understood it, but females—particularly the females back in high school—always seem to go for the inflated look.

Back in high school, you really wanted to hate R.L.'s guts, but he was such a nice guy he wouldn't let you. R.L. was always laughing, always joking, always the one you could count on to loan you his study notes if you were in a bind. Of course, studying R.L.'s notes was pretty much the same as not studying at all, but it was the thought that counted.

For a while, I couldn't understand it. How had R.L. ended up being so nice—with a father like Jacob? I finally decided that, like all teenagers, R.L. was rebelling against his dad—which meant that R.L. ended up being just about the nicest guy you'd ever want to meet.

Apparently, R.L. didn't notice me, because he didn't even glance in my direction when he came through the door. Instead, R.L. walked straight over to the receptionist's desk, picked up a stack of mail, and starting thumbing through it.

I glanced at my watch. It was almost 10:15. Since I strongly doubted that R.L. had had any pressing poultry appointments first thing this morning. I would bet that this was the hour R.L. usually showed up for work.

This sure sounded like the R.L. I remembered.

I glanced over at Jolene, expecting to see the expression on her face that I remembered from high school. Every girl at Pigeon Fork High had always looked at R.L. the same way.

As if he were something she'd just found under her Christmas tree.

Jolene, however, must've been used to R.L. by now. She barely glanced at him and went on with her typing. I started to feel better. It wasn't just me she ignored. Lord, if Jolene wouldn't look at R.L., she wouldn't look at anybody. The woman obviously wasn't well.

R.L. noticed me then. For a split second, he just stood there, frozen, staring at me. As if he couldn't, for the life of him, figure out what in hell I was doing there.

Right away, though, R.L. put down his mail and headed toward me, grinning to beat the band. "Haskell? Haskell Blevins? Well, as I live and breathe—"

Back in high school, R.L. always said hello to you by hitting you on the arm. I got up out of my chair and started backing away, but it was too late. R.L. was already there, hammering me on my left arm with one of his big ham-hock fists. "Well, how in the world are you?" He sounded real friendly and all, but his eyes were traveling from my face to Priss's office door. His handsome face looked uneasy.

"I reckon I'm doing just fine, R.L.," I said, rubbing my arm. I didn't have much time for rubbing, because R.L. was now grabbing up my hand, pumping it vigorously. You'd have known R.L. was an ex-football player just by his handshake. He was still trying to crush, kill, and destroy. I watched my fingers turning blue and tried not to wince.

In addition to pain, I was also feeling something else. Puzzled. R.L. was acting as if he hadn't seen me in years. And yet I'd run into him a few times on the street—and in Elmo's Drugstore—since I'd been back.

43

All those times he'd just nodded at me and gone on past.

Now he was acting as if we were long-lost buddies or something. Which was odd. I mean, he and I hadn't been enemies or anything, but in high school we hadn't exactly been pals. For one thing, jocks didn't generally hang around with the non-jocks. I'm not sure why that was. Maybe the jocks were afraid they might hurt the rest of us.

It was a distinct possibility.

"So, uh, what brings you all the way out here?" R.L. said, still pumping my blue fingers. R.L.'s smile stretched from ear to ear.

"I'm out here doing a little investigating for your dad," I said, reclaiming my fingers from captivity.

R.L.'s eyes got a little wider. "You don't mean to tell me that the old man is taking that note *seriously?*" R.L. ran a ham hock through his dark hair. It was a gesture, as I recall, that used to cause the Pigeon Fork High cheerleaders to squeal. "When Dad called me at home this morning, right after he received that dumb note, he told me he thought it was just a prank. You don't really think somebody's trying to, uh, grab Priss, do you?"

R.L. looked a lot more upset at the idea than Jacob had. "To tell you the truth, I don't know," I said. "But I'm going to be keeping an eye on her for the next few days."

R.L. shook his head, as if to clear it. "I can't believe that somebody is really—" His voice broke off, and then he added, "I mean, uh, it sounds like some high school joke, now, don't it?"

Come to think of it, it sounded a whole lot like the kind of pranks R.L. himself used to pull in high school. More than one teacher had found themselves sitting smack dab on chewing gum—and more than one of my fellow students had found their cars out in the school parking lot completely covered in toilet paper—courtesy of R.L. and his sense of humor. R.L. always was a real knee slapper.

R.L. didn't look like he was about to laugh now,

though. "I tell you what, Haskell," he said, "if anything should ever happen to Priss, I—I just don't know what I'd do. She's pretty special, you know."

I had to agree with him. Only *special* wasn't exactly the word I would've used.

"It'll probably turn out to be just some kid's idea of a prank," I said. I hoped I sounded reassuring, because R.L. was starting to look pretty upset. There didn't seem any delicate way to put my next question. "You don't happen to have any idea who might be behind this, do you? I mean, is there anybody who's been particularly hostile to Priss lately?"

In light of Priss's saintlike disposition, I half expected R.L. to mention most of Pigeon Fork, but he just shook his head. "Nope, nobody," he said. R.L. blinked a couple of times, glanced toward Priss's door, and then lowered his voice. "In fact, the only person who's been nasty to Priss here lately has been Dad."

I stared at him. "Jacob?"

R.L. moved a little away from Priss's door and nodded. "Yep, Dad called us into his office yesterday morning and told us he was, uh, making some changes."

"Changes?"

R.L. nodded again. "Dad's getting ready to retire with his new wife, you know, so he decided it was time—as he put it—to hand over the reins."

R.L. swallowed once before he went on. "He said he was going to transfer half of his shares in Vandeventer Poultry to me and give me absolute control of the company."

For a man who'd just been handed a successful company on a silver platter, you might've thought that R.L. would've looked more excited. What he looked was stunned. Like maybe he'd just been hit with a two-by-four.

Of course, if all this happened just yesterday, R.L. probably *was* still in shock. And, I'd guess, he was also feeling a little guilty. From what little I'd seen so far this morning, it seemed to me that if anybody deserved to be handed the company, it was Priss. I might've been jumping to conclusions a little, but it sure looked like there was every chance that Priss might just work a little harder than her brother.

This would explain why Priss had looked so strange when I'd asked her if anything had happened lately to make someone angry. Something had happened, all right, and Priss *herself* was the one who was angry.

R.L. ran his hand through his hair again. "Dad told Priss right in front of me that he wouldn't have a woman heading up his company. That folks would think he was a damn fool." R.L. sighed and added, "He also told her that she needed to find herself a man and settle down."

Lord. I bet that one went over like the *Hindenburg*.

R.L. stopped then and stared past me. He seemed to be looking at a remembered horror. "Boy, was Priss mad."

That was, no doubt, an understatement. I asked then what I thought was a logical question. "Is she mad at *you?*"

R.L. looked surprised that I'd even think such a thing. " 'Course not. I didn't do nothing."

I just looked at him. That I could believe.

"Nope," R.L. said. "The one Priss blames is Dad."

I nodded. I didn't want to think what I was now thinking. But wasn't it very possible that Priss could've sent the kidnap note herself? To increase her value in her father's eyes? The note had been mailed yesterday, and there had been all the time in the world yesterday afternoon, after Jacob had broken his happy news, for Priss to get to the post office.

Maybe there was a real good reason why Priss was so all-fired sure that the note was a prank. Because she herself was the prankster.

CHAPTER
4

For the rest of the morning, I kept sitting outside Priss's office, pretty much doing nothing except watching Jolene type. This is the part of a private detective's job that you never see on television. The part where you sit and sit and sit until your rear end gets numb.

I did decide during that time that my suspicions were right—Priss apparently *was* doing the majority of the work at Vandeventer Poultry. Jolene disappeared time and time again into Priss's office, only to reappear carrying mounds of paper to be typed or filed or what have you. I didn't know what Priss was doing in there, but whatever it was, it sure generated a lot of paper.

It also generated a certain amount of respect on my part. Some of the phone conversations I caught snatches of during the infrequent times when her door opened showed Priss to be a savvy businesswoman. Strong and competent. I had to admire that. The only thing my ex-wife Claudzilla had been competent at was applying makeup and extracting money from my wallet.

What R.L. was competent at, though, I wasn't sure. Although R.L. went into his office right after we talked, Jolene didn't seem to get any work from him. All the phone calls that came in were for Priss. In fact, the only call that came in for R.L. turned out to be from Lizbeth.

R.L.'s job, as best as I could tell, was warming a chair.

Much like mine, come to think of it. By noon I was so bored, I was almost wishing there *would* be a kidnapping attempt. It would give me something to do.

It also occurred to me about this time that maybe the kidnapping note should be taken a little more seriously than everybody seemed to be taking it. Kidnapping Priss might cripple Vandeventer Poultry. Maybe *that* was what the kidnapper had in mind.

Along about noon, however, someone a whole lot worse than a mere kidnapper walked through the Vandeventer Poultry front door. Wearing a calf-length mink coat that my ex-wife Claudzilla would no doubt have fought her for, Lizbeth Vandeventer went straight to the receptionist's desk, pointed a crimson-tipped finger at Jolene, and said, "Get R.L." No "please," no "thank you," no nothing. Just get him. Lizbeth had apparently attended the Leona Helmsley School of Manners.

Jolene looked flustered, as if maybe it was the pope—cleverly disguised as Lizbeth—standing in front of her desk, demanding an audience with Pigeon Fork's chicken baron. "Oh, right away," Jolene said, her voice agitated. *"Right away."*

Lizbeth looked bored. While Jolene was summoning R.L., Lizbeth glanced around the room with all the warmth of Simon Legree looking over the slave quarters. Unfortunately, she spotted me.

One of the slaves.

Lizbeth immediately arranged her crimson-tinted mouth into a tiny smile—the kind, no doubt, that Leona herself wore when she was about to stoop to talk to one of "the little people." Then, too, Lizbeth has got to be at least five-foot-ten in her stocking feet, so I would reckon that most everybody in her eyes is "little" in more ways than one.

Adjusting her mink, Lizbeth moved purposely toward me. As she did so, not a hair on her head moved. She must've had enough hair spray on her frosted blond head to turn it into concrete.

With her concrete hair swept back from her face, Lizbeth looked as if she were constantly heading into a stiff wind. She also looked as if—at the ripe old age of thirty-one—she'd already gotten herself one of them face-lift jobs that all the celebrities are getting. Either that, or they'd discovered the Fountain of Youth on the Vandeventer property. I'd swear Lizbeth's face had fewer lines now that it had had in high school. Her eyes looked different, too. They'd been big in high school, but now they were open so wide, Lizbeth looked perpetually surprised.

Of course, maybe she was just real surprised to find a wind blowing that hard in the house.

"Why, hello there," Lizbeth said, extending a diamond-laden hand. "I'm Lizbeth Vandeventer." She pronounced the name "VON-deventer," with heavy emphasis on the first syllable. I stared at her. This was a new one. Most everybody in Pigeon Fork pronounced the Vandeventer name as if it were spelled "Vandy-venter." "And you?"

Apparently, Lizbeth didn't remember me at all from high school. Things like this could really hurt a guy's feelings.

I got slowly to my feet, knowing full well—after the charming conversation we'd had the night before—that saying my name was going to be like pulling the pin on a grenade. "I'm Haskell Blevins." I pronounced my name "BLEH-vins," emphasizing the first syllable just like Lizbeth had. This subtlety, however, was lost on Lizbeth. She was too busy snatching back her hand so quick you might've thought my hand was a snake.

"You," she said. *"You."* That seemed to be all Lizbeth could say for a second or two. Being as how I'm just barely six foot, and Lizbeth's high heels had added a couple of inches to her height, we were looking at each other pretty much eye to eye. I stared back at her unblinking, the way you used to when you were a kid and a bully on the playground challenged you. Finally,

Lizbeth managed to get out, "You—you're the one with that *beast!*"

I gave her a smile I hoped looked tolerant. It didn't seem like good form to get into a big fight with the daughter-in-law of a client. Particularly with the client right down the hall. "Well, now, Lizbeth," I said, "I wouldn't go so far as to call Rip a—"

Just like on the phone, Lizbeth interrupted. "Oh, it's a beast, all right," she said, waving her hand. Her diamonds glittered merrily. "A garden-destroying *beast!*" Lizbeth's big eyes now looked like blue saucers. She gave her concrete an angry toss. Once again, not a curl moved. "That damn dog of yours ruined my tulips!" Lizbeth turned to Jolene as if expecting sympathy. "Can you believe it? He dug them all up!"

Jolene looked like a rabbit caught in the hypnotic glare of some predatory animal. She just sat there, apparently too terrified to make a sound, her eyes showing the whites all around.

I, on the other hand, wasn't feeling the least bit terrified. In fact, what I was feeling was an almost overwhelming urge to mosey on up to Lizbeth's mansion and dig up her garden personally. "Lizbeth," I said, "it wasn't my dog." My tolerant smile had vanished. "Like I told you—"

Lizbeth didn't even pause. Apparently, she was going for a record: most interruptions in a twenty-four-hour period. "Well," she said, "I guess I've put a real scare into you if you're up here trying to get on Jacob's good side."

I just looked at her. Jacob *had* a good side? This was news. "Look, Lizbeth, I—" That was all I got out.

"It's not going to work, you know." Lizbeth interrupted once again. We could be reading about her in the *Guinness Book of World Records* any time now. "If you think you can waltz in here and talk Jacob into putting pressure on me to forget all about this—this *outrage,* you've got another thing coming!"

Lizbeth had obviously misunderstood the reason I

was there. "Actually," I said, "I'm working for Jacob. I'm here to—"

"What?" Another interruption. Lizbeth was showing real skill under pressure.

"I'm Priss's bodyguard," I said. I started explaining real patient-like the exact nature of my job here, but Lizbeth apparently was in no mood to listen.

"Are you kidding me?" she said. "Jacob is paying out good money because some fool wrote a *note?* Why, everybody knows that silly thing is a prank. When R.L. told me about that note this morning, right after Jacob called, why, I told him—" You get the gist. Lizbeth went on and on. In the middle of her tirade, Lizbeth once again looked over at Jolene for support. This time Jolene bore a remarkable resemblance to a deer caught in the headlights of an oncoming car.

Lizbeth was making no effort to keep her voice down. Just as Lizbeth glanced toward Jolene, the door to Priss's office opened. I reckon Priss must've heard the ruckus. Hell, folks in *Louisville* probably heard it. Priss stood there, looking from Lizbeth to me and back again to Lizbeth, a question in her eyes.

Before Priss could put that question into words, however, Lizbeth hurried on. "You haven't heard the last of me, Haskell Blevins," she said, wagging her finger in my face.

I hate that. I really do.

"You're going to *pay* for my garden," Lizbeth went on. "I've called up my attorney, and as soon as he calls me back, you'll be sorry!"

I stared at her. I already was sorry. I was sorry I'd ever laid eyes on Lizbeth Vandeventer. Of course, there was every chance that Lizbeth's attorney, Alton Gabbard, felt the same rush of warmth toward her that I did. Maybe he wouldn't ever call her back.

R.L. was coming out of his office, too, by then. His eyes widened when he saw the entire group of us standing there.

Lizbeth's back was to R.L., so she didn't see him heading toward us. Her eyes were glued on Priss.

"Well, well, well," Lizbeth said. "Look who's joined us. I was afraid you were going to hide in your office until I was gone." Lizbeth apparently had a real knack for saying exactly the wrong thing. Priss's gray eyes started looking like molten lava.

Lizbeth's eyes, on the other hand, were now glittering as much as her diamonds. "I've been meaning to ask you, Priss dear, is it really necessary that R.L. go to all these late-night meetings? I mean, there were two last week, and two the week before that, and now the one last night—are all these meetings *really* necessary?"

Priss took a deep breath before she answered. Her voice was so calm, it made you nervous. You felt like you were listening to the eye of a hurricane. "Why, I don't know, Lizbeth. Why don't you ask your husband?"

R.L. had joined us by then. He stood there, looking from his sister to his wife, totally at a loss for words. R.L. was somebody I could identify with.

Lizbeth went over and linked her arm through R.L.'s. "R.L.'s already told me, *you're* the one who calls the damn meetings. I mean, really, Priss, you'd better get used to the fact that R.L. has responsibilities other than Vandeventer Poultry."

Priss's eyes were slits.

Lizbeth gave her a tight little smile. "You don't need your hand held every minute, do you?"

For a second there, I thought Priss might lunge for Lizbeth's throat, but Priss just blinked a couple of times and said nothing. Her slit eyes, however, were saying volumes. They traveled to her brother.

R.L. showed himself to be equal to the challenge. He looked at the floor and cleared his throat. "So," he said brightly, turning to Lizbeth, "are we ready for lunch?"

This courageous gesture on R.L.'s part left *me* standing there with Priss, the human time bomb, watching R.L. and Lizbeth walk out the front door. "There they go," Priss said through her teeth. "The happy couple." Somehow, I got the feeling that Priss was not being sincere. She looked over at me. "Tell me, Haskell, don't you think it's sweet the way Lizbeth comes in every single day to go to lunch with her adoring husband?''

I stared at Priss, fairly sure that this was a trick question. "It does seem nice," I said uneasily.

Priss gave me a look that said loud and clear, how dumb could you be? "Haskell, Lizbeth is just protecting her investment. It's not that she can't bear to be away from R.L. She's just making sure nobody else gets the chance to latch on to her meal ticket."

I continued to stare at Priss. What a lovely sentiment. There didn't seem to be any end to the kind things the Vandeventer family had to say about one another. Why, if you didn't know better, you'd think you were with the Waltons.

Lunch for me and Priss turned out to be burgers at Frank's Bar and Grill. Right after Lizbeth and R.L. left, Priss and I, too, headed outside, toward my truck. I don't mind telling you, when I gingerly opened the front door of Vandeventer Poultry, I was more or less mentally preparing my nose for another assault. It took me a second to realize that the smell was now almost nonexistent. The wind must've shifted while I'd been inside. I drove toward Frank's with the renewed appetite of someone who'd just narrowly escaped grievous bodily injury.

Located about seven miles south of Pigeon Fork at the junction where Main Street turns into a state road, Frank's Bar and Grill used to be a feed store. The feed store went bankrupt, though, some years back. That's when Frank Puckett bought the thing and turned it into a feed store and watering hole for people instead of animals. It's still real rustic inside, with exposed oak rafters overhead and wide plank flooring under foot. Frank's left up all the old metal signs from the feed store, too. Colorful signs advertising things like Friskies dog food and Mail Pouch tobacco and Aubrey's Red Feed are scattered here and there on the rough-hewn walls. Frank's also has the distinction of having the only neon sign in Pigeon Fork—a small red one in the front window that says "Say Bull." It sure doesn't look like much to me, but Frank seems real proud of it.

Priss's and my lunch was punctuated only by the sound of both of us chewing our burgers. I idiotically tried to break the silence a couple of times, but the looks Priss gave me started spoiling my appetite.

If Priss didn't have a single word for me, she seemed to have stored up quite a few for R.L. by the time we got back from lunch. As soon as R.L. walked in, Priss followed him into his office. I would've followed—after all, from the quick glance I got of the interior, it appeared that R.L.'s office *did* have windows—but I got the impression Priss wanted to talk to R.L. alone. I got this impression right about the time Priss slammed the door in my face. We private detectives are real good at picking up on this kind of subtle nuance. Fortunately, I picked up on this nuance just in time, narrowly escaping getting my face flattened.

I also picked up on something else. R.L.'s title wasn't the only thing that was real different from Priss's. With grass cloth on the walls and deep plush beige carpeting on the floor, R.L.'s office had not one but two floor-to-ceiling windows. R.L.'s view out his two windows wasn't any great shakes—he could sit in the dark green leather chair behind his large maple desk and watch the shadows play across the chicken barracks at all hours of the day—but compared to Priss's view, R.L.'s was downright awe-inspiring.

Standing just outside R.L.'s office, I could hear Priss yelling her head off at R.L. on the other side of the door. It wouldn't be polite to go barging in, I decided. Besides, I was pretty sure that if I walked in, I just might be included on the receiving end of that yelling.

I felt real dumb, though, standing there like some idiot sentry. Across the way, Jolene was still at her desk, typing away. She didn't once look up, but I could tell she knew very well that Priss and R.L. were fighting. I watched Jolene type for a second. She probably didn't miss much that happened around here. Jolene might be someone I'd like to talk to—if I could ever get her to actually form words.

The door to R.L.'s opened right then, and Priss came barreling out, her face looking like she'd just chomped down on a jalapeño pepper. "—better cut it out, you hear?" she was saying over her shoulder. "I mean it, R.L. I want to be left out of it!" She stomped into her office without looking at either me or Jolene. And, of course, she slammed the door.

At this rate, Priss's door was going to be nothing but splinters by five o'clock.

I sat back down outside Priss's door and thought about what I'd just heard. What exactly did Priss want R.L. to leave her out of? I glanced toward Priss's closed door. It didn't seem real likely that if I asked Priss to elaborate, she'd be happy to oblige.

I looked back over at Jolene. She saw my glance, and her own eyes immediately widened. Picking up the phone, she started dialing. No doubt, suddenly remembering an all-important phone call she *had* to make.

I slumped a little in my chair. My avenues of inquiry seemed to be pretty much shut down. This kidnapping case was getting to be a lot bigger pain in the neck than I'd ever thought it would. So far, all I'd really done on the case was chase Priss through the halls. And sit. I shifted around again. Metal chairs could probably have been put to good use during the Inquisition. This one was starting to kill my back.

Twenty minutes later, that chair was way beyond *starting* to kill my back. In fact, I was pretty sure that chair was in a homicidal rage. I'd just decided that if I didn't get up and move soon, my back was going to need CPR, when the doors to Priss's and R.L.'s offices opened almost simultaneously. Without a word, both Priss and R.L. hurried toward the corridor that led to Jacob's office.

I figured they'd both been summoned by Jacob himself. On the intercom. For what I had no idea, but I was determined to find out. I got up and followed Priss and R.L. down the corridor. Just as we got to Jacob's door,

Priss stopped dead, turned to me, and said, "Wait here."

Her tone was none too friendly.

The silver-haired woman at the desk in front of Jacob's door—the one I mentioned earlier whose ears had been gobbled up by grapes—looked at me with real sympathy.

I smiled at her. Wearing a tailored gray suit and a lavender blouse, Grape Ears looked as if she took the title of secretary real seriously. Why, she even had a dog-eared *Secretarial Handbook* right on top of her desk. Along with a dictionary and a thesaurus. All these books looked worn, as if she actually referred to them. Often.

I couldn't help thinking of Melba, my secretarial cross-to-bear. If Melba even *owned* a copy of the *Secretarial Handbook,* she was probably using it as a doorstop.

Grape Ears was still looking at me sympathetically.

"Haskell Blevins, P.I.," I said.

"Inez Evitts," she said. Her voice was brisk and businesslike.

I smiled at her. "Glad to meet you."

Inez gave a little nod of her head, without replying. Evidently, she hadn't yet fully made up her mind if she was glad to meet me.

Fifty years old if she was a day, Inez Evitts was not what you'd call an attractive woman. Neat and schoolmarmish, yes. Attractive, no. In fact, Inez looked a lot like she'd recently stuck her face in a pencil sharpener. Her nose was pointed, her chin was pointed, and the way she'd pulled her silver hair back from her long, thin face into a bun emphasized the points. It didn't help any that she was very thin. I'm pretty sure I've seen more curves on a tongue depressor.

Inez also appeared to have opted for the natural look. No lipstick, no mascara, no nothing. I myself don't particularly like a lot of makeup on a woman, but in Inez's case, I would've made an exception.

"I'm sure Priss didn't mean to sound so snippy, Mr. Blevins," Inez said, patting self-consciously at her bun.

"She's just terribly busy, you know. I don't think she realizes how rude she sometimes sounds."

I just looked at Inez. There wasn't a doubt in my mind that Priss knew exactly how she sounded. Being rude was probably one of Priss's life goals.

"You can call me Haskell," I said.

Inez acknowledged what I'd just said with a quick, tight smile. You could tell, however, that I'd said the wrong thing. It was as if I'd suggested she start wiping her nose on her sleeve. Apparently, calling a man you just met by his first name simply wasn't done.

Inez's small hazel eyes were now on her desk. "Priss has been real tense lately, *Mr. Blevins*." Did I imagine it, or did she put a slight emphasis on the "Mr. Blevins"? "There've been so many of these closed-door meetings lately," Inez went on. "There's a lot of changes going on." Inez said this last sentence the same way you might say, "There's a lot of bubonic plague going around."

Obviously, then, Inez was well aware of the changes Jacob was planning to make, and she was every bit as delighted about them as Priss. I nodded, trying to look real sympathetic myself now. I opened my mouth to ask her if she knew anything about the kidnap note, when the door to Jacob's office swung open and cracked itself against the wall. Both Inez and I jumped as if we'd been shot. Right away, Priss—no surprise—burst through the doorway and headed toward her office.

There was nothing else for me to do but catch up with her. I was real sorry I did, though. When I got up to her, Priss was using language that would've been a little strong for some sailors I know.

"Priss, is there something wrong?" Yep, I really said that. My only excuse is that I was caught off guard.

Priss stopped in mid-curse. "Wrong? What could be wrong? My dad is an asshole! A damn male chauvinist pig! But what on earth could be wrong?"

I decided that was one of them rhetorical-type questions. So I didn't bother answering her. I wouldn't have had much time anyway. We were right in front of her office by then, and Priss immediately disappeared inside. Once again, of course, taking her fury out on her door. The entire reception room echoed with the slam.

The way things were going, there could probably be an earthquake here at Vandeventer Poultry, and no one would notice. Everybody would think it was just Priss, being herself.

Everything was relatively calm after that. In fact, it actually got to be hard keeping my eyes open. A little after two, R.L. left his office for a while, heading back down the corridor to Jacob's office. He was only gone about fifteen minutes, and shortly after he returned, Jolene took off for a few minutes, carrying a sheaf of papers, also heading toward Jacob's office.

Around three-thirty, R.L. left for good. He came out of his office, obviously making for the front door. Halfway there, though, he apparently reconsidered and walked back over to where I was sitting.

"Uh, I always leave about this time on Wednesdays," he said. His eyes looked uneasy. You might've thought he was trying to get out of study hall in high school. "I got all my work done," he added. That one sounded familiar. I think I'd tried that one myself to get out of study hall. As I recall, it hadn't worked.

I just looked at R.L. What did he want from me? A hall pass? It certainly wasn't any of my business if he left at *noon,* but R.L. kept standing there, staring at me, as if he expected me to give him my blessing.

"Good for you," I said.

"I let my secretary leave, too. It's one of them, uh, company perks."

I looked over at Jolene, and sure enough, she was getting her stuff together, putting on her sweater, getting ready to go.

"It's OK," R.L. went on. "Uh, nobody minds."

I nodded and smiled. I mean, what was I supposed to say? *I don't mind, either?* I really didn't. In fact, he could take my word for it, I couldn't care less.

R.L., however, was overstating the case a little when

he said *nobody*. Because right away I could guess that there probably *was* somebody who did mind.

Just looking at Priss's face when she came out of her office about an hour later—and saw the empty desk where Jolene had been sitting—told me that I was right on the money. For once, though, Priss tried to cover her irritation. I wasn't sure why. Of course, it *was* almost four-thirty. Maybe by this time, Priss was getting all tantrummed out. Or maybe she, like me, was getting a little concerned about how much punishment her office door could take.

"Oh, that's right," she said to me, her mouth curved in a totally unconvincing smile. "It *is* Wednesday, isn't it?" Priss kind of shuffled the papers she had in her hand—the ones, no doubt, she'd intended to give Jolene to do something with—and then turned to go back into her office.

"Kind of an odd day to get off early, isn't it?" I said. "Wednesday afternoon isn't exactly one of your standard recognized holidays, is it?"

I was just trying to make conversation, that's all. I really didn't care one way or the other, but Priss looked at me as if I were questioning whether they ought to take off on *Christmas,* for God's sake. "R.L. always takes off early on Wednesdays." Priss's voice could've frosted a beer mug. "Anyway, by this time of the day, I generally don't have anything for Jolene to do, anyway." The papers she was holding in her hand sort of made a liar out of her, but I didn't say anything. My eyes did wander to those papers, though, in spite of myself.

Priss gave me a level look. "Look, I'll be in the ladies' room," she said, apparently changing her mind about going back into her office. Nature must call for her real sudden-like. "You don't need to follow me in *there,* do you?" Priss added. "Or do you think someone sinister might be lurking in one of the stalls?"

The answer to that one, of course, was, "I sure hope so." I didn't say that, though. I just gave Priss a look as level as her own.

While Priss was gone, I got up and called Melba on Jolene's phone to see if by any chance the moon had turned blue since this morning, and she'd actually found Rip's papers.

"No, I ain't found 'em." Melba's tone implied that it was a ridiculous thing for me to ask.

I couldn't help wondering if she'd even start to look. Melba is not real good at working without supervision. Come to think of it, she's not real good at working. Period.

Melba must've heard me start to hyperventilate, because she changed the subject real quick. "I did take a message for you, though." She sounded as if this might be cause for celebration.

"You did?" I tried not to sound doubtful.

"Some woman called you." Melba actually sounded proud that she'd gotten this much information.

"Some woman?" I said. I felt like I'd bitten down on that same jalapeño pepper Priss had been chewing on earlier. Because all of Melba's messages are like this. Some woman. A man. This guy. Sometimes I wish she wouldn't even tell me. Other times I think she's doing it on purpose. Just to torture me.

"Yeah," Melba said. "Some woman, all upset."

I gritted my teeth. "Did you happen to get her name, Melba?"

"Nope. I figure if she was all that upset, she'll be sure to call back," Melba said.

Now how can you argue with logic like that?

Melba apparently didn't want to hang around and find out, because she hung up almost as soon as the words were out of her mouth.

Right after that, Priss came back from the ladies' room, disappeared back into her office, and I continued to sit outside Priss's door, feeling guilty for wishing bodily harm to a woman who is the sole support of five kids. When Priss's door opened again, about an hour later, she was carrying a briefcase and her purse. "Guess I'm calling it a day," she said.

What I would call it was a *rotten* day, but I decided that was better left unsaid. I nodded, getting to my feet.

Priss stared at me. "You're not following me *home*, are you?"

I stared back at her. Lord. Not this again. I took a deep breath. "Well, yes, I reckon your dad wants you watched everywhere you happen to be."

That was generally how bodyguarding worked. It didn't seem all that difficult a concept to grasp.

Priss, however, didn't look as if she were grasping it. She dropped her briefcase on the floor. "This is too much. On top of everything else. It's just too much."

I didn't know what she meant by "everything else," but I tried for a conciliatory tone. "Look, Priss, I know you're upset about your dad leaving R.L. in charge of the company and all, but—"

Priss now dropped her purse. She dropped it evidently so she'd have her hand free to jab her finger in my face. Have I mentioned how much I hate that? "Now, YOU LOOK," Priss said. "You don't have any idea how I feel! GOT IT? And I'm telling you right now, you are FIRED! I don't need a bodyguard. I've never needed a bodyguard! I won't have you following me around like some crazy puppy dog!"

Now wait a minute. Hold the phone. She was making it sound as if I *wanted* to be following her around. Like maybe I had some kind of weird crush on her. Oh sure. I'm wildly attracted to the sound of slamming doors. Was she *kidding?* I couldn't help myself. Before I knew it, *my* finger was jabbing in *her* face. "Look, sister, you can't fire me!" I said. "Jacob's the one who hired me, and only HE can fire me!"

For a split second, Priss's mouth went open and shut like a fish out of water. Then, unfortunately, sound returned. "Oh yeah?" she said. "Well, we'll see about THAT!"

She turned and headed down the corridor to Jacob's office. This time I was ready for her. I was on her heels the entire way. In fact, a couple of times I think I could actually have *passed* her.

Inez Evitts was still sitting at her desk. Apparently, if Jacob was still at work at five-thirty, he expected his secretary to be there, too. Inez was typing away, but her silver head jerked up as Priss and I went by.

The second Priss went through Jacob's door, though, she immediately slowed down. In fact, she came to such an abrupt halt, I almost plowed right into her. As it was, I had to sort of veer off to the left to avoid mowing her down.

"Oh dear."

That was all Priss said. A short, mournful "Oh dear."

I was still off-balance, so the first thing I did was look over at Priss. "Why in hell did you stop so—" As soon as I saw Priss's face, though, my voice stopped even more abruptly than she had. Priss was staring transfixed toward Jacob's desk, her eyes wide.

I could tell right that minute that whatever it was that Priss was looking at was not something that would make a rotten day any better. I followed Priss's eyes, my mouth already going dry.

It was Jacob.

The old man was slumped sideways in his desk chair, both arms hanging limp by his side. With his arms askew like that, you could see real clear the dark red bull's eye spreading across the middle of his chest. Not to mention the wooden handle of the knife, sticking out like an arrow right in the middle of the bull's eye.

CHAPTER

5

I reckon, being away from homicide for the last eleven months, I must be out of practice at seeing folks in the condition Jacob was in. Or maybe it's something you never really get used to. Looking at Jacob, I started breathing fast, and for a moment, all I could hear was my own heart sounding like waves crashing on rocks in my ears. I couldn't seem to do anything but stare at the dark red stain spreading across Jacob's shirtfront.

Jacob was staring, too. Sort of. His head had lolled back, and his eyes were open, looking at the ceiling. Unblinking.

I rushed over to the desk, and felt Jacob's throat for a pulse. As soon as I touched him, though, I knew it was hopeless. There were steaks in my refrigerator warmer than Jacob.

I took a long breath. Poor old guy. Jacob definitely would never have won any Mr. Congeniality contests, but he sure didn't deserve this.

Nobody deserved this.

Now that I was this close to him, I could see that, in addition to the red stain on his chest, Jacob had this real nasty place on the right side of his head. Dark red and sticky, it looked like raw meat, matted with Jacob's black hair. It didn't take two seconds to figure out how Jacob had come by this. Lying on the floor, right in back of Jacob's chair, was the bronze statue of the Vandeventer Brown he'd gestured with earlier. Its Mona Lisa smile was now smeared with red. Apparently, in addition to being stabbed, Jacob had been clobbered with his own chicken.

I stared at the old man, swallowing hard. Whoever had killed Jacob had definitely wanted to make sure he stayed dead.

Behind me, Priss cleared her throat. "Is he—is he—" Her voice sounded shaky.

I took a step toward her before I answered. Getting ready to comfort her if maybe she broke into tears, or perhaps to catch her if she fainted. "I'm afraid so," I said. I got ready to move fast if I had to.

As it turned out, moving fast wasn't exactly what was required. In fact, crying and fainting were evidently way down on Priss's list of possible reactions. The reaction she apparently decided to go with was just giving me a hard, level look. She stepped around me, moved closer to the desk and stooped over to peer at Jacob. Dry-eyed. "Are you sure?" she said.

Obviously, the woman was broken up.

I just looked at her. I wasn't exactly the county coroner or anything, but if Jacob wasn't dead, he'd probably be up for an Academy Award this year. "I'm sure."

"Oh dear."

This seemed to be a real versatile phrase for Priss. Useful for a variety of occasions—like discovering your dad's body all the way to finding out he really was positively dead.

I couldn't help it. I kept staring at her. I mean, I've seen folks coming out of *Ghost* who were a lot more upset than Priss here. And *that* was just a movie. "We better get out of here and call the sheriff," I said. "Don't touch a thing."

The last part of what I said—the part about not touching anything—I'm pretty sure Priss didn't hear at all. It was completely drowned out.

Evidently, Inez had taken it upon herself to follow me and Priss into Jacob's office. Maybe she thought Jacob was going to give her a few more letters to type or something. Whatever her reason for being there, Inez must've just caught sight of him and realized that Jacob was probably not going to be dictating anything anytime soon. You could pretty much guess to the split second the exact moment Inez laid eyes on Jacob, because that's when she started screaming.

And screaming.

And screaming.

I was impressed. The woman could, no doubt, find part-time work as a civil defense siren. She'd be particularly good when a tornado is coming, doing that real annoying, pulsating sound that comes and goes. Believe me, you'd have no trouble hearing Inez over a little thing like thunder.

"Inez," I said during one of her semi-lulls, "calm down now. Let's get on out of here."

Apparently, Inez didn't hear a word I said. Which wasn't hard for me to believe. I couldn't hear me, either.

For a woman in her fifties, Inez had remarkable staying power. Every time she'd start to calm down, sort of sagging against the back wall of Jacob's office, she'd glance back over at Jacob and get inspired all over again. It was amazing. The last time I heard somebody holler that loud for that long without taking a breath, Claudzilla had just found out she was over her MasterCard limit.

"Come on, Inez," I said. I started trying to get her to move out of there, but it was like trying to push a statue through the door. Her legs wouldn't work. "Inez," I said, taking her elbow, "listen to me, you don't need to be in here. *Let's go.*"

For an answer, Inez started up her civil defense siren again.

Priss evidently wasn't anywhere near as impressed with Inez's remarkable ability as I was. This time when Inez revved up, Priss turned to her and shouted, "Oh, will you SHUT UP!"

Apparently, in times of stress, Priss could not be counted on to be a calming influence.

Inez's eyes went white all around, and her siren went into even higher gear.

I was starting to be afraid my hearing was going to be affected. There was every chance, too, that my insurance wouldn't cover it. Hearing loss on account of standing too close to a hysterical woman, I'm pretty sure, isn't on my policy. "Inez, really," I yelled. "Let's get OUT OF HERE!" I turned up my own volume as Inez increased hers. I had Inez turned around by then and pointed toward the door. I thought we were making real progress, too, but Priss apparently didn't have any patience left. If, indeed, she'd had any to begin with.

"Inez!" Priss shouted. "INEZ! Hey!" All this hollering sounds a lot less kind than it was. Inez's siren was at its peak at that particular time, and Priss and I had to shout or Inez probably would never have heard either one of us. "INEZ," Priss yelled, "if you don't shut up, I'm going to have to hit you! I MEAN IT!"

Now, if *this* sounds less than kind, it's because it was. I got the distinct impression that if indeed Priss did have to hit Inez, Priss might enjoy it. Particularly when—to show Inez she meant business—Priss doubled up her fist right in front of Inez's pointy nose.

This was apparently the kind of argument that got Inez's attention. Her siren tapered off. Instead, she whimpered.

Inez's legs seemed to in working order after that, so I herded her and Priss out of the room and, using the phone on Inez's desk, called up Vergil. With Inez's siren no longer sounding, it seemed strangely quiet as I dialed.

Vergil Minrath, the town sheriff, used to be my dad's best friend. Starting back when they were kids and all through high school. I reckon they'd still be best friends today if my dad hadn't died a little over nine years ago. He died of a heart attack the year after my mom died of cancer. I've always believed that Dad just couldn't bear to live without her.

With both my parents gone now—and being as how I can't rightly remember a time in my life when I didn't know Vergil—I sort of view Vergil as family these days. Near-family, anyway.

Vergil took my news with the kind of sympathetic support you'd expect from near-family. "Oh shit," I believe, was his first reaction. "*This* is a fine kettle of fish," Vergil went on. "Haskell, how in hell did you let a thing like this happen?" Vergil always sounds like he just got back from a funeral. This time, though, he managed to sound real sad and real angry all at the same time.

"Vergil," I said, "I didn't *let* it happen. Jacob got himself murdered without any help at all from me."

Vergil grunted. "Well, this is awful. Oh yeah. Lordy mercy, this is a crying shame."

Vergil seemed to have Priss beat bad in the grief department. I was pretty sure, though, that it wasn't Jacob's passing that was upsetting Vergil so much. I've heard Vergil frequently refer to Jacob Vandeventer using the same less-than-fond nickname my dad used to use. *Asshole*. As a matter of fact, as I recall, when Vergil heard about Jacob landing the Chick Delish account, Vergil told me mournfully, "You know, it could've happened to a nicer guy."

No, I was pretty sure it wasn't Jacob's *death* that had Vergil all in a dither. It was Jacob's *murder*. Vergil takes crime real personal. Particularly crime committed in his jurisdiction. I think Vergil sincerely believes that the culprits are just doing these things to spite him.

"This is just terrible, just terrible—" Vergil was saying.

I broke in. "Vergil, can you get right over here?"

Vergil acted as if he hadn't even heard me. "I just cain't believe there's been another murder. *Right after* the other one. I ain't been doing nothing lately 'cept investigating homicides!"

Now, this was a slight exaggeration. The only murder Vergil had investigated lately was the unfortunate demise of Eunice Krebbs's grandmother, which I believe

I mentioned earlier. That particular murder happened last March. Thirteen months ago.

Still, in a town the size of Pigeon Fork, you don't get many homicides. So, I reckon, counting Grammy, this made two whole murders in less than a year and a half. And if you included Grammy's pets, that made *four* murders. For Pigeon Fork, this was a crime wave.

Vergil was still muttering to himself on the phone. "Lordy, Lordy, this is just a real shock, a real shock." He seemed to remember then that I was still on the other end, because he took a deep, ragged breath and said, his tone tragic, "OK, I'll be right out there, Haskell. Don't you be touching nothing, you hear? *Nothing.*"

Vergil is always doing this. Talking to me as if I were still about six years old. *Instructing* me. I expect him to start teaching me my ABCs any minute. "You mean I shouldn't touch a thing?" I said. "Not anything? Really?"

Vergil evidently was too upset to reply. He hung up on me.

While I was waiting for him to show up, I decided this would be a real good time for me to go back into Jacob's office and have another look-see. I owed Jacob that much. The old man may not have actually hired me to look into his own murder, but I was pretty sure that—as penny-pinching as he was—Jacob would really appreciate getting two jobs for the price of one. It was the least I could do for the old guy.

I was going to have to do my looking around real quick, though, before Vergil got there. Even if Vergil *is* near-family, lately he's gotten himself into a real snit about me horning into his investigations. Seems he's got this dumb idea that I think I'm some big-shot ex-homicide detective from the Big City trying to show him how to do his job. The last time we worked together—and I got threatening notes and my truck tires were slashed and I was almost killed, along with my dog—Vergil took it real bad. He thought I was grabbing all the glory. For a while there, I thought I might have to make a couple of attempts on Vergil's life just to even things up.

He's calmed down some since then, but you can tell Vergil's nose is still a little out of joint. So I knew, sure as anything, once Vergil got there, I wouldn't be allowed back inside Jacob's office until the yellow caution tape came down. Maybe not even then.

Priss had gone and found Inez a Coke, and she was sitting in the chair next to Inez's desk, making sure Inez drank it. "The only reason I said all that was to get you to calm down," Priss was saying, nodding her dark head for emphasis. "You *were* hysterical, you know."

Seated behind her desk, Inez drank the Coke, dabbed at her pointy nose with a Kleenex, and nodded. But, I noticed, the silver-haired woman never took her eyes off Priss. As if maybe Inez were afraid that any minute Priss might haul off and smack her anyway. Just for fun.

When I went into Jacob's office, I carefully closed the door behind me. I sure didn't want Inez getting inspired again.

Poor Jacob was just as we'd left him, of course. I stared at the old man for a second. Without his bird's nest eyebrows all jammed together in a frown, he sure didn't look natural. In fact, in death Jacob looked to be in a better mood than I'd ever seen him.

I started walking around the room. Walking on the burgundy plush carpet was just like walking on velvet. There were only two doors cut into the mahogany paneling—the one I'd just walked through and one on my right that I found opened into a tiny kitchen. Complete with a sink, a refrigerator, and a stove. And one of them butcher block things for holding knives. It was sitting right next to the sink, on the imitation-marble Formica cabinet top. One of the slots in the butcher block was empty. Apparently, the killer had not only hit Jacob with his own chicken, he'd also stabbed Jacob with his own knife.

That seemed real mean.

Of course, if Jacob hadn't been the victim, he probably would've found something to admire here. Jacob

probably would've thought it was a real good idea on
the murder's part not to go to all the extra expense of
buying a weapon. Which would probably just be used
once and then locked up in an evidence room somewhere. Nope, the murderer had looked around and used
whatever was at hand. Sort of like recycling. Jacob, no
doubt, would've been downright pleased that the murderer was so frugal.

If, of course, he himself had not been the victim. That
little fact might've changed Jacob's opinion some.

I headed out of the kitchen, back into Jacob's office.
There were two long, narrow windows in back of Jacob's desk, and there had been one small window in the
kitchen. All the windows, however, had been painted
shut. None showed any signs of tampering.

It sure looked like whoever had come in here and
given Jacob a double dose of death had to have walked
right by Inez. If, in fact, Inez had been at her desk at the
time. I remembered that, on my way here, I'd passed a
door in the long corridor leading to Jacob's office. That
door opened directly to the outside of the building, but
even if you came in that, you'd still have to walk by
Inez to get into Jacob's office. I went back outside, wondering if Inez felt up to answering some questions.

The Coke must've been a good idea, because Inez
was looking normal again. Actually, she was looking a
little better than normal. Apparently, seeing a dead body
was just the thing to put a little color in her pale, thin
cheeks.

I reckon, though, that was not the sort of beauty tip
she'd recommend to her friends.

Priss was on the phone when I walked out, apparently
notifying Jacob's next of kin. I stopped, listening, wondering who it was that Priss was talking to with a voice
that could've sliced through barbed wire. I had a couple
of good guesses. Sure enough, it turned out to be one
of them. "—happened sometime this afternoon," Priss
was saying through clenched teeth. There was a pause,
and then Priss added, "Look, Willadette, I don't know

anything about the will. You'll have to talk to Alton Gabbard about that."

She also added, "—you damn bitch," but only Inez and I heard that. Priss said that part right after she hung up the phone.

I would've expected Inez to look shocked. It didn't seem likely that a woman who wouldn't call a man she'd just met by his first name would consider it socially acceptable to call recently bereaved widows ugly names, but I could tell Inez was trying not to smile. She pressed her thin lips into an even thinner line, while the look she gave Priss was clearly one of approval.

Priss looked at me as if daring me to say something.

I didn't say a word. Anything she had to say to her stepmother certainly wasn't any of my business. Pulling up a chair, I started questioning Inez. I didn't particularly want to question her in front of Priss, but it didn't look as if I had much choice. I wasn't about to let Priss out of my sight. I was still employed as Priss's bodyguard for the next two days, whether my employer was dead or not.

The first thing I asked Inez was if she'd been away from her desk for any extended length of time. It was apparently a bad way to start things off, because Inez looked as if I'd accused her of stealing from the payroll. She drew herself up, reached over, and picked up a pencil off her desk. "Mr. Blevins," Inez said, pointing the pencil at me, "I *pride* myself on my efficiency. I never leave my desk. *Never.*"

For emphasis, Inez stuck the pencil into her bun. I stared at her, wondering if she was too rattled to realize what she'd just done. Or was that where she kept her pencils these days? "Besides, if Mr. Vandeventer ever came out of his office and I wasn't at my desk," Inez went on, "why, I know he'd fire me. Without batting an eye." Having said this, Inez's own eyes immediately widened. Apparently, for a second there, Inez had forgotten that Jacob wasn't in any condition anymore to fire anybody. Batting his eyes was pretty much out of the question, too. Inez's thin hand went to her mouth, as if she'd just let a curse word slip. She looked around, her small hazel eyes confused. "Um, I don't mean, that he was—well, that he was—um—not a nice person."

Inez evidently was one of those folks who believed you should never speak ill of the dead, even if what you had to say was the truth.

"You were here all afternoon?"

Inez looked even more insulted. "Of course I was. Except for my fifteen-minute break. That one I'm allowed to take by law, you know. So it's OK."

I stared at her. This woman actually believed that she needed a good excuse to leave her desk. She really did. I could only imagine how Melba would feel about Inez's attitude. Melba would, no doubt, think Inez was a disgrace to her profession.

Inez's account of the events of the afternoon pretty much matched my own recollection. Around two o'clock, about a half-hour after Jacob had summoned R.L. and Priss into his office, R.L. returned and met with Jacob again. "He was only in there about fifteen minutes, though," Inez said.

"Did you hear anything that was said?"

Inez looked affronted again. Apparently, suggesting that she eavesdropped was as bad as suggesting she occasionally left her desk. "Why, of course not, Mr. Blevins. A good secretary *never* listens in." She pulled the pencil out of her bun, stared at it, and put it back in again. "Besides, the door was closed." It seemed to occur to Inez then what all this questioning was getting at, because she added real quick, "But, um, I could hear them *both* in there. I mean, um, I couldn't actually make out what they were saying, but I could hear them both talking."

I nodded, and Inez hurried on, glancing over at Priss anxiously. "After R.L. left, Jolene arrived with the daily status report. Just like always."

"The daily status report?"

I immediately wished I hadn't said anything, because Inez launched into a detailed explanation of how all the broiler sales are kept track of on this report. And how it's kept up to date every day. And how it plots sales and compares it to the same time last year and all. Inez actually talked about it as if it were really interesting, like maybe it was an epic novel or something, chronicling the comings and goings of several generations of chickens. The *Forsyte Saga* of the poultry world.

I stared at Inez. This woman must lead a very sheltered life.

I interrupted her. "And how long would you say Jolene was in there?"

Oddly enough, Inez reddened and looked away. "Oh, only a very few, *few* minutes." Her eyes were now on her desk. "Um, none of the women ever stayed in Jacob's office very long, because he was a—a little too *familiar.*" This last word Inez whispered. Her face now looked as if she'd applied a bright red blush all over it. Pointy nose and pointy chin, too.

I must've looked sort of blank, because Inez looked irritated. Like she'd just told her life secrets to somebody who didn't understand the language.

"Jacob Vandeventer was a bit too *familiar with the ladies.*" Her thin cheeks were very red. "If you get what I mean."

Inez's tone implied that she thought there was every possibility I wouldn't get it this time, either. But I got it, all right. What Inez was telling me was that Jacob was your basic dirty old man.

I glanced over at Priss. This didn't seem to be news to her. She met my eyes with a flat gray gaze. As if to say, see, *the man was slime.*

I stared back at her. The man, after all, was *dead.* And Jacob *was* her own father. Even slime deserves some respect, doesn't it?

No one would ever confuse Priss with one of the children on "Father Knows Best." But then again, I reckon you'd never confuse Jacob with Robert Young, either.

Inez was leaning toward me now, her voice confidential. "Why do you think I stopped wearing makeup?" She lifted an unplucked eyebrow as if she expected me to answer.

The obvious answer, of course, was: Because you decided it was hopeless? I didn't say a word, though. Not a word.

Fortunately, Inez didn't seem to have any idea what I was thinking. "Because it wasn't safe to look good around that man!" she said, answering her own question. "It really wasn't!"

For a second I didn't say anything. Was Inez actually suggesting that if she happened to put on a little mascara and some lipstick, it might have driven Jacob wild? Staring at Inez's long, thin face, into her small hazel eyes, I decided that Inez was probably wrong about this. I also decided that this was something I probably didn't want to pursue any further. "You didn't hear any voices in there when Jolene was leaving, did you?"

Thank goodness, Inez didn't seem to notice I'd changed the subject. "Matter of fact, I did hear Jacob's voice when Jolene was in there. I, um, couldn't make out what he was saying, but I heard him, all right. And after that, I went on my break, right around three."

It would appear then if Inez were telling the truth, Jacob had been very much alive right up until three.

Inez was taking a long sip of her Coke now, and acting as if that was all she intended to say. Obviously, however, she'd left out a major chunk of the afternoon. Like, for example, the two and a half hours from three until Priss and I walked in and found Jacob. I waited.

Inez stared back at me.

"And after three, when you got back from your break?"

Inez glanced toward Priss. "Well, um—"

For a woman who'd demonstrated so much energy in the screaming department, Inez seemed to have slipped into low gear. "Yes?" I prodded.

"Um—" Inez said, her eyes still on Priss.

"Yes?"

"Um—" Inez repeated.

I was starting to think it might be easier to talk to Jacob. "Look, Inez, did anybody else come by this afternoon?"

Inez's blush deepened. "Well, um, just one person.
But it really doesn't mean anything. She wouldn't hurt
a fly—"

OK. OK. I'd keep that in mind. I leaned forward.
"*Who* wouldn't hurt a fly?"

Inez looked miserable. "Ruby."

The minute Inez said the name, Priss gasped. "*Mama?*
Mama was here this afternoon?"

This was getting interesting. The woman Jacob had
dumped after umpteen years of marriage? *Ruby Vandeventer* had dropped by this afternoon? Now, maybe I
was jumping to conclusions, but it seemed to me that
Inez was probably right. Ruby wouldn't hurt a fly. But
from what I'd heard around Pigeon Fork, Ruby just
might not hesitate to give Jacob a merry send-off with
the very chicken she'd given him for Christmas.

What I was thinking must've been mirrored in my
face, because both Inez and Priss started talking at once.

"Now, wait a minute, Haskell, Mama *couldn't* do a
thing like this—"

"Ruby was only in there a few minutes, Mr. Blevins," Inez said. "Just a very few minutes. Hardly any
time at all."

It was like listening to a stereo. With each speaker on
a different station. I held up my hand. "Look, I'm not
making any accusations here. I just want to know when
she came by. That's all."

Inez now looked at her lap. "A little after four
o'clock," she said real low. "But I tell you, I've been
friends with Ruby for thirty years, and she's the sweetest, the nicest, the kindest person you'd ever want to
meet."

I'm sure a lot of his friends had similar things to say
about Ted Bundy. I nodded anyway, just like I believed
every word. "You didn't happen to hear anything of
what was said when Ruby was in Jacob's office, did
you?"

Inez looked as if I'd slapped her. Her eyes, oddly
enough, sort of slid toward the *Secretarial Handbook*
on her desk. As if maybe she could find the answer on

how to handle this particular office situation in that hefty volume. For a second I thought Inez might actually reach for it. Like she truly expected to find, sandwiched in between "Proper Phone Etiquette" and "Dealing with Business Correspondence," a chapter on "How to Answer Questions After Your Boss's Murder." Sure. This sort of thing had to come up all the time.

Inez finally stopped staring at the *Secretarial Handbook,* audibly sighed, and looked back over at me. "Well—" she said.

"Yes?" I said.

"Um—"

Oh no. Not this again. I was starting to wish Priss *had* belted Inez one earlier. I leaned forward again, trying to sound soothing. "Look, Inez, you're going to have to tell what you know to somebody. Either here or down at the sheriff's office."

I probably shouldn't have told her that. Obviously rattled, Inez reached for the pencil in her bun again, stared at it just like before, but this time when she tried to put the pencil back where she'd gotten it, her aim must've been a little off. She almost jabbed the thing in her ear.

I just looked at her, trying to hold my face perfectly still. No reaction at all. Like maybe I didn't notice what she'd done.

Having finally put the pencil back in her bun with her hearing still intact, Inez said, "Mr. Blevins, I—I couldn't possibly go down to the sheriff's office. There's nothing but the worst sort of people down there. Drunks. And—and riffraff."

I sincerely hoped she didn't say anything like this in front of Vergil. It would definitely hurt his feelings. My luck, he'd think I put her up to it.

Inez gave one final glance over at Priss and then sighed. "I—um—did hear one teeny, tiny, little thing."

"Yes?" I thought I sounded real patient under the circumstances.

"Just as Ruby went into Jacob's office, I heard her say, 'I'm not going to let you get away with this!'"

Priss turned pale. "That doesn't mean anything, Haskell. It really doesn't mean a thing!"

Of course it didn't. Like maybe a mushroom cloud doesn't mean a bomb just went off. Right.

I had another question for Inez. "What did Jacob say after Ruby said that?"

Inez gave her *Secretarial Handbook* another anxious glance, a "Where are you when I really need you?" look in her eyes. Then, looking back over at me, she said, "Well, that's—um—just the thing. I didn't actually hear Jacob say anything while Ruby was in there."

I stared at her. "Nothing?"

Inez looked defensive. "Well, Ruby closed the door right after she went in. And, um, I wasn't really listening, anyway."

I didn't say anything, but I knew right then she was lying. The ex-wife comes stomping into her boss's office, and Inez doesn't even *try* to listen? Did Inez expect me to believe that? Why, Melba would've been lying flat on the floor, her ear pressed against the crack under the door. Folks would've had to step over her to get in and out.

Inez looked uncomfortably aware of how things were now looking for her friend Ruby. "Maybe Jacob was talking real low? And that's why I didn't hear him?"

And maybe—just maybe—Jacob wasn't talking at all. At least, not after his ex-wife picked up that chicken.

CHAPTER
6

Inez looked real upset. "Just because I didn't hear Jacob talking to Ruby doesn't mean anything."

Priss looked outraged. "Why, the very idea, that you'd even think for a minute that my mother—of all people—honestly, Haskell, you've got to meet her. Then you'd know that she could never, ever—"

Meeting Ruby sounded like a real good idea. One I definitely intended to take Priss up on.

While Priss was going on about her mom, Inez's face was brightening. As if she'd just thought of a totally convincing argument. "Mr. Blevins," she said, interrupting Priss in her eagerness, "Ruby wasn't in there any time. I don't think she had the time to—to—" Apparently, Inez could not bring herself to describe what exactly had been done to Jacob. Particularly without the help of the *Secretarial Handbook*. Inez's voice trailed off.

I just looked at Inez. How long does it take to hit somebody with a chicken and stick a knife into him? I can't say I've actually timed such a thing, but it doesn't seem like a whole lot of minutes had to go by to get the deed done.

Inez evidently realized that her argument wasn't ex-

78

actly holding water, because she swallowed real quick and hurried on. "And, um, when Ruby came out, she didn't look upset. At least, not much."

I gave Inez a look. *Not much?* "Exactly how upset was she?" I tried to make my tone conversational, but I guess I didn't do too good a job of it. Priss's gray eyes met mine. They didn't look happy.

Inez waved a thin hand in the air. "Well, I guess Ruby *was* a teeny bit shaky. And a little nervous-acting. But she had a good reason."

I agreed. Killing an ex-husband could get a person real rattled.

Inez's eyes widened as she realized what she'd just said. She hurried to explain. "No, um, what I mean is that Ruby was all flustered because she couldn't find her car keys."

Oh, well, *that* explained it. Of course. The last time I lost my own car keys, I shook like a leaf. Doesn't everybody?

Inez was nodding her pointed face up and down emphatically. "And I know for sure she really did lose them because Ruby stood there for a while, right in front of my desk, rummaging through her coat pockets and her purse, looking for them." Inez raised an eyebrow, as if to say, See?

I can't say I was bowled over by Inez's logic. Just because Ruby had actually gone through the motions of looking for her car keys didn't necessarily mean they were really missing. It stood to reason that if you were going to fake losing your keys, you really ought to do it up big and actually *look* for them.

Inez went on, looking really confident now. "Finally, Ruby decided she must've locked them in her car. So I got her a coat hanger, and we both headed out to the side parking lot."

It was Priss's turn to look confident now. "—and there they were, locked in Mama's car?" she finished for Inez.

Inez looked away. "Well, no, not exactly. Once we

79

got out to the parking lot, Ruby found her keys in one of the side pockets of her skirt.''

Priss's face fell. Evidently, she was thinking what I was thinking. That this didn't look good. In fact, what it looked like was that there was every chance Ruby had made up the story about the missing keys. Either to cover up why she suddenly looked so flustered or just to get Inez away from her desk for a few minutes. So it would look as if *anybody* could've come in and gone into Jacob's office without being seen.

I was staring at Inez. "Didn't you find that odd? Her finding her keys all of a sudden like that?"

Inez looked at me as if I were speaking a foreign language. "For Ruby? Of course not! Maybe for someone else, but Ruby, well, she's always forgetting things." Inez leaned toward me, lowering her voice. "Mr. Blevins, Ruby's a little—" Here Inez paused, glancing over at Priss, as if reluctant to say something bad about Ruby in front of her daughter. "Ruby's a little, um, scatter-brained. She's a—um—she's a—"

I think the phrase Inez was looking for was *total ditz*. Inez apparently gave up trying to think of a complimentary way to say it. Her voice trailed off again.

Priss, surprisingly enough, didn't look at all offended. Apparently, her mother's reputation as the town ditz must've been common knowledge. In fact, while Inez was talking, Priss's own face had brightened a little. "That's right, Haskell," she said, her own voice as eager as Inez's had been. "Why, Mama could never actually *plan* something like this. Lord, if Mama ever did want to commit murder, she's the sort who'd forget the murder weapon!" Her voice, believe it or not, sounded fond. As if she were recounting some cute idiosyncrasy.

I didn't say anything, but this particular cute idiosyncrasy *did* seem to be in keeping with this particular crime. If you'd forgotten to bring your own weapon, a bronze chicken and a borrowed butcher knife might come in real handy.

It turned out I didn't have to say anything, because

all this seemed to dawn on Priss almost as soon as she spoke. Her smile slowly faded.

There was a short, uncomfortable silence which was interrupted by a voice I immediately recognized.

The voice sounded like static in the distance. Static that was moving rapidly down the corridor toward us. "Well, I don't care what you say," the voice was saying. "I think we deserve some kind of explanation. I mean, he was paid good money, and now *this!*"

Following in the wake of this static was R.L., still in the same gray pin-striped suit he'd worn to work that day. He shambled along in back of Lizbeth, not looking at any of us.

Lizbeth was wearing yet another mink coat, this time a dark brown calf-length one, thrown over a burgundy running suit. Either Lizbeth had dressed in a hurry, or she was starting a whole new look in leisure wear. She was moving fairly fast toward us, her Reeboks slapping the hardwood floor rhythmically.

Even in sneakers, Lizbeth was still real tall, and being as how I was sitting down, she looked like a giant of a woman hurtling toward us. I hurriedly got to my feet, watching her uneasily.

Once again, not a concrete hair on Lizbeth's head moved. Apparently, she was still heading into that invisible wind she'd been heading into earlier. With her hair swept back from her face like that, you couldn't miss her eyes. They had narrowed into wide blue slits. "So— what do you have to say for yourself *now?*"

Lizbeth's slits appeared to be directed at me.

I stared back at her, not quite sure what she meant. Did she think I had something to do with Jacob's death? Was I supposed to break down and confess? I scrambled in my mind for a reply, but Lizbeth evidently wasn't about to wait to hear what I had to say for myself, anyway. "Weren't you hired to be a bodyguard?" There was a "Queen Elizabeth questioning the Palace Guard" tone to Lizbeth's voice.

"Well, sure," I said, "but I was supposed to be body-guarding Priss here." I glanced pointedly over at Priss.

As everybody could plainly see, Priss was perfectly fine. So what exactly was Lizbeth's point?

Lizbeth wasted no time at all cluing me in. "Did you really think that Jacob meant for you to guard Priss and let HIM get killed?"

That was a cheap shot. "Just a cotton-picking minute," I said. "I had no idea that Jacob was in any danger, or I certainly—"

Lizbeth continued the tradition she'd started earlier and interrupted. "And *you* call yourself a bodyguard?" She snorted. "Come to think of it, I guess you should call yourself that. Because now you've sure got yourself a *body* to guard!" Lizbeth glanced around at the others, smirking at her little joke.

That did it. I took a step closer. "Look," I said, "I didn't *let* anything happen to Jacob. I spent all day keeping an eye on Priss here—"

"—while Jacob was getting himself killed," Lizbeth finished for me.

I almost winced. I realized right then why I was being so defensive. It was because I really did feel awful about what had happened to Jacob. Practically under my nose. Maybe it was true that I hadn't been hired to guard *him*, but Lizbeth was right. If Jacob had known somebody was planning on murdering him, he no doubt would've included that in my job description. My voice was a little weaker than I would've liked when I said, "Look, Lizbeth, I was doing what Jacob told me—"

Lizbeth didn't wait for me to finish. Dismissing me with a contemptuous toss of her concrete, she turned to Inez. "And I suppose *you're* going to tell me that Jacob never did get around to signing his new will?"

Inez, at that moment, looked a whole lot like I suppose the guy in the *Titanic* public relations office must have, the day after the boat went down. She sank down a little lower behind her desk and began to fiddle with her grape earrings. "Well—" Inez said.

"Well what?" Lizbeth's voice was not gentle.

"Well, um, Mr. Vandeventer's appointment with Mr. Gabbard wasn't until tomorrow."

Inez's voice was very low, but apparently Lizbeth didn't miss a word. Lizbeth's face flushed deep red.

"Um, I did have all the papers typed." Inez's point evidently was that *she* wasn't to blame. She'd done all she could to get the new will signed.

Lizbeth didn't look at all moved by this obvious display of efficiency on Inez's part. She gave Inez a dark look, and wheeled on R.L. "See?" Lizbeth said. "What did I tell you? I knew it! I knew it!" For a minute there, I was sure Lizbeth was going to stomp her foot. "Damn!" she said, pouting. "Now everything stays just like it is! Damn! Damn! Damn!"

Lizbeth's slits now turned toward Jacob's office. "Are you sure he's really dead? Maybe he just *looks* dead."

I stared at her. If Jacob was just doing an impression of dead, the man was a comic genius.

Lizbeth took a step toward Jacob's office. For a split second I had an almost overpowering impulse to let Lizbeth barge on in there and see Jacob's comic genius for herself, but at the last second I thought better of it. Even Lizbeth didn't deserve that. Besides, she probably had a civil defense siren that could outdo Inez's. I stepped in front of her. "You don't want to go in there," I said.

Lizbeth stared at me. For at least thirty seconds. Then, apparently making up her mind, she gave her concrete another toss and turned to R.L. "OK, R.L., *you* go in there and check Jacob out. Maybe Haskell doesn't know how to tell if somebody's dead any better than he knows how to bodyguard."

Now *that* stung. I immediately started rethinking my decision not to let Lizbeth go on past me.

R.L., however, looked a lot more stung than me. In fact, the last time I think I'd seen this particular expression on R.L.'s face was back in high school, when the Pigeon Fork football coach sent him in to block the biggest linebacker in Crayton County. R.L. stared open-mouthed at Lizbeth, the blood slowly draining out of his handsome face. "Now, honey, I don't know any more about dead folks than Haskell here." R.L.'s voice was pleading. "Haskell here is the—the *professional*."

I think R.L. had me confused with the coroner, but I decided that this might not be a good time to point out what my duties as a private detective usually entailed.

Lizbeth gave R.L. a look of pure contempt. "Nonsense! What kind of man are you? You go on in there and check Jacob out! Who knows, maybe Jacob can be CPR'd back to life. I've seen them do it on TV all the time. I mean, it might not work for permanent, but all we need is a couple of seconds. So Jacob could sign the will—"

R.L. looked like he was the one who needed CPR. He glanced anxiously toward the door to Jacob's office and then turned back to me. "You're pretty sure, aren't you, Haskell?"

Somehow, I knew R.L. was ready to take my word for it. I nodded. If Jacob wasn't dead, he now held the world's record for holding your breath. "I'm real sure, R.L. I'm sorry."

R.L. didn't look sorry. In fact, he looked relieved. Turning to Lizbeth, he said, "See?"

Lizbeth looked disgusted. "No, I don't see, and *you* don't see, either! Now you get your butt in there and—"

I decided I'd better help R.L. out before Lizbeth shoved him bodily into Jacob's office. "We're not supposed to go in there anyway," I said. "Sheriff Minrath told me to keep everybody out of the office. So's we don't touch anything. He was real particular about that."

This was a slight exaggeration of what Vergil had actually said, but the look on R.L.'s face told me I'd done the right thing. For a second I thought R.L. might drop to his knees and kiss my feet.

Lizbeth, on the other hand, looked as if she might want to find out if the kind of wounds Jacob had sustained were really life-threatening. By trying them out on me.

I decided I'd better distract her. "While we're all standing around, waiting for the sheriff to get here, I've got some questions. Do you all happen to know of anyone who hated Jacob enough to want him dead?"

Lizbeth looked at me as if I'd just asked if she knew anybody who didn't like Hitler. She gave her concrete hair yet another contemptuous toss. "Are you kidding?" she said. "If you've got a couple of hours, we could give you their names."

Priss nodded in agreement. "Jacob Vandeventer didn't exactly know how to win friends and influence people."

I glanced toward the closed door to Jacob's office. The old man's eulogy was evidently going to be a real piece of creative writing. "Well," I went on, "do you all know of anyone who had anything to gain if something happened to Jacob?"

I was looking at Lizbeth, but it was R.L. who answered. "Nope. Nobody," he said.

Lizbeth gave R.L. a look that could've, if not killed, then at least maimed. I couldn't tell if it was because she was angry that he'd jumped in and answered for her, or if she was still irritated over his reluctance to take a look at Jacob. "Nonsense!" Lizbeth said. "That little money-grabbing tramp had a *lot* to gain."

I didn't have to ask Lizbeth who it was she was talking about. In fact, I don't think anybody in the room had any doubt as to the identity of the particular money-grubbing tramp Lizbeth was referring to.

"I mean," Lizbeth went on, waving a manicured hand in the air, "*now* Willadette gets the money, and she doesn't have to put up with Jacob anymore. If *that* isn't a motive for murder, nothing is."

Lizbeth had a point. She wasn't through yet, though. Lizbeth now directed a lethal look at Priss. "And let's not forget Priss here. Lord knows, Jacob's dying isn't the worst thing in the world to happen to *her*."

Priss stood up. "What exactly are you trying to say, Lizbeth?"

Lizbeth's tone was spiteful. "I'm not *trying* to say anything. I'm outright saying it—" Lizbeth went on, explaining in a voice louder than necessary that since Jacob had not been able to change his will—and now would never be able to change it—Jacob's death clearly benefited Priss. "Because *now* you get to keep as big a share of Vandeventer Poultry as R.L." Lizbeth's look grew even nastier. "In fact, Priss, I bet deep down you're really tickled pink about this, aren't you?"

I noticed, while Lizbeth was going on, that Priss's gray eyes had started doing their molten lava routine again. Now Priss took a step toward Lizbeth, clenching her fists.

I stepped in front of Priss. "Wait a minute now," I said.

I don't know what I thought I was going to do. I may have outweighed both women, but I believe I've already mentioned that Lizbeth was nearly as tall as I. And though Priss was several inches shorter, she'd already proved she was in better physical shape during our earlier workouts, running down the hall. So I'm not at all sure that I could've stopped them from fighting if they had their minds set on it. Fortunately, as it turned out, it didn't come to that. Right at that moment, sirens started sounding out front. At the sound, Priss blinked a couple of times and turned away.

I breathed a sigh of relief. I don't know how I would've explained it to Vergil if, right about the time he came walking down the hall, Priss and Lizbeth were rolling on the floor, trying to scratch each other's eyes out.

You could hear Vergil and his entourage outside real plain, tires squealing as they all screeched to a stop. There must've been at least ten cars. It sounded as if every car that had a siren was using it. I wasn't quite sure why they were making all that ruckus. There wasn't exactly any big rush now, being as how Jacob wasn't going anywhere. I suspected, however, that the sirens were Vergil's idea. If he hadn't been able to prevent this murder, then he sure as hell was going to make sure that everybody—including the murderer—knew that Vergil Minrath was on the case.

And that he was pissed.

Fury and grief seemed to be warring in Vergil's face

as he came walking down the long corridor to where we stood. In his crisply pressed tan sheriff's uniform, Vergil would've looked downright dapper, if it hadn't been for the fairly good-sized gut hanging over his belt buckle. Instead of looking dapper, Vergil looked more like he'd fought the Potato Chip Wars and lost.

By the time he'd gotten up to us, it was grief that seemed to have won out in Vergil's face. This wasn't exactly a new look for Vergil. In fact, Vergil always looks as if somebody he cared about has just died. Because he always looks like this, there aren't many times when the expression on Vergil's face seems appropriate. This time, though, he was right on target.

Vergil's tanned face is crisscrossed with spider web lines, but they deepen the sadder he gets. That afternoon, as he walked toward us, the lines at the sides of Vergil's mouth looked like canyons. Vergil's thinning salt-and-pepper hair was real messed up, too, like maybe he'd dragged his hand through it about a million times on his way here. "Lord, Lord, this is awful," he said by way of a greeting. "Just awful."

Nobody argued with him.

Watching Vergil and the guys from the crime lab and the coroner and Vergil's deputies swarming all over Jacob's office like ants at a picnic brought back memories for me. I can't say it brought back *happy* memories, but it sure made me remember once again why it was that I'd up and decided to move back to Pigeon Fork not quite a year ago. Not that I've ever really forgotten, of course. After eight years of seeing folks at their worst, I reckon I got pretty sick of the whole scene. When you're working homicide, you don't run into very many really nice folks.

And you get real tired of seeing folks in the condition poor Jacob was in.

I reckon it wasn't that hard of a decision to come back home and open up my own detective agency, just like I'd been dreaming about for years.

Of course, today wasn't exactly like old times. For one thing, just like I'd expected, Vergil wouldn't let me go back into Jacob's office again. For another, this time it wasn't me asking the questions, it was Vergil asking me. "You were here?" he said. "Right in the building when this happened?"

We were sitting at Inez's desk, Vergil having commandeered it for questioning. Vergil had opened up a small notepad and was scratching away with a Bic pen. I knew very well that Vergil already knew the answer to his question, but I said it anyway. "That's right. I was down the hall, sitting out in front of Priss's office."

"Acting as a *bodyguard?*" Vergil added. There was disbelief in his tone.

I stared at him. Vergil evidently wasn't going to be doing a thing to make me feel any better about all this. Matter of fact, I got the feeling that Vergil just might be enjoying my discomfort some. Oh, he still looked mournful and all, but there was a gleam in his sad eyes that hadn't been there when he first walked up to us.

"Yeah, Vergil," I said. "I was acting as a bodyguard. To *Priss.*" I emphasized that last word.

Vergil didn't look at all impressed. "A *bodyguard*, you say?" he repeated.

"Right." I gritted my teeth.

It didn't help any to hear Lizbeth right at that very moment. Vergil had moved all the family members and Inez out into the corridor, to wait for their turn to be questioned. He'd stationed one of his deputies at the far end of the hall, and another one right next to the side door in the middle of the hall so's nobody would even think of trying to leave. Vergil's two deputies were two guys you didn't much want to argue with, either—the Gunterman twins, Jeb and Fred. At the Crayton County Fair one year, part of the entertainment was watching Jeb and Fred lift a truck between them.

Lizbeth right then was standing across from Fred, clutching her brown mink coat so tight around her you might've thought it was some kind of security blanket. She was quite a ways down the hall, but her voice carried loud and clear to where Vergil and I were sitting. "R.L., can't we sue him for malpractice? I mean, when doctors end up letting somebody die, don't they get sued?''

It didn't take a detective to figure out who it was Lizbeth was talking about.

Whatever R.L. said back to her, I didn't get. I did, however, notice that the gleam in Vergil's eyes got a little brighter. For a split second there, I could've sworn that Vergil was actually going to smile. He managed to get control of himself, though, scratching a little more in his notebook without looking up at me.

I sank a little lower in my chair. This was getting real embarrassing.

After that, it didn't take long for Vergil to get everything he wanted to know out of me. I did, of course, forget to mention that right after talking to Vergil on the phone, I'd poked around in Jacob's office a little. No use causing Vergil any more grief than he already had. Right away, it seemed, Vergil was putting down his Bic and nodding at me. "Tell that secretary—Inez Somebody—that I want to talk to her next." Vergil made it sound as if this were tragic news.

Inez reacted as if she thought so, too. Standing in the corridor across from Priss, the thin woman gave a little start and then moved forward toward Vergil, looking as if she were walking toward the electric chair.

I leaned back against the left wall of the corridor, watching Inez go. Priss was standing just down from me, and R.L. and Lizbeth a little further down from her. I looked at all of these folks, and I suddenly got this weird feeling. Like something was missing. What was it?

It came to me right away. Tears. *That's* what should be here but wasn't. There was a dead man down the hall, and these folks were all his relatives. And yet none of them was crying. Not a single one.

I stared at all of them. Priss, R.L., Lizbeth. And down there with Vergil, Jacob's secretary, Inez. Not one of them looked all that perturbed that Jacob was gone. Annoyed, maybe. Terribly inconvenienced. But upset? Not really.

The only one who looked even close to tears right that moment was Inez. Apparently, it had just occurred to her that she no longer had a boss. And that if she no longer had a boss, it stood to reason she no longer had a job. "Oh my God," I heard her to say in a loud voice to Vergil. "I guess I—I'm *unemployed* now!" She made it sound like something unclean.

Priss evidently heard Inez, too. Right after Inez mentioned the word *unemployed,* Priss came over to stand next to me. "Well, Haskell," she said, "I guess you and Inez have a lot in common."

I stared at her. It wasn't hard to guess what she was getting at, but I thought I'd play it dumb. "How do you figure?"

Priss stared back at me. "The way I see it, if you don't have an employer anymore, you're not employed." Her tone implied she was explaining something to someone with the IQ of a preschooler.

So far I'd had a real bad day—not as bad as Jacob's, of course, but still pretty bad—so I reckon my voice sounded angrier than I meant it to. "Look, Priss, Jacob paid me for three days, and that's exactly how long I'm going to be working on this case."

Priss's mouth actually dropped open. She took a couple of deep breaths and said, "Oh no you're not."

She turned on her heel and started to walk away from me, but I grabbed her arm. "Priss, did it ever occur to you that there's still a possible kidnapper out there? That Jacob's murder and the kidnapping note aren't necessarily related?"

Priss stopped and blinked at me. "That—that's a little farfetched, don't you think? You don't even know for sure if there ever *was* a kidnapper."

I still held on to her arm. "If you think that's farfetched, how about this? Maybe the murder and the kidnapping threat really *are* related. Maybe what we've got here is a kidnapper-turned-murderer. You just might need a bodyguard *now* more than ever."

Priss wrenched her arm away, but she didn't move. She just stood there, looking at me. I thought I could see alarm in her gray eyes for the first time. I was positive of it not a second later when we both heard, plain as day, Inez repeating to Vergil almost word for word what she'd told us earlier.

All about Ruby and how she'd lost her keys.

Priss took one look at Vergil's suddenly alert, interested face, and she looked alarmed, all right. Very, very alarmed.

CHAPTER

7

Priss's wide gray eyes were still focused on Vergil's face when we all heard the sound of footsteps heading toward us. Priss blinked, took one quick look down the hall in back of us, and her mouth tightened up. Like she'd just bitten down on an unripe persimmon.

"Oh, for crying out loud," Priss said.

Crying out loud was exactly what Willadette Sweeney Vandeventer was doing. The new widow was bawling up a storm as she headed toward us, dabbing at her heavily mascaraed eyes with a lace handkerchief.

Judging from appearances, Willadette had gone through her closet in a hurry, looking for something suitable to show up at the murder scene in. What she'd come up with was the right color, all right, but I don't know if I'd exactly call it *suitable*. Willadette had poured her ample curves into a pair of black stretch knit pants—the kind I think they used to call toreador pants back in the sixties.

The toreador pants in themselves, however, weren't what had every eye in the immediate vicinity trained on Willadette. In fact, this is something you get used to right away around these parts. Every day you see clothes that haven't been seen anywhere else in at least

twenty-five years. Any minute now I expect to see somebody walking around downtown Pigeon Fork in a Nehru
jacket.

No, it was how *tight* those toreador pants were that
made them an eye-grabber. Willadette's toreadors were
so tight you could see the lines of her bikini panties, if
you bothered to look. Glancing around me, I couldn't
help noticing that every male within looking distance of
Willadette did seem to be bothering. Particularly Jeb and
Fred Gunterman, Vergil's twin deputies. They were staring at Willadette, openmouthed.

I was willing to bet that it wasn't just Willadette's
toreador pants that had Jeb and Fred all agog. To complete her funereal ensemble, Willadette was also wearing
a black knit long-sleeved sweater with sparkly black
beads all across the front. This sweater wasn't anywhere
near as tight as her knit pants, which I figure was real
good planning on Willadette's part. If that sweater had
been even *close* to as tight as her pants, poor Willadette
probably would've strangled to death right before
our eyes.

The sweater was still pretty tight, though. The black
sparkly beads across the front seemed to be holding on
for dear life, stretched precariously across what were—
according to Melba and the rest of Gossip Central—two
of the biggest reasons Jacob Vandeventer had married
Willadette.

These two big reasons bobbled up and down as Willadette hurried down the corridor toward us. I noticed
that the eyes of the twins and those of R.L. also bobbled
up and down in perfect synchronization.

If you didn't count her reasons, Willadette was a tiny
little thing. She couldn't have been more than five feet
tall, but she made up for it by wearing her red hair in a
style that a lot of the women are still wearing here in
Pigeon Fork, including, as I mentioned before, my secretary Melba. Apparently, Melba and Willadette and the
others all feel that this one style is tried and true—the
beehive. Willadette had herself quite a massive one, too.
Her beehive added a good three inches to her height.

As if all this wasn't enough, the not-so-merry widow was also wearing three-inch high heels. On the hardwood floor, her heels made a noise like tiny firecrackers going off as she hurried toward us. About halfway, Willadette apparently realized that everybody in the place was staring straight at her, because she stopped in midflight, lifted one trembling hand to her forehead, and said, "Oh God, oh-h-h GOD."

This woman was good.

If Melba hadn't told me that she'd overheard Willadette referring to Jacob more than once as "that old coot I married," I might've thought Willadette was really broken up over this.

Willadette managed to regain her composure some and moved on past me and Priss. For a second there, I actually thought Priss might stick out her foot and trip Willadette. I think the thought must've crossed Willadette's mind, too, because—even though she didn't look directly at her stepdaughter—I noticed that Willadette gave Priss a real wide berth as she went by.

This close, you could see things about Willadette that weren't immediately evident when she was all the way down the hall. For one thing, even if Willadette had been trying out for a rock band, her makeup would've been a little overdone. Blue eye shadow covered both lids all the way to her eyebrows—eyebrows which, by the way, had been plucked so many times, there didn't look to be any hair left up there at all. In fact, as best as I could tell, watching her go by, Willadette's eyebrows were bald.

To make up for the lack of hair *above* her eyes, apparently, Willadette had decided to wear a little extra hair *around* her eyes. Long, unnaturally black eyelashes fringed both. Unfortunately, Willadette's eyes were on the small side, so it looked as if something dark and furry had nested on her lids. She'd outlined her lips a good eighth of an inch all the way around in a dark red pencil, coloring them inside with a slightly lighter red. From a distance, this made Willadette's mouth look real full and distinctly pouty. Up close, though, you could tell where her real lips ended. It gave the impression that Willadette didn't know how to color between the lines.

Even with that much makeup—or maybe because of it—Willadette was none too pretty in the face, but as I glanced around, it was real clear that none of the men in the corridor cared. Most of their eyes still hadn't gotten above Willadette's black sparkly beads anyway.

Even Vergil, who has sort of sworn off women ever since his wife Doris left him a couple of years ago, had stopped talking to Inez at Willadette's approach, and was now staring fixedly at Willadette's beads. It looked like maybe he'd gone into a trance, hypnotized by the rhythmic motion of black sparkles.

Willadette scooted right past everybody in the hall and made a beeline straight for Vergil.

"Oh, sheriff, tell me it isn't true—" Willadette's voice broke at this point. She shook her red beehive as if she couldn't go on, clutching her handkerchief tight to her mouth.

Did I mention this woman was good?

Vergil, I reckon, hadn't expected Willadette to single him out. His eyes were still on her beads when she spoke. He tried to cover it up, though, by hurriedly getting to his feet. It didn't help, though, that Virgil was flushing guiltily the entire time, looking exactly like he'd just been caught coming out of a porn film. "I—I'm real sorry, ma'am," Vergil said, his eyes now on the floor.

I'm fairly sure that Vergil was referring to the recent demise of Jacob. And not apologizing for being unable to drag his eyes away from Willadette's black sparkles. Although I couldn't be positive.

Whatever Vergil meant, that was apparently all he needed to say, because Willadette suddenly flung herself into his arms, weeping uncontrollably. "Oh, sheriff," she said. "O-o-oh, sheriff!"

Vergil looked like he might cry, too. He stood there, ramrod stiff, patting Willadette's back, while his face turned beet red. I would've sworn that even his pepper-gray hair now had a slight tinge of pink as Vergil's eyes traveled frantically around the room.

Vergil needn't have worried. It was obvious that if he himself wasn't getting a kick out of holding Willadette while she shook with sobs, there were quite a few folks in the corridor who would be glad to volunteer for the duty. Starting with Jeb and Fred *and* R.L. All three of these men moved closer to Inez's desk, just in case Vergil got ready to hand Willadette off to somebody.

"This—this is such a shock," sobbed Willadette. "Su-u-uch a sh-o-o-ock!"

"Uh—uh—uh—" Vergil said, his eyes getting even more frantic.

That Vergil. He always has had a real way with the ladies.

Vergil's frantic eyes lighted on me for a second, but I looked away. I may have been wrong, but tiny Willadette looked to me like she might be a lot more trouble than she was worth.

Which, come to think of it—considering just exactly how much she had only just recently become worth—was saying a *lot*.

R.L., however, didn't seem to have any of my reservations. He was definitely inching closer, cutting off the Gunterman brothers like the football player he used to be, positioning himself for the hand-off. Of course, I'm sure R.L. was only concerned about offering his poor, sweet little stepmother some comfort in her time of need, the way any caring stepson would.

Lizbeth evidently was equally convinced. As soon as R.L. started moving, Lizbeth did, too, beating him to Willadette's side by a good half-second.

"Oh, Willadette," Lizbeth said, holding out her arms, "you poor thing!"

I don't know. Maybe tears were catching. Or maybe it just hadn't occurred to anybody to actually cry until Willadette gave them the idea. Whatever the reason, large, wet drops were suddenly leaking out of Lizbeth's eyes.

Vergil looked as if he'd been dancing with Lucretia

Borgia and someone had just cut in. Relief flooded his lined face when Willadette pulled away from him and turned to Lizbeth. Holding on to Lizbeth's mink-draped shoulders, Willadette sobbed even louder. "Isn't this just dreadful?" Willadette said.

I had to agree with her. Dreadful *was* the word for it.

Lizbeth apparently tried for a sob, too. It wasn't anywhere near as convincing as Willadette's, but I reckon it was the thought that counted. "Oh, yes," Lizbeth cried, patting Willadette distractedly, "and it was so—so sudden! R.L. had no more than walked in the door when the phone rang, and it was Priss telling me the awful news. It—it was just *such* a shock!"

"A shock," Willadette repeated. She broke off in mid-sob to look Lizbeth straight in the face. She had to lean back some, being as how Lizbeth was at least seven inches taller. "By the way, had Jacob made up his new will yet?"

Lizbeth's eyes teared up all over again. "No," she said, shaking her blond concrete from side to side. "No, he hadn't."

This brought fresh wailing from Willadette. In fact, I thought it was right after this exchange that both Willadette's and Lizbeth's sobs sounded the most genuine of all.

"You poor, poor little thing," Lizbeth soothed. "The first thing I thought of after I heard the awful news was *you*. And what a terrible, terrible shock this was going to be for you. I just can't tell you how sorry I am—"

This was the woman who moments before had referred to Willadette as "a money-grubbing tramp"? Somehow, it made you doubt Lizbeth's sincerity.

Of course, it didn't take a genius to figure out why Lizbeth had evidently decided that money-grubbing tramps were just the sort of people she wanted to hang around with. Obviously, Lizbeth knew which side her bread was buttered on. And Willadette—who had just become a major shareholder in Vandeventer Poultry—no doubt had quite a quantity of butter.

Beside me, Priss was looking distinctly nauseated.

She noisily cleared her throat. "I don't know whether to laugh or applaud," she said.

Her comment was directed at me, her voice not a bit loud, but I was pretty sure both women heard her.

"Come on, Haskell," Priss went on. "Let's get out of here. I want to go see Mama right away, and I think I've had all I can stomach of this."

I stared at Priss, a little surprised that she was now including me in her plans. Maybe I'd convinced her after all that she really did need somebody to watch out for her for the next few days.

Vergil was staring at Priss, too. Evidently, he'd also heard her every word. The lines beside his mouth looked even deeper. "Nobody leaves here until I say so," he said. "Understand me? I still haven't talked to everybody yet." Vergil's tone implied that his not having done this yet was one of the great tragedies of his life.

Priss's gray eyes narrowed, but she didn't say a word.

While Vergil was talking, I noticed Willadette glance up from sobbing all over the front of Lizbeth's mink and shoot Priss a real dirty look. I reckon Willadette was still reacting to Priss's crack about what all she wasn't able to stomach. Oddly enough, when Willadette looked up, her eyes were bone dry. It was downright amazing how fast that woman's tears could dry up. Or maybe she just had so many tears in stock, and she'd just run out.

Willadette's eyes immediately traveled from Priss's face to mine. Moving away from the still weeping Lizbeth, who evidently hadn't used up her own tear supply yet, Willadette said, "Hey, ain't you the bodyguard Jacob hired? All the way from Louisville?" For a woman in mourning, her voice sounded downright belligerent. Willadette sniffled once, dabbed her nose with her handkerchief, and then said to no one in particular, "Jacob called me this morning and told me he'd hired some guy who looked like Howdy Doody." She squinted at me. "That's you, ain't it?"

Now it was *my* turn to look nauseated.

"Jacob did hire me to guard Priss here," I said

evenly. "I *used* to live in Louisville. I now live right here in—"

Interrupting must be a Vandeventer family trait. Even folks who *married* into the family had it. Willadette turned back to Vergil. "Can you believe that Jacob hired this clown to be his bodyguard? And that he just started *today?*" She glanced around now at everybody else in the hall. Jeb and Fred, I noticed, returned her glance eagerly. "Jacob never had a bodyguard in his life," Willadette went on, "and the one day he does, somebody murders him."

Lizbeth nodded, still weeping. "Don't that beat all?" she said.

My face was getting warm. What was worse, folks around me were starting to actually look *sorry* for me. Inez, R.L., even *Priss.* "I wasn't Jacob's bodyguard," I said. For what seemed like at least the millionth time. "I was bodyguarding Priss."

Apparently, no one was listening. Inez, R.L., and Priss continued to look excessively sympathetic. "Don't worry, Haskell," Priss said, patting my arm. "I know you did your best."

I looked at her. Priss was actually trying to be nice. She was. This was definitely a side to her I hadn't seen before. At least, not anytime today.

I was not, however, at all comforted by what she'd said. What I was, in fact, was embarrassed. Bone-deep embarrassed. I was also getting more and more convinced that all this was getting to be a matter of pride. I had to find out who did this to Jacob. I owed it to him. And I owed it to *me.*

Besides, if I didn't find the killer, I might be the first private detective laughed out of Pigeon Fork.

Even Vergil was looking uncomfortable for me. Which was even more embarrassing—and I wouldn't have thought that was possible. Clearing his throat, Vergil said, "Mrs. Vandeventer, did Jacob have any enemies that you know of?"

You could tell Vergil was just trying to change the subject real quick to help me out. Maybe Vergil was more near-family than I thought. Still, I can't say I felt all that grateful. I mean, thank you very much, Vergil, but I can take care of myself.

Willadette didn't even have to think about Vergil's question. "Oh, of course he did," she said brightly, turning away from me to face Vergil. "Jacob had *lots* of enemies." Willadette made it sound as if it were something to be proud of. She nodded her head emphatically, causing her red beehive to bob up and down with as much energy as her black beads earlier. "The poultry business is dog-eat-dog, you know."

Vergil nodded slowly and led Willadette over to Inez's desk. Either he had finished talking to Inez, or he wanted to get Willadette out of my vicinity. Whatever his reasons, Vergil started questioning Willadette in earnest. I would've liked to have listened in, but Jeb and Fred immediately started herding all of us back down the hall. They were none too kind about it, either. I think they were taking out on us their disappointment at not getting the chance to comfort Willadette personally.

I moved along with everybody else, but my eyes were still on Willadette. Dog-eat-dog, she'd said. The poultry business is dog-eat-dog.

Her choice of words, of course, couldn't help but remind me. It was getting way past Rip's suppertime. It was also getting way past time for his nightly visit to my front yard. And yet there was nothing I could do about it. I wasn't about to let Priss go anywhere unaccompanied—I hadn't been blowing smoke when I told her about her possibly being in even more danger now. There really could be a kidnapper/murderer on the prowl around here. After what had happened to Jacob, I wasn't about to take a chance on losing Priss, too.

Besides, it occurred to me as I stood there in the hall next to Priss, maybe I haven't been doing Rip any favor all these years, carrying him up and down steps. Maybe I'm one of those what-you-call *codependents* that they're always talking about on TV these days. It could be that I'm some kind of an enabler, and I've been making it too easy for Rip to remain neurotic. I could be one of the reasons he's never faced his problem and tried to conquer it.

Be that as it may, as soon as Vergil settled himself back behind Inez's desk again and started interviewing Willadette, I whispered to Priss that I'd be right back. Then, of course, I hurried out front and dialed up Melba again. This time I called Melba at her home. As I was dialing, I thought about all the faithful secretaries in all those detective shows on television—all the Della Streets who were always on call, always willing to go the extra mile to help out their bosses.

Apparently, Melba hadn't seen any of those shows.

"You have GOT to be kidding," Melba said, as soon as I explained what I wanted her to do. In the background, I could hear whooping and carrying on. And occasionally, a crash. It sounded like Melba's five kids were holding a demolition derby in her living room. "No way am I going to wrestle that hundred-pound brute down a flight of stairs," Melba added. "NO WAY."

"Melba, all you have to do is carry Rip down the steps. And he doesn't weigh a hundred pounds. Only sixty. He isn't a brute, either. He's a real nice dog."

"No way. *No frigging way,*" Melba said.

There was suddenly an even bigger crash in the background. "Look, I've got to go," Melba added, her voice now real agitated. "The kids are playing checkers, and somebody could get hurt."

I stared at the receiver. *Checkers?* From the sounds in the background, checkers for Melba's hellions must be a full-contact sport. Of course, knowing her kids, that wasn't exactly a surprise.

I hung up the phone, feeling kind of let down. For one thing, I don't think Della Street ever used the word *frigging*.

Turning around to head back toward Jacob's office, I was surprised to find Priss standing there. Apparently, she'd heard every word. "Having problems with your dog?" she said.

By the time I'd finished explaining, Priss was smiling. I reckon it was the first time I'd seen her smile since, well, since high school. I couldn't help staring at her, Priss Vandeventer sure looked like a different person when she smiled. A real pretty person, surprisingly enough.

"Tell you what," she said. "Right after we talk to my mother, we'll go feed Rip. OK? But we ought to leave right now. I don't want Mama finding out about this on TV."

"You didn't call her when you called the others?"

Priss shook her head. "I want to be there when she finds out about Dad. You never know, she might take it real hard. After all, she *was* married to the man for over forty years."

I hated to bring it up, but— "Well, we can't leave now. You heard the sheriff. Vergil made it real clear that he wants us to hang around for a while longer."

Priss just looked at me and smiled again. She *was* a real pretty woman when she did that.

Not ten minutes later, we were on our way out the front door. Priss was looking triumphant, and I was feeling a little uneasy. I wasn't quite sure why. What Priss had done was harmless enough. We'd walked back into the corridor, and then, when we'd gotten close enough to Vergil so that he couldn't miss the full impact of the entire dramatic scene, Priss up and fainted.

As fainters go, Priss was a pretty good one.

She dropped like a rock. Inez immediately started running around, getting a cold, wet cloth for Priss's head, and one of the folks from the crime lab came over and took Priss's pulse.

Priss kept her eyes shut only about a minute. When she opened them again, the first thing she said was, oddly enough, "Sheriff, can I go on home now? I— I'm really not feeling at all well." Priss's voice sounded genuinely woozy. I was impressed.

Vergil hesitated, looking at me. Like maybe he wasn't buying any of this.

"Sheriff," Priss added, "my father has been murdered. I—I need to get away from all this—this horror."

In Priss's eyes, for a second there, you would've sworn there was heartfelt grief.

I jumped in. "I'll take her home, Vergil. Don't worry about it. I won't let her out of my sight."

Vergil didn't look totally convinced, but he agreed anyway, real reluctant-like. "I'll be around later to talk to you both, so don't you be going anywhere that I can't find you right away."

Priss actually batted her eyes at him, still lying on the floor where she'd fallen. "Thank you so much, sheriff, I'll never forget this," she said. "You're a real gentleman."

"Hm," Vergil said, giving her a long look. But he let us go ahead and leave.

It was on our way to see Priss's mother, driving down the two-lane state road away from Vandeventer Poultry toward downtown Pigeon Fork, that it finally hit me why I was feeling so uneasy. It was because I was now no longer completely sure what kind of thing Priss *would* do. Watching her talk to Vergil, watching her lie, I was pretty amazed at how well she pulled it off. It takes real talent to look straight into somebody else's eyes without blinking and lie your head off.

Priss had been appallingly good at it.

I also couldn't help remember, heading down that blacktop road with Priss sitting right beside me, that Priss *had* gone to the ladies' room for a few minutes this afternoon. It had been shortly before we'd gone into Jacob's office and discovered his body. I didn't remember exactly what time it had been, but I did know it had been when I'd phoned Melba the first time. I swallowed, gripping the steering wheel a little tighter than necessary.

The time Priss was gone could easily have coincided with the time when Ruby took Inez away from her desk.

It made you wonder. Maybe the reason Priss was no longer objecting to having me around wasn't so much that she wanted me to keep an eye on *her* but that— while I was investigating Jacob's murder—she wanted to keep an eye on *me.*

CHAPTER

8

We'd already reached the outskirts of Pigeon Fork before Priss finally decided to start giving me directions. Turn right here, left at the next stop sign, right at the next one after that—Priss gave the directions as if by rote, her mind clearly elsewhere. Which was understandable. I reckon if you had to tell your mom that your dad's been murdered, you'd have to gear yourself up for it some.

So I kept quiet, concentrating on my driving. I figured out where we were headed a couple of turns before we got there. The Griswold Apts.

Being as how the Griswold Apartments is the only apartment building in Pigeon Fork, folks around these parts just call it the Apts. They actually pronounce the abbreviation *Apts.* as if it were spelled *Apse.* I've never been able to figure out if folks think they're being funny, or if they really believe that's how you pronounce it. I've never had the heart to ask anybody to their face, either. All my life, I've just gone along with the gag.

"You should've just told me your mom lived in the Apts.," I said as we pulled up. I looked out almost affectionately at the white frame building heavily laden with gingerbread. "I sure don't need directions *here.*"

Three stories high, the Apts. is the closest thing to a high-rise that we've got here in Pigeon Fork. Converted from a big, old Victorian-style farmhouse into six apartments, it's a Pigeon Fork landmark.

Years ago, this old farmhouse with its domed cupola and iron weather vane had been the center of the huge Griswold farm to which most of the land that now made up Pigeon Fork once belonged. There wasn't a doubt in my mind that every native-born Pigeon Forkian knew exactly where the Apts. was located. In fact, for me, not knowing where the Apts. was would've been like a native Philadelphian not knowing how to get to the Liberty Bell.

Priss was reaching for the door handle on her side. "Actually," she said, "Mama isn't the only one who lives here. She's been sharing my apartment with me ever since her divorce."

Priss didn't wait around for my reaction to that one. I didn't even get the chance to open her door for her. Priss was already headed up the walk by the time I'd gotten out and come around to her side. I actually had to run a little to catch up with her.

I must've had a question written all over my face—a question that went something like *What in the world was a thirty-three-year-old woman doing still living with her mother?*—because Priss answered just as if I'd actually put it into words. "I insisted Mama move in with me. She was so lost after the divorce. I mean, Mama had never even written a check by herself before. My father had taken care of *everything* all those years they were married. And then, one day he leaves her. It was just like leaving a child—" Priss's voice trailed off.

I stared after her. Obviously, Priss must love her mother an awful lot to take her on as a roommate. The thought made me feel kind of uneasy. Because if Priss loved her mom that much, then how much more must she have hated her father for what he did to her mother?

We headed up a steep, narrow staircase with a highly polished wood banister. Apparently, the current Griswold landlords were every bit as frugal as Jacob himself had been. Or else the Griswolds had carried being energy-conscious to a new extreme. One small sconce at the very top of the landing offered the only light there was. Outside it was just getting dark, but in the Apts. hallway, it might as well have been midnight. I followed Priss, feeling my way gingerly up the stairs, hoping that no one before us had left anything like, say, a roller skate on the steps. If someone had, Priss and I were goners.

Priss's door on the second floor opened to a small living room filled to overflowing with Early American maple furniture. Colonial prints showing Minutemen in the act of shooting covered the couch and both side chairs. Gold eagles with lamp shades on their heads perched on each maple end table, and above the couch hung a large gold eagle with a couple of arrows in its mouth. The eagle had a wildly unhappy look in its eyes, like maybe it didn't realize that arrows could taste that bad.

I couldn't help it. For a second, I stopped dead in my tracks. This sure didn't look like the kind of decor I expected Priss to have.

Priss gave me a quick glance over her shoulder as she headed into the hall off the living room. "My mother redecorated my apartment for me right after she moved in. It was a surprise for my birthday." Her eyes dared me to say anything.

"No kidding" was what I decided to say. I didn't think I could get any more noncommittal than that. I followed Priss through the room, zigzagging around the maple coffee table and a couple of needlepoint footstools. *This* must've been some surprise, all right. *Shock* probably would've been a better word for it. I started feeling even more uneasy. If Priss could stand idly by while Ruby filled her apartment with eagles, then Priss must *adore* Ruby.

I took another quick look around. The way I saw it, there was a strong possibility that Priss had totally hated her father's guts.

Priss's sixty-something-year-old "child" was out in

the kitchen, stirring something in a pot that smelled suspiciously like beef stew. Wearing a white ruffled bib apron embroidered with blue pansies and tied with a bow in the back, Ruby did look a lot like an oversized little girl. She was just standing out there in the kitchen in a blue calico dress and fuzzy blue bedroom scuffs, stirring and humming to herself.

She was also doing something else.

Smiling.

Either Ruby Vandeventer was enjoying some private joke, or else stirring beef stew had put her in a real good mood.

I reckon it was the humming that Ruby was doing that kept her from hearing me and Priss come in. Humming and stirring and smiling, Ruby didn't once glance our way for several seconds. It gave me a chance to really look at her. Up to that moment, I might as well admit, I'd pretty much put Ruby Vandeventer at the top of my list of suspects. Particularly after what Inez had told me about Ruby's afternoon visit. Now, looking at Ruby, I knew why Priss had told me earlier that if I'd ever met Ruby, I'd never think she could be capable of murder. Round-cheeked, round-bodied, with hair that looked exactly like gray cotton candy, Ruby Vandeventer had the face of an elderly cherub. An elderly cherub with a red gingham oven mitt on one hand and a wooden spoon in the other.

Just looking at her, I couldn't picture her doing anything, to anybody, that wasn't nice. Lord. Accusing this woman of murder would be like trying to pin a homicide on Shirley Temple.

When Ruby finally raised her head and saw us, I noticed that Ruby's eyes exactly matched the shade of blue of the embroidered pansies on the bib and side pocket of her apron. Ruby's eyes crinkled, and her cherubic smile immediately widened, dimpling both cheeks. "Why, sweetie," she said, looking at Priss with teasing disapproval, "you didn't tell me you were bringing home a gentleman caller." She patted her gray cotton candy hair with the hand still in the oven mitt. "And I look a fright."

I braced myself for Priss to say, "Oh, no, Mama, you got that wrong—Haskell's no gentleman," but Priss let that one slide. Maybe she was too intent on what she had to say. "Mama, I—I've got some bad news."

Ruby blinked, the wooden spoon poised in midair, looking first at Priss and then at me. "Bad news?"

Judging from Ruby's reaction right after Priss finished cluing her mother in on what had happened to Jacob, the word *bad* had probably been a slight exaggeration on Priss's part. When Priss next paused for breath, her mother was still smiling. "Do tell," Ruby said.

Priss and I both blinked at Ruby's reaction. Even for an ex-wife, it seemed a tad cold. On the other hand, of course, I have no doubt that if Claudzilla were ever to be told of *my* unfortunate demise, they'd have to give her something real strong to calm her down. Oh, yes. She'd be laughing *that* hard.

"Mama, did you understand me?" Priss said. "Somebody has *murdered* Dad."

Ruby patted her hair with her oven mitt again, still smiling. "Of course, dear," she said sweetly. "I understood you perfectly."

Evidently, Priss's worry over how Ruby would manage to shoulder the awful news had been a tad premature.

Ruby turned to me then, her smile as cherubic as ever. "It *is* too bad, of course. But something like this was bound to happen." Ruby pointed at me with the wooden spoon. "That man was such an asshole," she said sweetly.

I just looked at her. There probably wasn't much chance that they'd be calling on Ruby to deliver the eulogy.

Priss tried again. "Mama, somebody hit Dad over the head with that bronze chicken you gave him for Christmas." I think Priss was going for maximum impact this time.

It worked, sort of. This last bit of news got the biggest reaction so far. Ruby's mitt went to her mouth. "Oh dear," she said. "Did it hurt the chicken?" Two exclamation marks had suddenly appeared between Ruby's gray cotton candy eyebrows, but her mouth smiled on. "I paid quite a chunk of change for that bird," Ruby said to me, by way of explanation, "and it would be a real pity if something happened to it." Her smile didn't dim. "A *real* pity," she repeated.

I believed her.

While Priss was assuring her mother that the chicken itself had suffered no permanent damage, while the same could not be said of Jacob, I looked around the kitchen. The Early American decor had not been continued out here. Maybe Priss had stopped Ruby in time. It was just your average kitchen with yellow linoleum, yellow floral wallpaper, yellow-gold appliances—and notes. There were small yellow paper squares stuck all over everything. Notes with scrawled messages that said, "Tuesday is garbage day." "Pick up: Milk, bacon, bread." "Call for dental appointment." These were the ones that seemed pretty run-of-the-mill. The notes that worried me were the ones that said: "Did you shut the refrigerator door?" "Make sure the tap is turned OFF!" and "TURN OFF THE STOVE!!!" This last one was posted on the range hood right above the gas range that Ruby was now cooking on. It gave you a real feeling of confidence. I stared at that last note. Evidently, the rumors of Ruby's forgetfulness had not been exaggerated.

Ruby had apparently lost interest in the current condition of the bronze chicken because she turned her dimples toward me. "You'll be staying for dinner, won't you? We've got *plenty*," she said, waving her wooden spoon again. "Besides, it's about time Priss had herself a boyfriend over."

Priss's eyes widened. For a second there, I thought she might actually be embarrassed, but I decided it had to have been the setting sun shining in through the kitchen window over the sink, giving Priss's cheeks that reddish glow. "Mama," Priss said evenly. "Haskell here was *hired* by Dad. This morning. To watch out for me for a little while."

Ruby's smile, believe it or not, didn't even dim while Priss told her all about the kidnap note, and why it was that Jacob had decided to hire me. Ruby just kept nodding her cotton candy head, taking in every word, her eyes getting a little bigger.

When Priss was finished, Ruby swallowed once, reached over, and patted Priss's hand with her gingham oven mitt. "Now, hon," she said, "don't you be getting all scared now. That note don't have nothing to do with your daddy's death. It's just a prank. That's *all* it is." Ruby, amazingly enough, smiled throughout this little speech, too.

I decided then and there that Ruby must be one of that rare breed in this day and time—a Perpetual Smiler. You see one every once in a while. They're the women who have taken a little too much to heart all the TV and magazine ads you see all the time showing all those ever-happy models. Perpetual Smilers, even when they're relaxing—even when they think nobody's looking—don't ever let their smiles slip.

If I needed any more evidence to support my theory, I got plenty while we ate dinner. Throughout the meal, Ruby's smile didn't fade once. After a while, it got to be a kind of game, trying to catch Ruby when she wasn't smiling. I kept darting quick glances to Ruby's face—while she ladled out the stew, while she buttered her biscuit, while she talked to Priss. It was no use. I didn't win the game once.

Even when Ruby started telling me, between spoonfuls of stew, how she'd always known Jacob would get his one day, because he was such "a lecherous old fuddy duddy," Ruby practically beamed at me. It was as if her mouth couldn't hear what her voice was saying.

"Why, that man didn't have a faithful bone in his body, you know," Ruby said. Her pansy-blue eyes twinkled merrily. "Willadette wasn't the first, and she wasn't the last, neither. Oh no. Jacob had to have his fun."

I stared at Ruby. *This* was news. "Then you really think that Jacob was running around on *Willadette?*" It

seemed a tad farfetched. I mean, Jacob *was* in his sixties. If he had had the energy to run around on the
voluptuous Willadette, that man had been an inspiration
to us all.

Still, if Ruby was right, Willadette might have herself
more than mere money for a murder motive.

Priss was giving me a sharp look, and obviously trying
her best to head Ruby off. "Oh, my, this is such good
stew, Mama. You've outdone yourself."

Ruby went on as if Priss had said nothing. "Why,
of course, Jacob was running around on Willadette!
Believe you me, if Jacob Vandeventer is breathing,
he's chasing some skirt!" Ruby's smile looked a little
crooked for a split second, as she apparently realized
that, as a matter of fact, Jacob was not doing any breathing any longer. Her smile, however, straightened itself
up right away. "The younger they were, the better
Jacob liked them," she went on cheerily. "Lands, I was
afraid one day he'd come home with a kindergartner!"
Ruby was seated across from me at the maple kitchen
table, and now she slapped the arm rest on the side of
her chair as if she'd just said something hilarious. She
even giggled a little, covering her pink mouth with the
oven mitt she still wore.

Priss was now not even bothering to be subtle about
trying to shut Ruby up. Apparently, she was determined
to get her mother on another subject. One, perhaps, that
wouldn't give Ruby a motive for murder. "Mama, you
know you don't have to wear that mitt to the table."

Ruby blinked at that, but her smile—of course—didn't
dim. Staring at the mitt on her right hand as if she
couldn't quite remember why on earth it was there, she
nodded. "I was wondering why one of my hands felt so
warm," Ruby said.

I couldn't help it. I stared at her.

"Oh, my, yes, that's better," she went on, pulling off
the mitt and putting it carefully beside her plate. "That's
much better." She beamed at me again.

I couldn't help glancing toward the stove. Just to
make sure Ruby hadn't forgotten to read the note on

the range hood. I would've hated to end the evening—
and, incidentally, my life—by being blown to
smithereens.

Now I understood why Inez said forgetting her car
keys wouldn't be odd behavior for Ruby. Lord. Forgetting the entire *car* might not be odd for her.

I was starting to wonder if maybe Ruby was ill.
Maybe she had Alzheimer's, or maybe she'd had a
stroke.

What it turned out she'd had, however, was Jacob.

When Ruby left the room a little later to get some
red wine, which she insisted was "just what this meal
needed," Priss leaned over and whispered, "I know
what you're thinking, but Mama's perfectly all right. I
make sure she has a physical every year." Priss looked
fondly toward the door through which Ruby had disappeared. "Mama's always been like this, as far back as
I can remember—always sort of vague. I think it was
her way of dealing with my dad and his temper all those
years. It was her defense."

It was a defense, I reckon, that probably would've
worked real good. If you couldn't avoid your husband
physically, you could sure avoid him mentally.

Staring after Ruby, I felt sorry for her. Ruby of the
Perpetual Smile and Jacob of the Eternal Frown. Hers
and Jacob's marriage probably ranked right down there
with mine and Claudzilla's. Marriages made in hell.

Claudzilla told me the day she walked out on me that
one of the women's magazines she was always reading
had a column called "Can This Marriage Be Saved?"
She said she'd been wanting to get that magazine to do
one of those columns on *us* and all our problems. She
said it would be the shortest column ever. It would be
just one word: *No*.

That woman had a real sense of humor.

Apparently, Ruby had one, too. After she came back
with the wine and some glasses and poured us all a little,
Ruby started giggling. Actually giggling, like a five-year-
old. I thought for a minute it was the wine, but then
Ruby said, "You know, I just realized that I told Jacob

today that he wasn't going to get away with what he was doing to Priss—and now look, he isn't! Ain't that funny?'' she said.

Evidently, Priss thought it was a real hoot. She immediately began to choke on the last spoonful of beef stew she'd put in her mouth.

Ruby stared at Priss, her eyes concerned, her mouth still smiling. ''Sweetie, are you OK?''

Priss nodded, coughing. I gave Priss a long look myself, deciding right away that she probably wasn't going to need the Heimlich maneuver. And if she was, I'd get to it in just a second. Right now, this was too good a chance to pass up. I'd been wondering how I was going to go about questioning Ruby about what Inez had told us—without it sounding too much like an interrogation—and here she was, starting to talk about it all on her own. ''You told Jacob that this afternoon?'' I said.

Priss's eyes started speaking volumes, but she was still choking some, so she couldn't say a word.

Ruby blinked. ''Well, no, I told him that this morning. On the phone. But he hung up on me, you know.'' Ruby shrugged here and wrinkled her nose. You got the feeling that Jacob hanging up on her probably wasn't that rare an occurrence. ''So I up and decided to go into his office and *make* him listen!'' Ruby nodded her head emphatically. ''Somebody had to tell him what's what, and after Priss called me up yesterday morning and told me that Jacob was going to put *R.L.*, of all people, in charge of the company, why, it made me so mad I couldn't see straight!''

Ruby didn't seem to have any reservations at all about confessing that she was furious with a murder victim on the very day he was killed. Either the woman was so innocent she couldn't conceive of anyone thinking she was guilty, or maybe it was just one more problem with her memory. Maybe she'd simply forgotten that murderers could generally be narrowed down to those folks who actually *did* have a motive.

I hated to think it, but this sweet-faced woman could obviously be numbered among this last group.

"It was just so unfair," Ruby went on, "for Jacob to pass Priss by after all she's done. Priss has put her life-blood into Vandeventer Poultry—and now this! The nerve of that old man!" Ruby was still smiling, but it was an excited sort of smile now. "So I made up my mind that I'd go right down there today and tell him what I thought of him for once. I mean, it was ridiculous—R.L. has no head for business! I love the boy dearly, but everybody knows that he cain't possibly head up a company!"

Everybody, apparently, except Jacob.

Priss was now gulping down wine, trying to be able to talk. Her face wasn't anywhere near as red as it had been, so I knew I didn't have much time before Priss finally got her throat cleared and could jump in to shut Ruby up. "So, what did Jacob say when you told him all this?" I said.

Ruby's eyes went to her lap. "Jacob said, 'Butt out.'" Ruby's smile now looked a little uncertain.

I myself didn't quite know what to say to that. Jacob seemed to have had a real way with words.

Ruby lifted her head and looked directly at me. "Of course, that was what Jacob always said to everything."

It sounded as if conversations with Jacob must've been short and somewhat less that sweet.

Priss was really glaring at me now. She'd gotten her voice back, too. It was still a little scratchy, but Priss managed to say, clear as anything, "Mama, you didn't happen to see anybody *else* heading toward Jacob's office after you left, did you?"

Ruby smiled wider. "Oh, no, love," she said. "I thought I'd locked my keys in my car, so me and Inez went out to the parking lot for a while." Ruby looked over at me. "So anybody—anybody at all—could've gone into Jacob's office." Her pansy-blue eyes were as guileless as a child's. "*Anybody* at all," she repeated.

I stared back at her. Wishing, of course, that I really could believe every word she was saying. Unfortunately, Ruby—unlike her daughter—was not real good

114

at deceiving folks, and—unless I missed my guess—this cherubic woman wasn't telling all she knew.

True to *his* word, Vergil showed up just as we were finishing with dessert. When the doorbell rang, I was still sitting at the kitchen table, savoring Ruby's home-made pecan pie with genuine melt-in-your-mouth crust. The whole time I was chewing, though, I was thinking about Rip. It was the pie that reminded me of him. That dog is crazy about pecan pie. So I sat there, chewing away, trying not to feel guilty about that dumb dog, who was no doubt whining that very minute on my deck, wondering where in hell I was.

Ruby jumped up right away to answer the doorbell, and misinterpreted Vergil's intentions right from the start. "Why, Vergil Minrath," I heard her say, "you sweet old thing. How nice of you to stop by!" Ruby was actually acting as if this were a social call.

"I came by to offer my condolences at your—" Vergil had obviously prepared a somber little speech, but Ruby didn't let him finish it.

"Why, ain't this nice of you, dropping by like this!" From where I sat, Ruby's voice sounded positively de-lighted. Apparently, the solemnity of the occasion was completely lost on her. "Come right on in and let me get you a piece of my pecan pie."

Evidently Vergil managed to make his way unevent-fully through the Early American obstacle course out in the living room. Following Ruby solemnly into the kitchen, he nodded in mine and Priss's direction and pulled out a chair for himself. I reckon Vergil would've spoken, except I could see that his mind was completely preoccupied right that minute, no doubt trying to decide whether or not it was unethical to accept dessert from a possible murder suspect. Evidently, Vergil worked it out with his conscience because he finally said, "Thanks, Ruby, a piece of pie would be right nice."

Of course, from the way Vergil said it, you might've thought he expected the pie to be poisoned. Ruby must've been used to Vergil, though. She just beamed at him and bustled off, immediately returning with his plate. I couldn't help noticing that the piece Ruby cut for Vergil was bigger than any of the ones the rest of us had had.

"Here you are," Ruby said. Her smile was a lot bigger now, too. As she put the pie down, she put her arms around Vergil and gave him a little hug. "Oh, it's so good to see you, Verg. It's been too long!" She waggled a chubby finger at him. "You're going to have to stop by more often, you know. You cain't be that busy!"

Vergil must've seen my eyes widen, because he looked over at me as if he thought he'd better say something. Before I jumped to some awful conclusions—like maybe he was carrying on with a woman more than a dozen years older.

"Ruby and I go way back," Vergil said, picking up his fork. "She used to babysit for me when I was knee-high to a grasshopper."

Ruby nodded her cotton candy head. "Can you believe that?" she said, wiping her hands on her apron. "I used to babysit for the sheriff!"

Vergil nodded, too, only real solemn-like. He took a couple of bites, then cleared his throat and said, looking over at me and Ruby, "Uh, would you all mind giving me and Priss here a few minutes by ourselves?"

Vergil is not real good at working up to things. He generally seems to prefer the blunt approach.

Ruby looked over at him, smiling indulgently, as if he were talking nonsense. "Oh, Verg, whatever you have to say to Priss, you can say in front of us."

Vergil stared at her. "It's not what I got to say to *her*, Ruby. It's what she's got to say to me. I need to talk to her about what happened today. Official business, you know."

Apparently, for a second there, Ruby didn't know. Unbelievably, she stared at Vergil real blank. Then it seemed to dawn on her exactly what it was that Vergil was talking about. "Oh," she said, her blue eyes crinkling. "Of course. What was I thinking of?"

That, of course, was the question of the year.

I stared at Ruby's round, smiling face. Could it really

be that it had momentarily slipped her mind that Jacob had been murdered? Lord. She was going to need a lot more yellow notes.

Ruby and I moved on out into the living room. The kitchen door was left standing wide open, and I might've been able to hear what all Priss was telling Vergil if it hadn't been for Ruby. Ruby evidently thought that it was her job to entertain me until Priss got back, so for the next few minutes, she gave me a play-by-play account of how it was that she'd managed to find every stick of furniture in the room. Ruby had just started telling me what a real bargain the eagle over the couch had been—something that didn't surprise me a bit—when Priss appeared to tell Ruby that it was her turn in the kitchen.

Ruby's eyes lit up. You might've thought she'd just been asked to dance. "Oh, yes, of course," she said to no one in particular, hurrying past Priss.

This time Vergil got up and shut the door. Standing there in the middle of the living room, Priss stiffened. "Well, what do you suppose that means?" Priss said.

I had a pretty good idea, and I was pretty sure Priss herself probably did, too, but I shrugged my shoulders as if I didn't. I thought I'd let Vergil explain it to Priss. Which, of course, he did, in his own way. He came walking out of the kitchen about fifteen minutes later, looking even more grim than usual, his eyes on the floor, the lines at the sides of his mouth like canyons again. Priss had been sitting in one of the side chairs, but at Vergil's entrance, she got hurriedly to her feet. Staring at Vergil, Priss had the same expression on her face that I'd seen on the next of kin in hospital emergency rooms. Right when the doctor finally shows up.

Vergil's diagnosis wasn't good.

"Uh, Priss," he said, his voice very low, "just to be on the safe side, I think Ruby should talk to a lawyer."

Priss's eyes looked suddenly like gray satellite dishes.

It was a good thing Vergil's voice was low, because Ruby came out of the kitchen right behind him. She bustled up, smiling as always, and gave Vergil a final hug before he went out the door. "Now, Verg, you come on back now, real soon. You promise?"

Obviously, Ruby had no idea that Vergil's next visit might not be something to look forward to.

Vergil looked at the floor. "I promise," he said, his tone mournful.

With Ruby in front of me and Priss right next to me, I stood there at the door, watching Vergil make his way real slow down those dark stairs, and something started niggling at the back of my mind.

Something I'd heard today didn't quite make sense. What had it been?

CHAPTER
9

As soon as Vergil went out the door, Ruby turned to me and Priss, her blue eyes twinkling. "Well now, wasn't that nice of Vergil to drop by?" Ruby went over and settled herself into one of the Minutemen chairs, her perpetual smile even wider than usual. "That Vergil always was a real thoughtful boy."

Like a fool, I found myself nodding in agreement. That Vergil. What a considerate soul.

Unbelievably, Priss was nodding, too. "Vergil's a doll, all right," she said absently. Priss's eyes traveled to mine, and then back to her mother. "I've got to make a phone call. Be right back." With that not terribly smooth exit line, Priss disappeared into the kitchen, closing the door behind her.

I, knew, of course, what phone call Priss was making. She was dialing up Alton Gabbard, the Vandeventer family attorney, just as Vergil had suggested. Evidently, Priss had no intention of including Ruby in the discussion. She was going to protect her mother until the last possible moment.

Which was kind of admirable.

I wasn't sure how long Priss could pull this one off, though. If Vergil showed up to haul Ruby off to jail, how would Priss explain it? That Vergil still needed a babysitter?

I don't think even Ruby would buy that one.

Ruby's eyes followed Priss out of the room. I swallowed and sat myself down in the other Minutemen chair, bracing myself for Ruby to start pumping me about who all Priss suddenly needed to phone.

I was way off base. Ruby, as it turned out, had other fish to fry. Once the door shut behind Priss, Ruby gave the kitchen door a long, hard look, as if making sure it was totally closed. "You're not married, are you?" Ruby said, leaning toward me.

Oh dear. If I'd seen this one coming, I might've been able to head it off. As it was, I felt like I'd been blindsided by a truck. I don't know what it is about the women in Pigeon Fork, but I figure they must have some kind of sixth sense. They can home in on an unattached male the way bees go after pollen. It's amazing. I expect any minute now for the entire Pigeon Fork female population to show up on "Unsolved Mysteries."

"As a matter of fact, I'm divorced," I said, trying not to clench my teeth.

Ruby looked as if she was trying not to break into applause. "You know, my Priss is divorced, too."

I stared at her. "No kidding," I said. Matter of fact, I didn't even know Priss had been married.

Ruby was clucking her tongue, shaking her cotton candy head ruefully. "My Priss has been single now almost two years."

Ruby said this last sentence in much the same way she might've told me that Priss had a terminal illness. How Ruby managed to look so mournful and still maintain that perpetual smile was beyond me.

"Really?" I said. "Two years, huh?"

Ruby nodded, her eyes a lot more unhappy than when we'd told her about Jacob. She leaned a little closer. "I probably shouldn't say this—but, I do declare, you and Priss make the cutest couple."

I gave Ruby a weak smile.

Her dimples deepened. "It wasn't Priss's fault, neither, her having to get a divorce and all. Why, her husband Chuck turned out to be an asshole—just like Jacob," Ruby said sweetly. "I do declare Priss was just about the best wife any man could ever want, but did Chuck appreciate her? Not a bit—"

Ruby went on and on. I started sort of squirming around in my chair, knowing full well that if Priss happened to come out here and overhear what all Ruby was telling me, Priss might start slamming doors again.

The door to the kitchen opened just as Ruby was filling me in on what a real good cook Priss was. "You might not know it to look at her, but that girl can make the best meat loaf you ever tasted. It melts in your mouth—" The second the door opened, Ruby immediately shut her own mouth and sat up very straight, smoothing a nonexistent wrinkle in her embroidered apron.

Priss had apparently decided to change out of the navy blue tailored suit she'd worn all day. Now dressed in form-fitting faded jeans, an oversized gray sweatshirt, and scuffed suede walking shoes, she sure looked a lot more like the old Priss I remembered.

One look at Priss's face told me she had a pretty good idea what all Ruby had been talking about in her absence. Priss's eyes narrowed. "Mama," she said, "Haskell and I are going over to his house for a little while to see about his dog. We won't be gone long."

I stared at Priss, amazed. Up to that minute, I was sure she'd completely forgotten what she'd told me earlier about going to take care of Rip. Lord knows, she'd had other things to think about since then.

Ruby looked positively *thrilled* that my dog needed to be fed. "Oh, that's wonderful," Ruby said, clasping her plump hands together. "You two young folks run along now. And have fun!"

I stared at her. *Fun?* Feeding my dog? Apparently, Ruby was reading more into this dog-feeding excursion than there really was.

Behind Ruby, Priss rolled her eyes.

As we were getting in my truck, Priss said, "Alton

Gabbard's going to come by my office at eleven tomorrow morning—but, Haskell, don't mention it to Mama, OK? I'm not going to have her getting all upset over nothing."

I nodded. I wasn't sure, however, if *nothing* adequately described the situation.

We were putting on our seat belts, when Priss added, not looking at me, "By the way, you'll have to excuse Mama. Ever since my divorce, Mama's been real anxious to pair me up with somebody again. I half expect her to start running an ad in the *Pigeon Fork Gazette*."

I turned on my headlights and pulled away from the curb, feeling real uncomfortable. I mean, what was I supposed to say? *Lots of luck?* Instead, I said, "I didn't know you were divorced."

What a conversationalist.

"Yep," Priss said. Apparently, she was every bit as impressive a conversationalist as I was. I was real relieved, though, to be talking about something other than Ruby's plans for the two of us.

"I'm divorced myself," I said. "For almost a year and a half, you know."

The expression on Priss's face told me that she *did* know, no doubt having heard about it through the everdiligent Pigeon Fork grapevine. Priss smiled a little, not meeting my eyes. "I hear tell your ex was a pip," she said.

I shrugged. I wasn't sure what a pip was exactly, but if it flirted with anything that moved and ran up large amounts on charge cards, Claudzilla probably qualified.

Maybe it was because neither one of us could think of anything else to talk about on the fifteen-minute ride to my house—or maybe it was because both of us wanted to avoid the topic of Ruby's possible involvement in Jacob's murder—whatever the reason, Priss and I ended up talking about our ex-spouses.

As it turned out, Claudzilla and Priss's ex-husband Chuck sounded as if they could be twins. Both blond, both good-looking, both with the same remarkable ability to spend a great deal of money with no accompanying ability to earn it.

And both unfaithful.

"Why, I think they belong together," Priss said. "Maybe we should introduce them."

Priss and I had both relaxed some by then. I reckon there's nothing quite so ice-breaking as two people getting together and sharing just how much each of them totally dislikes his or her ex-spouse. It's that kind of warm conversation that brings folks together.

Priss even had a fond nickname for her ex-husband, just like the one I had for Claudine. Priss called him "Up-Chuck."

I must admit, though, I wasn't completely convinced right off the bat—in spite of what Ruby had told me—that the reason Priss's marriage had died a premature death was entirely the fault of Up-Chuck. After all, this *was* the woman whom I'd spent the morning chasing through the halls, while she raced around being furious. A real calm demeanor like that doesn't exactly recommend you as a marriage partner. It wasn't until Priss mentioned one little thing that I started believing that Up-Chuck no doubt deserved his nickname.

"We'd probably still be together, I was *that* big a fool," Priss told me, "except for one thing—my father offered Up-Chuck twenty-five thousand dollars to get out of my life, and he took it."

I'd been driving along, watching the truck's headlights bounce along the road ahead of us and listening to her, feeling more and more at ease. Now suddenly my stomach tightened up. "Your dad did what?"

Priss shrugged. "Dad hated Up-Chuck from the start. He said Up-Chuck wasn't good enough for me—that all he was really interested in was the money. When I told Dad I was marrying Chuck anyway, Dad said we weren't going to live in the Vandeventer mansion. Can you believe it? *Lizbeth* Dad welcomed with open arms, but Chuck Dad wouldn't have under his roof."

I kept my eyes on the black ribbon of road up ahead, but my mind was going almost as fast as my truck. This was a slightly different version of events from what Jacob had told me earlier. Jacob had made it sound as if it had been *Priss's* idea to move out of the family home.

Beside me, Priss swallowed and then went on. "Turns out for once my father was right. He proved it by buying Up-Chuck off."

There was an awkward silence while I scrambled in my mind for something to say. There wasn't any getting around it. This definitely gave Priss one more motive. Even if Jacob *had* been trying to help his daughter out, buying off her husband was a pretty crummy thing to do. It could make a person want to take revenge. I swallowed, and almost wished Priss hadn't told me.

"Dad did me a favor, though," Priss added. "It was probably the only good thing he ever did for me. Dad helped me see the real man I'd married."

I took a quick glance at her face. Priss didn't look any too grateful.

Thank goodness, we were right at the bottom of my driveway by then, and right away Priss changed the subject. She changed it to what the subject always is whenever someone goes up my driveway for the first time. "Oh my God! How in the world do you get up this thing?"

My driveway *is* a little long. In fact, it's about a quarter of a mile, almost straight up through dense trees. Everybody who's ever come to visit me complains about it. Me, I don't mind it. Of course, I do have four-wheel drive. I reckon that could make a difference in your attitude.

My driveway makes a real sharp curve at the end, and then suddenly you're right in front of the small A-frame that Rip and I call home these days. Surrounded by huge old oaks and maples, we've got ourselves an ample helping of privacy here. This is real nice as far as I'm concerned, being as how we don't hardly ever get any visitors up here other than folks I've invited. It's not so great for Rip, though. He hardly ever gets the chance to bark.

I reckon that's why Rip decided a long time ago to put in his barking time whenever I show up. I could already hear Rip doing his thing when we were no more than halfway up the hill. Barking. And howling. And carrying on.

You'd have thought we were a gang of outlaws here to plunder the place.

I would've liked to have thought that the reason Rip was carrying on so bad was that he just couldn't recognize my truck, being as how it was so dark out. It *is* real black in these woods once night comes on. The only trouble with the Rip-doesn't-see-me theory, though, was that I knew very well that he carries on this bad in broad daylight, too. Then, too, I've got me two big porch lights on either side of my front door that switch themselves on once it gets dark enough out. Both porch lights, I could see, were on, lighting up my entire front yard and a good part of my driveway.

And Rip was still barking.

It's real irritating to have your own dog bark at you. Particularly in front of company.

Priss was grinning before we'd taken two steps toward the house.

"Doesn't he recognize you?" she asked.

"Why, of course he does," I said. "Rip, come on, boy. It's me. Rip, it's ME, boy. Now, STOP IT."

Rip totally ignored me. Sitting at the top of the steps, having moved as close as he dared to the edge of the redwood deck that surrounds the house, Rip now alternated between barking and whimpering. I think the bark was to let me know he was mad I was late, and the whimper was to let me know he was desperate.

Almost as irritating as being barked at is having to pick up your nutty dog and carry him downstairs to the yard. Again, in front of company. It makes you feel real foolish. Particularly when your dog is so overjoyed to see you that he keeps twisting and turning in your arms and trying to lick your ears.

"Rip, come on, boy. Stop it, now! CUT IT OUT!"

Rip, just like before, ignored me.

Priss was no longer grinning. Now she looked like she was trying real hard not to laugh out loud.

"My goodness," she said, "he does have a problem, doesn't he?"

"No, he doesn't," I said, finally depositing Rip, now in full hysteria, on my front yard. *"I'm* the one with the problem."

Priss turned away real quick, but not before I could plainly see that she was snickering.

As soon as Rip finished doing his business, he trotted back over to me and waited. He was waiting, of course, for me to pick him up and carry him back upstairs, as usual. This time, Rip must've picked up on my irritation, because he only tried to lick my ears once, and once he missed the first time, he gave up, settling into my arms like a sixty-pound lump.

Priss had already headed up the deck in front of me, and she was standing there at my front door, waiting for me to unlock it. She needn't have bothered. Out here, as secluded as it is, I never lock my doors. My neighbors don't, either. I reckon we all figure that if thieves show up all the way out here in the middle of the woods, they deserve a little something for their effort.

A little something is about all they'd get, too. I don't have all that much to steal. A color TV and a microwave. It would be a real small haul for the amount of time thieves would have to put into it.

I put Rip down, and we all moved inside.

Priss walked into my living room, and, wonder of wonders, when she looked around, her face didn't pale. My place isn't the Bermuda Rectangle that my office is, but I guess you'd say they were both done by the same decorator. Priss, however, didn't look stunned like some of my other guests have. She just stood there inside the door for a second, looking around, like she was trying to figure out where to sit down. That's all. Her mouth wasn't even pinched with distaste.

I was starting to kind of like this woman.

Of course, Priss didn't have much of a choice as to where to sit. It was either the plaid chair filled to overflowing with magazines or the couch covered in yesterday's newspapers. Priss probably should've kept moving. Her standing there, real still like that, gave Rip the chance to do what he always does whenever we have ourselves a guest.

He sniffed her shoes.

Being as how Rip is about the size of a German shepherd and has very large sharp teeth to match, I've had some women freeze stiff when Rip does this. I've also seen a few men look unnerved. "Rip, stop," I said, moving toward him, getting ready to grab his collar. "Don't be scared, Priss. He won't hurt you."

Priss gave me a look, laughed, bent down, and scratched Rip's ears, all in one smooth easy motion. "Well, of course, you sweet thing," she said. It took me aback for a moment, and then I realized she was talking to Rip. "Of course, you won't hurt me," Priss went on. "Why, I used to have a dog just like you when I was a kid!"

It was Rip who froze. For about a split second. He stared at Priss, as if he was sure she was out of her mind. Then, no doubt realizing that Priss and he had a lot in common, Rip started wriggling all over, his tail going like a triphammer.

So much for Rip doing his rendition of Fierce Guard Dog. Oh, he was scaring Priss to death, all right. The woman was putty in his paws.

I started to reach for Rip's collar, to haul his silly body away from Priss, but Priss held up her hand.

"Oh, come on now, Haskell, he's not bothering me," she said. "He's a great dog." She was still scratching Rip's ears, looking him straight in the eyes. "You're a sweetheart, aren't you, boy? You're just an old pussycat, aren't you?"

To any other dog, those no doubt would have been fighting words. Rip, however, apparently didn't realize that he was being insulted. In fact, you would've thought that dumb dog had never had his ears scratched before. Rip went into doggie nirvana. His tongue lolled out, and his eyes actually rolled back a little in his head.

I stared at him. This was one disgusting display if ever I saw it.

I decided I couldn't take it anymore. I left the room and busied myself filling Rip's dog bowls heaping full and getting together what all I was going to need to spend the night on Priss's couch. My toothbrush, my shaving kit, that sort of thing. I decided not to take a change of clothes, because I figured I'd be back here tomorrow morning anyway, and I'd change then.

I don't think Rip even noticed that I'd left the room. He was too busy staring at Priss adoringly. The pushover.

When I came back out, carrying my shaving kit and all, Rip was on his back, his legs askew, and Priss was scratching his stomach. At my entrance, Priss's eyes sort of wandered to the shaving kit I was holding. Rip's eyes, of course, didn't leave Priss's face.

I steeled myself for Priss to start in again. About how she didn't need a bodyguard, and wasn't I carrying this a bit too far.

Instead, Priss just shrugged. "You ready to get back to my place?"

I just looked at her, trying not to show my surprise. "Sure am," I said.

That was that. The parting scene between Priss and Rip was a bit much—Rip actually howled—but other than that, things went pretty smooth.

They went smooth the next morning, too. Ruby made all of us a real country breakfast—ham, sausage, eggs, bacon, toast, gravy, apple butter, and I don't know what all—the sort of breakfast that made you wonder how farmers ever made it out to the fields in the morning.

I thought Priss and I had made it pretty clear why it was I'd stayed overnight, but Ruby seemed to have come to an entirely different conclusion. She kept beaming at me and Priss. As I was eating my third biscuit covered with apple butter, Ruby said, "It's so nice to have a man around the house, ain't it, Priss?"

I stopped chewing.

Priss had been eating the last of her scrambled eggs,

but she stopped chewing, too. Swallowing fast, she said, "Mom, Haskell is here because that's his job. OK? He's been *paid* to do this."

I thought that put the entire thing into the proper mercenary light. Thanks so much, Priss.

Ruby just smiled vaguely at both of us. "Oh, of course, sweetie," she said. "Of course."

Instead of looking angry, though, Priss actually smiled. She tried to cover it with her napkin, but I saw her smile, all right. "We better be leaving soon," she told me. "The office doesn't open until eight, but I like to get a head start on the day. I try to get to work at least a half-hour earlier than anybody else, to open the place up and maybe go through the mail. Or whatever."

She was still smiling a little when she said that, but when she mentioned work, her face tightened up some. I knew what she was thinking. That it ought to be real fun going into Vandeventer Poultry the day after Jacob was murdered there.

Priss blinked and went on. "—and we need to go by your place to see Rip, too, don't we?"

I stared at Priss. I had been priming myself to remind her that we'd need to take care of Rip again this morning, and here Priss was, reminding *me*. I was starting to feel I'd badly misjudged her. Anybody who could remember a nutty dog in the face of what all had happened just lately in her family was OK in my book.

At my place, Rip only barked a couple of times this time as Priss and I got out of my truck. Both these barks, however, were directed at me, which on the annoyance meter definitely rated a ten. The rest of the time Rip wagged his silly back end with such force that his legs lifted up off the floor. His wagging, of course, was directed at Priss. She seemed almost as delighted to see Rip as he was to see her. It was Priss who—even though she was wearing a dark gray tailored wool suit—picked Rip up and carried him down off the deck.

Evidently, Rip and I have something in common. Here lately, neither one of us has been touched by female hands anywhere near often enough. I thought Rip was going to have a heart attack from the sheer joy of it.

I might as well admit it. I was feeling distinctly jealous. Any minute now, I expected to find out that Rip and Priss were planning to run away together.

I left the two lovebirds alone while I went and changed into fresh clothes. While I was doing that, I couldn't help thinking about how different Priss was from how I'd first thought her to be. She seemed like a real nice, real down-to-earth kind of person. Right that minute, I could hear her out there in the living room, laughing and talking to Rip, while she wrestled with him on my couch. You might've thought Priss was a young girl out there, laughing as if she didn't have a care in the world.

For a second, I wondered which made me feel more jealous: Priss hogging all of Rip's attention or Rip hogging all of hers.

Evidently, Rip—the old scoundrel—could teach me a thing or two about how to impress the ladies. Who knows? Maybe I should learn how to let my eyes roll back in my head like he does.

I decided since I was going to spend the day in an office, I probably ought to wear something else besides the jeans and boots I'm usually in. I went through my closet and found a cream-colored dress shirt that didn't need ironing. At least, it didn't need it much. I also found a pair of lightweight brown wool slacks that miraculously still had a crease. This was real lucky since these particular slacks go fairly well with the only sport coat I own, a brown plaid job that a saleslady in Louisville convinced me five years ago was the latest style. Having put together this dapper fashion ensemble, I decided enough was enough and drew the line at wearing a tie. There was no use going hog wild. Besides, I sure didn't want folks mistaking me for R.L.

Fat chance.

I had put on my shoulder holster and was just buttoning my sport coat when the phone on my nightstand started ringing. I knew the minute I picked up the receiver that this had to be the irate woman that Melba had told me about earlier. Evidently, this particular irate woman had managed to stay every bit as irate as she'd been when she talked to Melba. "Haskell, this is Belinda Renfrow." Just saying her own name, the woman sounded furious.

The Renfrows, as I mentioned before, are my closest neighbors. They're the ones who live in the log cabin. My guess is that the Renfrows were hippies back in the sixties, and they've never completely gotten over it. They raise all their own vegetables, do all their cooking on a wood stove, and—like I said earlier—have a huge compost heap that Rip gets into every once in a while. I hoped that this last wasn't what had made Belinda so mad. Was it possible she'd had some rare antique compost that she'd been saving for years, and that Rip had destroyed it?

"Yes, Belinda, what can I do for you?" I tried to sound real cheerful, as if I didn't notice that Belinda sounded as if she were near meltdown. It's a technique I perfected when I was living with Claudzilla.

Belinda got right to the point. "Why in blue blazes didn't you return my phone call?"

That, of course, was a long story. "To tell you the truth, I didn't know you'd called."

"Of course you did," Belinda snapped. "I told your secretary!"

That did it. I decided right then to throw Melba under the bus. "My secretary didn't give me the message."

"Oh, sure," Belinda said.

Evidently, my believability factor here was zero.

"Well," Belinda hurried on, "I'm calling about that damn dog of yours. He came down here yesterday and killed two of my ducks. *Two* of 'em!"

For a minute, I was so surprised I couldn't talk. I swallowed a couple of times and finally said, "Belinda, it couldn't have been Rip. You know Rip never gets off my deck."

The Renfrows, like all my neighbors, have heard me talk about Rip's stairs-o-phobia. In fact, my neighbors themselves all talk about Rip, too. And—from what I've heard—they *laugh*.

"Your dog does too get off your deck," Belinda said. "I saw him. He jumped my damn fence, and he got to my damn ducks. I want them replaced, damn it, every single one of them!" *Damn* apparently was one of Belinda's favorite words. She sounded breathless, she was so angry. "And Haskell?" she added. "You know damn well there's only one thing you can do with a dog that starts killing things. Once a dog tastes blood, it don't never stop killing."

My throat went dry. I wasn't sure if Belinda was right about the homicidal tendencies of blood-tasting dogs, but I did know for a fact that when a dog started killing poultry around these parts, farmers didn't feel any qualms at all about shooting it.

I could hear Priss still laughing out there in the living room with Rip. Rip, at the moment, was doing his mumble-barking. Rip knows he's not supposed to bark in the house, so when he gets excited, he does the next best thing. He mumble-barks under his breath. It sounds a little like *"Barmnf. Barmnf."* It's enough to drive you crazy. I've always thought it was Rip's way of punishing me for not letting him bark out loud in the first place.

I ran my hand through my hair, unable to decide which was the most farfetched—Rip as a cold-blooded killer or his getting off the porch on his own. "Belinda," I said, "you've got to be mistaken. It can't have been Rip."

Belinda Renfrow is in her early forties, and wears her straight gray-streaked brown hair in a long plait down her back. I've never seen her wear anything other than faded jeans, a madras shirt, and moccasins. Occasionally, when she dresses up, she wears a macrame necklace. This is a no-nonsense kind of woman. The kind of woman who takes personally the idea that she might've been mistaken about anything. I could hear over the phone a long drawn-out breath before Belinda said, "Look, Haskell, I'm not wrong. It was *your* dog. Sure as shooting."

I kind of wished she hadn't used that particular expression.

Priss had come to my bedroom door by then, her eyes widening a little when she saw what I was wearing. Now she stood there, looking first at me and then pointedly at her watch.

I swallowed. "Belinda, I can't talk right now, I've got to leave," I said, "but I'll be getting back to you on this, OK?"

Belinda apparently took this as if I'd told her my check was in the mail. "Sure you will," she said flatly. "Well, you'd better find another home for your damn dog, Haskell. Because if *I* see him again, he's going to be eating lead."

Belinda Renfrow must've been hell on wheels at all those hippie protests they used to have. "Belinda, I really will get back to you." I think I was being real calm here, considering that she was threatening murder.

"I want my damn ducks replaced," Belinda said.

"I understand," I said, "and I'll be getting back to you. Really."

Belinda made an ugly noise on the phone. *"I want my damn ducks replaced,"* she said—apparently in case I hadn't heard her the first time—and hung up.

Priss was staring at me now, clearly ready to leave, but instead I went over and scratched Rip behind the ears. And, just to be on the safe side, I checked Rip's paws. Looking for—you guessed it—the telltale signs of a homicidal rage. Or, say, compost residue. Rip's paws were as clean as any dog's who has spent the majority of his adult life lying on a redwood deck and being carried most everywhere he wants to go. There wasn't any mud, nothing. Rip's nails looked as if maybe they'd recently been manicured. "Good boy, Rip," I said, scratching his ears some more. "For a minute there, I thought you'd had yourself a miracle cure."

Rip looked at me as if *I* were the one who's nuts.

I explained Rip's problem to Priss on the way into Vandeventer Poultry.

Priss looked surprised. "I hate to tell you, Haskell, but Rip hasn't been cured. He's a nut. Really."

I stared at her. *That* was terribly reassuring to hear.

"By the way, Haskell," Priss added, now staring straight ahead, "this is a new look for you, isn't it?"

"Oh no," I lied. "I dress up every once in a while."

Priss, for some reason, grinned. "You look real nice," she said.

I wasn't sure if she was making fun of me or what, so I didn't say anything.

"No, I mean, really," she said, "you clean up real nice." After that, she gave me a real pretty smile.

I found myself smiling back at her without even being sure what I was smiling about.

Both our smiles faded as we pulled into the parking lot in front of the white Vandeventer Poultry shoe box. I parked the truck right next to the front door, and we both headed inside.

One reason I parked so close was that I was real afraid that the wonderful fragrance I'd enjoyed so much yesterday morning might've returned overnight. It hadn't. Oh, there might've been a faint tinge of it in the air, but it was nothing like what I remembered. In fact, I actually took a couple of deep breaths on the way in, wondering if maybe my nose was on the blink. Maybe it had sustained permanent damage during the assault yesterday.

It was real strange going into Vandeventer Poultry after what had happened the day before. Of course, Jacob's office *was* off down the hall a ways. From where I was sitting just outside Priss's office, you'd never guess that somewhere nearby, there was a room with a chalk outline on the floor.

I noticed Priss didn't even glance that way when she went into her own office. Neither did Jolene, when she showed up about thirty minutes later. Jolene, of course, didn't glance any way at all. She mainly kept her eyes glued to the thin green carpet as she took her place behind the receptionist's desk. Today she was wearing a pink dress every bit as pale as the green one she'd had on yesterday. I watched her, idly wondering if every dress Jolene owned looked faded.

Jolene's eyes remained on the floor when Inez arrived minutes later, with R.L. a couple of steps behind. Jolene not even glancing up when they came in was all the more amazing because Inez was talking to herself. Out loud.

"I don't know what I can do today. I doubt if anyone will call. And if they do, what on earth am I going to say? *He can't come to the phone right now. Or ever?*" Inez kept up a running monologue as she went past the front desk. "I probably should've just called in sick, but does a good secretary do that? I don't think so—"

Evidently, the current state of affairs had gotten to be too much for poor Inez. The skirt of her tweed suit was on so that the pleat in the back was off to one side, and she'd put on only one grape earring. When R.L. said good morning to her, Inez jumped.

"Oh my yes, good morning," she said distractedly.

You could tell Inez did not consider the morning good at all. She gave R.L. a shaky smile. "I didn't know if I should come in today or not, being as how I don't really have a job anymore, but, well, I thought I might as well—"

Priss had come out of her office with a stack of paper in her hands, just as Inez and R.L. were arriving. She stood there, watching, as R.L. put his arm around Inez. "Don't you worry, Inez," R.L. said. "You'll always have a job here with us."

Priss immediately frowned. Apparently, she didn't quite agree with R.L. on the availability of jobs for Inez. Priss opened up her mouth to speak, then obviously thought better of it. She turned around and went back into her office.

Inez made a move toward the corridor leading to Jacob's office, and then hesitated. "He's—um—not still back there, is he?"

Inez was just walking past where I had taken up my post outside Priss's office, and her question appeared directed at me.

135

"I'm sure he's not," I said.

Inez looked relieved.

"You don't have to sit back there at your desk," R.L. said, "if it makes you uncomfortable—"

This was a side to R.L. I hadn't seen. Back in high school, he hadn't exactly been known for being considerate. A lot of football players aren't. It's bad for their image, I guess. Of course, you would've had to have been a rock not to be a little sorry for Inez. The poor woman looked totally rattled.

"You could sit out here—" R.L. went on.

Inez, however, shook her silver head. "Oh, no, I'm fine. I should be at my desk, in case anyone calls. Or if anybody, um, needs me—" Her voice trailed off. Clearly, Inez was charting new ground in the secretarial world here. She headed determinedly down the corridor toward Jacob's office.

After that, it was business as usual. Or, at least, as close to usual as you could get, considering the circumstances. R.L. disappeared into his office. Priss busied herself, generating paper. Jolene busied herself, typing and filing and doing whatever. And me—I busied myself, doing pretty much nothing. Except, of course, mulling over everything. Thinking about Priss, and how she was turning out to be an entirely different person from what I'd expected. Thinking about Jacob and wondering how in hell he'd managed to get so many folks to hate him in only one short lifetime. And, of course, thinking about the Rip Dilemma. Why on earth was everybody, it seemed, suddenly accusing Rip of what was—for him—the unthinkable?

Shortly after nine, Jolene started sorting the morning's mail, and that gave me something else to think about. Jolene had no sooner carried a stack of envelopes into Priss's office and returned to her desk, when Priss appeared in the doorway beside me, a white envelope in her hand, her eyes very wide.

Priss extended the envelope toward me, without saying a word. Her hand was shaking.

Its address printed in all capitals in blue ballpoint pen,

the envelope looked exactly like the one Jacob had shown me yesterday morning in my office. Except for one thing. This time it wasn't addressed to Jacob—it said simply, "Vandeventer Poultry," and then the address.

I opened the envelope real careful, and pulled out a piece of white bond paper, trying to handle it only by its edges as best as I could. The note, like the first one, had been made by tearing words out of a newspaper and gluing them in place.

It read:

NEVER MIND.

CHAPTER

10

P riss's face had been almost as white as the note I held in my hands. After she read it, though, color started returning to her cheeks. "Haskell, what does this mean?" she said. She actually looked at me as if she expected me to know.

Fact was, I had no idea. Was the would-be kidnapper really calling things off? Or did he just want me to let down my guard, so he could get his hands on Priss?

Priss had apparently made up her mind on the subject. "Well, this is *great*," she said. She was actually smiling. "I guess this proves what I said all along—that the note was nothing but a prank."

I was looking at the envelope, not feeling at all like smiling myself. The envelope was postmarked yesterday, Pigeon Fork, Kentucky. Priss and I had found Jacob right around five-thirty. Since the one and only post office in Pigeon Fork closes on weekdays at five, then—in order for it to have been mailed yesterday—the note had to have been sent *before* Priss and I discovered Jacob's body. And yet whoever had sent this note had not addressed it to Jacob, as he had the first note. Had the sender already known—*before five*—that Jacob should no longer be included on any mailing lists? If so, how had he known?

Lord. Was it possible that whoever had sent this note was Jacob's killer? I must've looked kind of appalled, because Priss gave me an odd look and said, "What is it, Haskell?"

I explained what all I'd been thinking. After that, it was Priss's turn to look appalled. She stood there, staring at me, her mouth white, as I went into her office to call up Vergil.

Oddly enough, Vergil didn't sound any too happy to hear from me. "You still there?" he said. His tone implied that my continued presence on the Vandeventer Poultry premises was a personal affront.

"Jacob Vandeventer hired me for three days, remember?" I said.

"Hm," Vergil said.

I took a deep breath. If I didn't know better, I'd say Vergil was working himself up into a snit again—getting all bent out of shape about me horning in on his cases. Vergil, apparently, had not learned back in nursery school how to share. I decided, however, not to point this out to him.

Besides, Vergil seemed to forget to be irritated after I told him what it was that I was calling about. He didn't waste any time getting to Vandeventer Poultry, either. Less than twenty minutes later, he was pulling up in front of the building, which meant, of course, that he'd been speeding all the way. Once again, Vergil had his siren going full-blast when he pulled up.

Vergil must believe in the power of advertising.

As soon as the siren sounded outside, R.L. came running out of his office, looking pale. "What—what's happened?" he said.

Priss showed him the note, but all that evidently did was raise more questions in R.L.'s mind. "So what are the police doing here?" he said, knitting his brows together. "Why aren't we 'never minding'?"

I was still explaining it to him when Vergil walked in the front door. It took a while for R.L. to grasp what I was saying. Vergil had already gone into Priss's office and started questioning her by the time I was done. I still wasn't sure R.L. had gotten it. "You mean Jacob's killer coulda sent this here note?" he said.

I stared at R.L. No wonder Priss had been angry that she'd been passed over in favor of her brother. This guy would probably have trouble managing a lemonade stand.

Vergil's visit should've taken about fifteen minutes, tops. I mean, how long does it take to put a note and an envelope into a plastic evidence bag, and then take it off to be checked for fingerprints? Vergil stretched the whole thing out into an hour. Looking quite a bit less cheerful than Jacob had yesterday evening, Vergil first talked to Priss, then to me, and then finally to R.L. and Jolene.

When he talked to me, the first thing Vergil mentioned was the way I was dressed. "I didn't know you had a sport coat," he said. His tone implied that my having such a garment in my wardrobe was tragic news.

I decided that his comment didn't deserve an answer. "Is this what you're going to be wearing 'round town from now on?" Vergil said, his eyes mournful. "It looks kinda high-falutin', to my way of thinking."

I actually had to remind Vergil why he'd dropped by. Even then, the whole time I was talking to him, he kept eyeing my coat. Disapprovingly.

Vergil's talking to R.L. and Jolene was strictly window dressing. I would've bet money Vergil didn't really expect to get any useful information out of either one of them.

Jolene I felt sorry for. The whole time she was talking to Vergil, she looked as though every drop of blood was slowly draining from her face. Poor thing. There were probably rabbits out in the woods right that minute that were a lot less shy than Jolene. And what exactly was Vergil trying to find out from her? The note had been delivered with the rest of the mail. Did Vergil want to know if Jolene could pick the *mailman* out of a lineup?

Vergil even went back into Jacob's office and poked

around in there for a while. I followed him back there, and maybe I was getting a little touchy, but I thought Vergil gave me a real superior look when he stepped over the yellow caution tape still in place and headed inside.

Inez was, of course, sitting there at her desk when Vergil went in. She looked real sorry for me, the way you might a kid who hasn't been invited to play with the others. I smiled at her to show I didn't really care that Vergil was now in Jacob's office, no doubt uncovering all sorts of vital clues right that minute. Inez gave me a thin-lipped smile. "You know," she said, leaning forward, her tone confidential, "I heard the sirens and all, but I decided I'd better not leave my desk. It's not time for my fifteen-minute morning break yet, you know."

I continued to smile at her. This woman should be in the Secretary Hall of Fame.

I couldn't help but wonder, now that Inez was going to be out of a job, if she'd be at all interested in working for Elmo and me. Of course, it could be messy. It would involve one of us—either Elmo or me—actually telling Melba to her face that her services were no longer needed.

If, indeed, they ever were.

I couldn't be sure, but I strongly doubted if Elmo and I had it in us to fire a mother of five. If we didn't feel guilty enough about it all by ourselves, there was no doubt an ample load of public opinion in Pigeon Fork to help us out in that regard. Folks would be sure to think that anybody who'd put the sole support of five kids out of work was scum.

Not to mention Melba herself. Melba, in her own understanding way, could probably be counted on to send those particular five kids—the ones she solely supported—to express their individual opinions personally. No doubt in spray paint on Elmo's car and my truck. And maybe on the sides of our houses.

Inez leaned forward again. "I don't suppose you know why the sheriff's here again?"

Looking at Inez and realizing what a secretary-fanatic she was, I knew very well that whatever I told her would probably, in all likelihood, go no further. But I couldn't take a chance. Maybe Inez still had a trace of Melba in her. There was a slim possibility that whatever I happened to mention to Inez could very well be all over Pigeon Fork by nightfall. And if Inez told, Inez would no doubt also tell exactly where it was that she'd gotten her information. It didn't seem like a good idea to give the impression that as a private detective, I wasn't all that private. "I'm not sure," I lied. If Inez was going to hear about Priss's new note, she'd have to hear about it from somebody else.

"Oh." Inez looked disappointed. Clearly, she didn't have anything to do but sit there and wait for the phone to ring. She drummed her fingers idly on the desk. "You know, I just hate that icky yellow tape," she said, by way of making conversation. "Do you suppose it really means it?"

She had lost me. "Means what?"

Inez drummed her fingers on the desktop again. "Do you think it really means 'Do not cross'? I mean, if I can't even go into his office, I sure can't dust like I'm supposed to every single morning—and I can't straighten the stuff on top of his desk. Or water his plants. Or turn his desk calendar to today's date. I can't do any of the things a good secretary always does."

I tried to look sympathetic. Truth was, I didn't think Jacob was going to mind his desk calendar not being turned for once.

"They'll take down that tape soon," I said. "Don't worry."

Inez sniffed. "Well, I certainly hope so." Her tone was injured.

After that, I decided it would probably be best if I resumed my post outside Priss's door. If I talked to Inez much more, I might throw caution to the winds and start *begging* her to come work for me and Elmo.

Then, too, there was no use in my being out there

when Vergil came back outside. He'd probably go "Nyah, nyah, nyah" right in my face.

Besides, I pretty much knew what Vergil was up to in there. He was staking out his territory. I do believe that if Vergil could've put a yellow caution tape around the entirety of Crayton County, he'd have done it.

Before Vergil finally left, he came back by Priss's office. I had seated myself out front again, a position that put me at a distinct disadvantage, looking up at Vergil like a little kid. Vergil stared down at me, his face grim. "Haskell," he said, "don't you think it's odd that all these murders have started happening after *you* got back in town?"

I stared back at him. Exactly what was his point? Did he think a whole passel of criminals had followed me down here from Louisville? Or was he implying that maybe I was the leader of some kind of gang, importing cold-blooded killers into his formerly peaceful little town?

Apparently, Vergil didn't expect an answer, because he didn't wait for me to give one. He just went right on, his eyes now sadder than I'd ever seen them—and that was going some. "I hate to say this, I really do—"

I sat up a little straighter. Let me see now. As my near-family, Vergil apparently didn't hate implying that I was personally responsible for a crime wave, but, according to Vergil, it appeared now that there was, after all, *something* he minded telling me. This ought to be good.

Vergil cleared his throat. "When I talked to Ruby last night," he said, looking toward the floor now, "she told me she left here around four-fifteen or so yesterday. So, the way I see it, she had plenty of time to get to the post office after she left." Vergil sighed heavily. He studied his shoes for a good minute, and then he added, "You know, it don't take no time at all to tear two little words out of a newspaper."

Vergil had a point.

I nodded, starting to feel sad myself. Things sure

weren't looking any too good for Ruby. Could that cherubic little woman actually have committed murder?

Vergil's eyes looked as if they were looking at all the pain and suffering in the world. "Just thought I'd mention it," he added.

I nodded, without saying anything. I watched Vergil slowly head out the front door of Vandeventer Poultry, and I decided then and there that there was no real reason to mention to Priss what Vergil had just said to me.

She was upset enough as it was.

Evidently, her getting correspondence from a possible murderer had rattled her a tad. Priss was still looking pale when, at eleven o'clock on the dot, Alton Gabbard came walking through the front door.

It was a good thing I'd seen the man a couple of times before on the street, or my jaw probably would've dropped open the second I saw him. It was that hard to imagine that *this* was the guy that everybody I knew kept saying was Pigeon Fork's answer to F. Lee Bailey.

Alton Gabbard was five feet tall, tops. Weighing in at well over two hundred fifty pounds, he looked like a fireplug dressed in a navy blue designer suit. His hair was dark brown, graying at the temples, and it might've given him an air of distinction if it hadn't been so curly. As it was, Alton Gabbard looked like a fireplug in a designer suit with an Afro.

Looking at Gabbard, you couldn't help but wonder how in the world this guy managed to create any kind of commanding presence in a courtroom. At least, you wondered that right up to the moment Gabbard opened his mouth. "I'm here to see Miss Priscilla Vandeventer," he said, fingering the blue paisley handkerchief in his vest pocket. His voice boomed across the lobby.

I stared at him. Gabbard had the voice of a radio announcer. In fact, the radio was probably where he belonged. If you heard that voice and couldn't see him, you'd think he was six foot five and looked like Burt Reynolds.

Jolene colored as usual but managed to pull herself

together enough to buzz Priss and announce Gabbard's arrival. Minutes later, all three of us—Priss, Gabbard, and me—were seated in Priss's office, Priss behind her desk, Gabbard and I seated next to each other in two gray metal chairs, facing Priss. Gabbard looked annoyed the minute he sat down. I thought for a second that it was because he wasn't seated behind the desk—in the position of authority—but, as it turned out, Gabbard was mad because Priss had included *me* in the discussion.

Evidently, Gabbard felt that whatever he had to say was private family business. I picked up on this right about the time Gabbard said, "You know, what I have to say is *private* family business." Staring at me, as if I were a roach.

Priss frowned, giving Gabbard a less than cordial look. "I want Haskell to be here," she said. "He's a good friend of mine."

I couldn't help it. I glanced over at her, surprised. Did she really consider me a good friend? That was right nice to hear.

Apparently, Gabbard didn't feel the same way about it. He scowled at me, and said, "If you wish." He managed to say the words and sigh all at the same time. It was a technique that Vergil, no doubt, would envy.

Priss ignored him and went on, explaining about Ruby's growing predicament and how Vergil had suggested last night that Priss contact an attorney for her mother.

Gabbard's eyebrows went up at that.

"Ruby?" he said. "The authorities actually think that *Ruby*—" He didn't finish, but he didn't have to. Priss was already nodding her dark head, her gray eyes huge.

"Why, that's preposterous!" Gabbard said, his voice booming around us. It sounded as if the radio had been turned up a couple of notches. "Ruby couldn't possibly be a suspect!"

Gabbard didn't look quite so convinced by the time Priss finished telling him why it was that the police had reached such a conclusion. Priss pretty much covered it all—how, according to Inez, Ruby had been the last one to see Jacob yesterday, how Ruby made no bones about being furious with Jacob for handing the company over to R.L., not to mention Jacob's dumping her for Willadette a year ago. Ruby didn't actually use the word *dump,* but Gabbard got the gist, tapping a plump forefinger on his double chin the entire time Priss was speaking. The only thing Priss didn't mention was the terribly affectionate way in which Ruby referred to the deceased as an asshole. Evidently, though, Priss had told him enough.

"Oh my," Gabbard said. His voice didn't boom at all this time. Gabbard sat there beside me, tapping his chins for a few more minutes.

"Well, of course, you realize that I don't generally take *criminal* cases." Gabbard said the word *criminal* with obvious distaste. "But I will, of course, make an exception in this one instance. Since the Vandeventer family have been such dear, dear friends all these years." Gabbard was making it sound as if he were sacrificing his firstborn. He seemed to be neglecting to mention that there was also the very real possibility that if he didn't make an exception in this one instance, the fat fees he collected annually from the Vandeventers were history. "And I realize, Priscilla, my dear," Gabbard went on, "that you want nothing less than the very *best* handling this delicate matter."

Apparently, Gabbard was one of those men who believed that his bodily wastes do not give off an odor. To put it as, no doubt, he would have put it himself.

Gabbard looked from Priss to me as if he expected applause. I myself had never felt less like applauding in my life. Priss looked equally unmoved.

Since he wasn't getting the expected gratitude, Gabbard must've decided to move on. He cleared his throat and said, "I suppose you're both already aware that I had an appointment with Jacob this afternoon to get his new will signed. And to—ah—transfer a considerable number of Jacob's shares in Vandeventer Poultry to R.L. It would've given R.L. complete control." Gabbard gave Priss a quick, solicitous look, as if acknowledging that he knew he was on a touchy subject here.

Priss just looked at him, her face immobile.

"The new will would also have left a greater share of Jacob's estate to his—ah—*present* wife."

A muscle jumped in Priss's jaw, but that was the only reaction she had. I stared at her, amazed. Either this woman had only very recently learned to control her temper, or all this wasn't news to her. Remembering Priss's terrific self-control yesterday, I tended to believe the latter.

Gabbard's eyes were now on his lap. "Jacob explained that he felt that his—ah—primary allegiance had to be to his current spouse."

Or, to put it another way, as time went by Jacob was feeling less and less guilty about dumping Ruby for Willadette.

Something else also occurred to me. Lord. If Jacob had lived much longer, one day he might have written Ruby out of his will altogether. Ruby's best deal was, no doubt, in Jacob's *first* will. The one now still in effect because Jacob hadn't lived to sign a new one.

This was either the result of remarkable luck or real good planning on someone's part.

I moved around uneasily in my chair. There was no getting around it. This gave Ruby yet another motive.

It apparently didn't take a detective to figure this out. Gabbard cleared his throat and tapped a couple more times on his chins. "Of course, just because you have a motive does not necessarily mean you'll be accused of the crime."

Priss blinked and nodded her head. You could tell she didn't quite believe him.

It didn't help Gabbard's believability factor to have him say right then, "By the way, you'll call me immediately, in the event that your mother is—ah—taken in for questioning?" he said.

What a delicate way to put that. I was impressed.

Gabbard seemed to think he'd said all he needed to

say. He got to his feet and stuck his hand out toward Priss.

Priss shook it without speaking.

Gabbard even extended his hand to me before he left, but you could tell he was only doing it because Priss was standing right there, and he knew he'd better not insult one of her "good friends."

Shaking Gabbard's hand was like grasping a piece of raw liver. Only I think liver would've been a little warmer.

As soon as Gabbard was out the front door, I decided that this was as good a time as any to find out exactly what all Priss had known before Gabbard showed up here today. "I guess all that stuff about your father leaving more to Willadette in his new will wasn't exactly news to you, was it?" I said.

Priss had been looking sort of stunned. I guess actually hearing Gabbard talk out loud about the possibility of Ruby being taken in for questioning had brought the whole thing home to her. When I spoke, though, Priss's eyes became suddenly alert. "Yes, as a matter of fact, Dad told me and R.L. about the new will two days ago," she said, her tone cautious.

I nodded, my eyes on hers. That's all I did—I just nodded—but Priss started looking like maybe she was getting annoyed. "And *yes*, Haskell," she said, her tone a bit testy, "I *did* tell Mama that night what all Dad intended to do. That doesn't mean anything."

"If it doesn't mean anything, why didn't you tell me about it yesterday?"

Now there was no doubt. Priss was annoyed, all right. Lava flowed once again behind her eyes. "If you can't figure out why I didn't mention it, then you're not a very good detective, are you?"

I decided to let that one pass. Still, was that any way to talk to a good friend?

"Look, Priss, you've got to level with me," I said, "or I'm working at a real disadvantage here. Whatever you tell me doesn't necessarily mean I'm going to be jumping to any horrible conclusions, but I do need to know what I'm dealing with.''

"What you're dealing with is a mean old man who didn't care who he hurt as long as he got his way. *That's* what you're dealing with.'' Priss's voice was bitter. "A man who'd turn his back on the mother of his own children.''

"Is that why you were so mad at him yesterday afternoon?''

Priss looked away and shook her dark head. "Yesterday afternoon Dad told me I was to hand over all my files to R.L.—that I was to start training R.L. right away to do my job.'' Priss's voice sounded real tired. "Dad knew I loved my job—that I'd rather work here in the family business more than anywhere else. So see, Haskell,'' Priss finished, looking back over at me, "Mama's not the only one with a good motive, now, is she?''

What could I say? All of that did sound like a perfectly good motive for murder to me. And yet I couldn't help but wonder if Priss wasn't just telling me this now to divert suspicion from her mom.

I took a deep breath and cautiously moved on. "Is there anything else that you haven't quite gotten around to telling me?''

Something flickered in Priss's eyes. Something quick and furtive, a wild thing darting for cover.

I stared back at her, getting an uneasy feeling in my stomach. Great, just great. So Priss *was* holding something back.

I took another deep breath before I spoke again. This case was going to make me start gulping Rolaids again, just like I used to do back in Louisville. The last year I was on the force, I carried around the giant, economy-sized package of industrial-strength Rolaids in my unmarked car. "All right, Priss,'' I said, my voice now as tired as hers. "What is it? What else haven't you been telling me?''

Priss looked me straight in the eye. Without blinking once. "Haskell,'' she said quietly, "I've told you everything I know.''

Staring into those clear gray eyes, I knew—without a shadow of a doubt—that she was lying.

CHAPTER
11

Priss stared straight at me, her eyes real wide open. It was the kind of look a kid always gives you when you know he's guilty of something. "I'm not holding out on you, Haskell," Priss said. She managed to put an injured tone into her voice. "I can't think of a thing I haven't told you." She blinked those big gray eyes of hers a couple more times for good measure, and added, "I wouldn't lie to you, Haskell. I really wouldn't. Besides, what good would it do me?"

That last sentence is a real red flag. Because folks who are telling the truth don't generally think to tell you so. And they for sure don't ask you to wonder why they're lying. Truth tellers just naturally assume that you'll believe them because what they're saying is really so. It's only liars who insist they're telling the truth. And then try to divert your attention to something else. Like playing guessing games.

I swallowed a couple of times while all this ran through my mind. "Priss, why don't you just level with me?"

Which, of course, I shouldn't have said, because Priss said, "I *am* leveling with you," and I said, "Oh no you're not," and she said, "How in hell would you know?" and I said, "Because I do, that's all." And it went down from there. Until finally I was saying something totally dumb like, "If there's one thing I can't stand, it's not being told everything there is to know about a case I'm working on. I might as well be working blindfolded!"

To which Priss replied, breathing heavily, "Will you shut up? Everybody out in the lobby can hear you."

Priss's door *was* standing open, and I guess I was talking pretty loud. But seeing how upset Priss was about my talking so loud, I raised my voice a little louder. "Oh yeah? Well, if you think that was loud, how about THIS? TELL ME WHAT YOU KNOW."

Priss's eyes got real round. She did a quick glance toward the door, and then said, "Come on, Haskell. Let's go to lunch."

This I took to mean that she was giving in. That Priss, no doubt, intended to tell me what she knew in more private surroundings. Like while we ate, which was fine with me. "That's more like it," I said.

Lizbeth had evidently showed up for *her* daily lunch with R.L. while Priss and I were yelling at each other, because she was standing out there at the front desk when Priss and I walked out. Lizbeth was wearing yet another fur—this time a blue fox wrapped around her tall frame. It was getting kind of warm outside for somebody to still be wearing fur, but I had a hunch that Lizbeth probably wore a mink coat to the beach. As a bathing suit cover-up. She stared openly at me and Priss, her large blue eyes intense, as we headed past her.

Neither Priss nor I spoke. If Lizbeth wasn't going to condescend to speak to *me,* I certainly wasn't going to condescend to speak to *her.*

Priss and I walked to my truck. You'll remember I'd parked it only a couple of steps from the front door of Vandeventer Poultry. This time I was real glad I'd parked so close, because as soon as I walked outside, I realized two things. One, my nose was, unfortunately, in excellent working condition after all. Two, the Eau was back with a vengeance. I walked rapidly to my truck, intent on getting inside before my nose became suicidal.

It was a real pretty spring day—dogwoods were blooming here and there among the distant trees, like white popcorn against bright green foliage—but I barely gave them a glance. I had other things on my mind. Things like trying to get my truck door open in record time. Things like trying not to take any more breaths than I absolutely had to. Things like wondering why it was that the Vandeventers didn't even seem to notice the smell. Standing on the other side of truck, waiting for me to get in and unlock her door, Priss wasn't even wrinkling her nose. Or, say, gagging.

I don't know. Maybe your sense of smell is like your sense of hearing. If constantly hearing extremely loud noises can eventually make you deaf, maybe constantly smelling extremely bad odors can numb your nose. Priss's sense of smell must've been in a coma.

It seemed to take forever to get my key in the lock. I mentally kicked myself for locking my truck in the first place. You'd think that if I didn't lock my own house out here, I wouldn't bother to lock my truck, either. But, somehow, locking my truck is too ingrained. After living in a mid-sized city all those years, I can't seem to bring myself to leave it open.

I finally got my door unlocked and got inside, slamming it shut. Shutting the door helped a whole lot. The smell wasn't completely gone, but at least you could breathe naturally again without wanting to kill yourself. As I was reaching over to unlock the door on the passenger side for Priss, I noticed Jacob's White House on my right, sitting high up there on the hill in back of Vandeventer Poultry. The Vandeventer mansion seemed to be looking down on me with a distinct air of superiority. No pun intended. It couldn't be more than a five-minute drive away, and yet the Vandeventer home looked like it belonged to another world.

A cleaner, tidier world.

A definitely better-smelling world.

A world in which folks didn't get themselves murdered.

I froze, right in the middle of putting my key in the ignition, as Priss got in beside me. It suddenly hit me what it was that had been niggling at me since last night. Yesterday afternoon, R.L. had left the office at three-thirty—and yet, when he and Lizbeth had returned to Vandeventer Poultry last night, Lizbeth had told Willa-dette that R.L. had only just been walking in the door when Priss had phoned her with the news of Jacob's death. Priss's phone call had to have been after five-thirty.

So—the $64,000 question was, *where was R.L. all that time?*

The whole time I was driving into Pigeon Fork, I kept going over this in my mind. Where in hell *was* R.L. during the time his father was murdered?

Priss reached over and turned on the radio as soon as we pulled out of the parking lot, so I got the distinct impression that she wasn't in any mood right that minute to do any talking.

That was all right with me. I could be patient. For a while.

Priss and I had decided on Lassiter's Restaurant in downtown Pigeon Fork for lunch. However, it wasn't as if we had a lot of places in town to choose from. Once you went to Frank's Bar and Grill and Lassiter's, you either started over again or you went home and did your own cooking.

Downtown Pigeon Fork was crowded, like it always is at noon. Or, at least, it was crowded for Pigeon Fork. I counted all of ten cars and trucks parked up and down the block, and on either side of the street, near Lassi-ter's. Nearly every one of the old-fashioned parking me-ters that line Main Street had a car or a truck pulled up to it, too. In Pigeon Fork, you can park for two hours for a dime, so this isn't exactly a big source of revenue for the town. You'd never know it, though, to hear folks around these parts talk. I hear tell they've been com-plaining about the price of parking for the past five years—ever since the powers that be raised it up from a nickel.

Priss and I ended up parking on Mulberry, a side street, and walking back. On the way, Priss didn't seem any more talkative than she'd been in the truck. She nodded at Pop Matheny, who waved at us from inside his barber shop, and she lifted her hand in greeting to a woman across the street—who was a total stranger to me—but if you didn't know better, you'd have thought *I* was invisible as far as Priss was concerned. Even when she beat me by a couple of steps to the entrance of the restaurant, making sure I didn't get the chance to hold the door for her, Priss didn't say a word. She just walked on into Lassiter's Restaurant without so much as glancing my way.

Lassiter's Restaurant is something of a misnomer, but I don't reckon Cyrus Lassiter would get too many customers if he put on his sign exactly what his establishment really is—Lassiter's Greasy Spoon.

Even that doesn't exactly tell the whole picture, because Lassiter's spoons sure aren't the only things that are greasy. The plates, the bowls, the glasses—*and* the food—are all pretty well coated. Grease, you might say, is a Lassiter specialty. Still, Cyrus Lassiter does do one thing right—barbecue. The down-home hickory flavor of Cyrus's barbecue sauce makes you forgive him for everything else.

You even forgive the music he plays the entire time you're eating. Cyrus got himself religion a couple of months back, right after his brother died real sudden of a heart attack, so instead of the country ballads that used to blast out of the two speakers at either end of the room, now you've got to listen to hymns. It makes you a little nervous, listening to "Onward Christian Soldiers" and "Amazing Grace" while you're eating Cyrus's food. You can't help but wonder if maybe Cyrus knows a little more than you do about the quality of his cuisine, if he feels compelled to prepare you for the hereafter right while you're swallowing a big mouthful of his barbecued beef.

Priss and I slipped into one of the red plastic-covered booths near the door, and it was no time at all until Cyrus Lassiter himself came by and took our orders. I reckon that's what comes of being with Pigeon Fork royalty—you get waited on right away. A big, heavyset guy whose face was about as red as the catsup bottle sitting on our linoleum-topped table, Cyrus all but bowed in front of Priss. "Real sorry to hear about your dad," he said.

Priss muttered something I didn't catch, and immediately ordered her lunch. It seemed kind of abrupt to me, but Cyrus seemed to excuse her behavior under the general heading of grief. His small, deep-set eyes were filled with sympathy when he looked over at me.

I hoped he didn't look that sad because we both had chosen the specialty of the house—the barbecue platter. The platter comes with the works—strips of barbecued beef, a hunk of barbecued pork ribs, some barbecued chicken wings, french fries, and a huge dill pickle—and it seemed like a lot to eat for a slim girl Priss's size. Maybe, though, getting mad at me back at the office had given Priss an appetite.

After we gave Cyrus our order, I sat there and waited awhile for Priss to start in, telling me what all she hadn't enlightened me about before now. Before long, though, I got the distinct feeling that I would wait forever if I expected Priss to *volunteer* anything. Priss took a sip out of her water glass, fiddled nervously with the aluminum napkin holder, and arranged her silverware so that it lined up perfectly parallel with the sides of her red plastic placemat. She did all that, but she didn't say a thing. Not a thing.

I decided it was up to me to get the ball rolling. Moreover, I'd better do it now, rather than later in my truck. My reasoning here was pretty simple. In the truck, Priss could take my head off. At Lassiter's Restaurant, crowded with a good portion of Pigeon Fork's downtown population, Priss was a lot less likely to make a scene.

Particularly since, every once in a while, somebody

would come over to the booth and offer their condolences. It looks real bad for a person in supposed mourning to have a screaming fit in public. People in mourning, oddly enough, are actually expected to be on the subdued side.

I took a deep breath. "Well, Priss," I said, "do you have anything you want to tell me?"

Priss gave me a level look. "I don't think so," she said. She took a sip of her water, staring straight at me with her eyes real round and innocent-looking again, like they'd been back at her office.

Apparently, I had misinterpreted Priss's invitation to lunch. She hadn't been giving in at all. Priss had just been trying to get me out of the office, away from anybody who could overhear what we were talking about. Claudzilla always did say I didn't know one thing about women. More and more, I was starting to believe she was right.

I gave Priss as level a look as she was directing at me. "For starters," I said, "why don't you tell me where you think R.L. was yesterday afternoon? The way I figure it, he's got about two hours to account for."

I had hit a nerve. Priss's gray eyes blinked, and a bright spot of color appeared on each of her cheeks. "I—I don't know what you're talking about."

I was getting downright tired of playing this little game. "Look, Priss, you know something. Now spill it," I said. "The way I see it, R.L. had plenty of time to sneak back to Vandeventer Poultry, hide outside until Inez left with Ruby, and then go back in and—"

Priss was already shaking her head before I'd said ten words. "Haskell, you're seeing it wrong. R.L. getting home late yesterday has nothing to do with my father's death. *Nothing. Whatsoever.*"

"How can you be so sure about that?" It seemed a logical question.

Priss's answer wasn't quite so logical. "Because I am, that's all."

Cyrus showed up with our platters right then, and

Priss glared at me, practically daring me to say anything in front of him. Was it my imagination, or did Cyrus give Priss her platter with considerably more courtesy than he did mine?

I made up my mind that it wasn't my imagination right after Cyrus all but slapped my platter down in front of me. The platter landed so hard some of the barbecued pork fell off onto my red plastic placemat. "Oops," Cyrus said. Immediately, however, he turned to Priss. "Do you need anything else, Miss Vandeventer?" he said.

"I'd like a napkin to clean this up," I said.

Cyrus looked over at me as if surprised to see me still sitting there. "Oh. Yeah," he said. He handed me the bill and walked off.

Unlike grease, service is something that Lassiter's is not known for. Except maybe the *lack* of it.

Once our lunch arrived, I could tell that Priss was trying to keep her mouth consistently full so she couldn't answer any questions. Every time I tried to ask her something, she'd just shake her head and point to her mouth, doing a pretty good imitation of a cow with its cud.

I didn't buy it.

Besides, I didn't care how Priss answered me, as long as she answered. For all I cared, she could scribble her answers out on one of the handful of paper napkins Cyrus had thoughtfully given *her* but neglected to give me.

"OK, Priss," I said, "if you don't tell me what you know, I'm going to have to mention to Vergil that R.L. was missing for two hours yesterday—"

As soon as I said Vergil's name, it was amazing. Priss suddenly remembered how to swallow. "This is blackmail," she said.

"Matter of fact, it is," I said.

Priss stared at me, apparently going over her options in her mind. She evidently decided she didn't have any, because she finally said, "OK, OK, there's no need to bring the sheriff into this." Now it was Priss's voice that was sounding tired. "You're going to feel like a real fool, though, when I get finished telling you all this."

I just looked at her. Maybe Priss didn't know it, but she was talking to a guy who—even though he was a detective—had been the very last person in the world to find out that his own wife was cheating on him. In fact, this particular guy had only found out about it because his *wife* had decided to mention it to him on her way out the door. As sort of a parting gift. And now Priss actually entertained the notion that *she* could make me feel foolish? Was she kidding? To make me feel foolish these days, you have to go some.

Priss sighed and went on. "R.L.'s been having an affair for the last few months. That's where he was those two hours—with *her*." Priss wiped her mouth with one of her napkins. It needed wiping. "R.L. and I have always been real close—I guess because we're only a year apart, it's almost like we're twins or something—anyway, he confided in me a few weeks ago."

I didn't feel foolish, like Priss said I would, but—I'll admit it—I *did* feel surprised. R.L. was actually fooling around on *Lizbeth?* Was the man suicidal? Lizbeth didn't seem like the sort of woman who would take this kind of news graciously.

"Who's the lucky woman?" I said, taking in a big mouthful of barbecued pork.

I immediately regretted saying that so flip, because Priss's eyes narrowed. "I think I've told you all I intend to. Besides, all you need to know is that R.L. didn't sneak back to Vandeventer Poultry yesterday."

I swallowed. "Is it someone I know?"

Priss glared at me. "Haskell, believe me, you don't know her. And I'm not telling you anything more."

"Have I seen her around town?" Mentally, I was trying to think of any women in Pigeon Fork who might possibly be sneaking around with R.L. I couldn't think of a one. Except maybe Melba. She herself would no doubt be willing, but I think R.L. might object. Melba is no less than a hundred pounds overweight, and after meeting her five hellions, it is my opinion that Melba should not be looking for a husband. A *warden* is what she should be looking for. R.L. may not be any whiz kid, but I'm pretty sure he'd reach the same conclusion.

Priss was really looking exasperated now. "Look, Haskell, you can light matches under my fingernails, or stake me out over an anthill, or do whatever it is you private detectives do, but I'm *not* telling you who the woman is. Got it?"

The two options she suggested were real tempting, particularly in light of the tone Priss was using with me, but I decided Priss *was* probably telling the truth. Besides, she looked pretty determined. I could probably do all the bizarre things she'd mentioned, and Priss still wouldn't tell me. And I would've wasted all those matches for nothing. Not to mention scaring a lot of innocent ants.

"I got it," I said.

Priss took a bite of her dill pickle, chewed it slowly, and then added, "I guess you realize now that's why I was so mad at R.L. yesterday when we got back from lunch. He's been using me as an excuse for coming home late." Priss shrugged. "I mean, it's one thing for me to keep a secret for him, but when he starts telling Lizbeth that *I've* called a meeting, and that's why he's late—well, that's too much."

I remembered Priss yelling at R.L. yesterday to "leave her out of it." So *that* had been what she was talking about.

Priss was now lifting a forkful of barbecued pork to her mouth. "So, Haskell, *now* you know none of this has anything to do with my father's murder. And that there really wasn't any good reason for me to tell you."

"*This* was what you've been holding back all this time?"

Priss actually looked surprised. "Well, of course. Did you think there was something else?"

I shrugged, not wanting to say what I was thinking. Which, of course, was: There could be something else. For all I know. Now that I know you've been less than honest with me, how do I know when you're telling me the whole truth and when you're fudging a little?

Thinking all this made me feel real uneasy. I must've not done too good a job at covering up how I was feeling, either, because Priss started looking at me kind of strange. "You don't still seriously suspect R.L., do you?" Her voice was impatient. "I mean, Haskell, R.L. is the only one who clearly does *not* benefit from my father's death."

She was right. In fact, R.L. apparently had everything to gain, had Jacob lived just a day longer.

I nodded, concentrating now on one of my chicken wings.

Evidently, just nodding wasn't enough for Priss. She kept on stating her case. "I mean, even if R.L. *was* considering a divorce, well, being worth a lot more money ought to make it easier for him, shouldn't it?"

I nodded again, still chewing. What did the woman want from me? A signed affidavit?

Priss now nodded back at me. "Well, then," she said.

I had swallowed by then, and I decided that maybe she needed to hear me say it. "You're right. OK?"

Priss smiled at me. Lord, this woman really liked to win one.

Still, she was kind of cute, sitting there, smiling at me like that. It made me not want to tie her down over an anthill anywhere near as much as I had a couple of minutes before.

After that, we didn't do much more talking at all. We both mainly concentrated on making our barbecue disappear. Cyrus serves up his platters with homemade biscuits, which—while a little greasy, of course—were still real good. By the time Priss and I were headed on back to Vandeventer Poultry, I think the quality of our lunch had put us both in a much better mood.

The mood lasted right up until we pulled up in front of Vandeventer Poultry and we got out of my truck. Right away I noticed the smell didn't seem anywhere near as bad as when we'd left. Either the wind wasn't blowing as hard, or it had shifted directions, or my nose had slipped into a Vandeventer coma. Or maybe all of the above.

I hurried around the side of my Ford pickup, trying to get to Priss's door before she opened it, but she was already out the door by the time I got there. I followed Priss up the sidewalk, wondering if the woman was ever going to let me be a gentleman and get the door for her.

And then I heard it.

It was a sound that, if you've ever been a cop, you don't ever forget. It's like this particular sound is imprinted forever on your brain.

The sound of a gun being cocked.

"Priss, get down!" I yelled.

Naturally, instead of immediately dropping right where she stood, Priss turned around to look at me, her gray eyes puzzled. "What on earth—"

Whatever else Priss was going to say, she never got a chance to say it. I took a running leap and tackled her.

Somewhere between hitting Priss and hitting the ground, I heard the gun go off.

It was real strange. As Priss and I fell, one part of my mind was an absolute wreck, repeating, "Oh my God oh my God oh my God." And pretty much waiting to find out how a bullet feels when it rips into you. Another part of my mind was unbelievably calm, almost detached. It registered that the right side of my face was about to make painful contact with a concrete sidewalk. It registered that the shots seemed to be coming from the heavy shrubbery on the right side of the building. And it coolly counted off the shots.

One, two, three.

CHAPTER

12

Beneath me, Priss grunted. I'd hit her in the back, and I was now lying partially on top of her, my legs at an angle. The right side of my face was smarting some, on account of it going for a skate on the sidewalk, but as best as I could tell, that was my biggest injury. I wasn't so sure about Priss.

"Priss, have you been hit?" I whispered.

Having the breath knocked out of her must've clouded Priss's thinking a little, because apparently she misinterpreted what I was asking. She whispered back loud enough so that if indeed there was a killer still in the shrubbery trying to make up his mind whether or not to pump a few more bullets in our direction, he would've heard every word. "Yes, Haskell—"

My mouth actually went dry.

Until, of course, Priss went on. *"You* ought to know. *You* hit me."

I swallowed and decided maybe I'd better rephrase my question. "I mean, are you *shot?*"

"Oh. No." Priss tried to accompany this with a shake of her head, but lying flat on the ground hampered her head movement some. All she did was jerk her head back and forth a little.

162

I took a deep breath. Thank God she was OK.

I now turned my own head to the right, so that I could take a good look at the shrubbery on the side of the building. It was so thick, though, I couldn't decide if whoever had shot at us was still back there, hiding and watching. Or had he already left?

It wasn't the sort of thing you wanted to gamble with.

It was, however, real uncomfortable lying facedown on a sidewalk with somebody crumpled beneath you. In spite of that, oddly enough, I didn't feel at all inclined to get up just yet. Bullets whizzing by within inches of my ear make me get real cautious like that.

Priss seemed to feel exactly the same way I did. She lay there beneath me, not moving a muscle.

I figure we both might still be lying there, having folks who wanted to go in the front door of Vandeventer Poultry step over us, if I hadn't heard footsteps running away in the distance. The shooter had apparently taken off the second Priss and I hit the sidewalk.

I scrambled to my feet, got out my gun, and took off after whoever it was. What I failed to reckon on was how thick that shrubbery was. And how many thorns grew on those bushes. Lord. Who in the world would actually plant shrubs like this? Two names, of course, immediately came to mind. The Marquis de Sade. And Lizbeth.

Huge thorns grabbing at my slacks and hanging on to my socks and, not incidentally, scratching up my legs slowed me down quite a bit. By the time I'd gotten the Shrubs de Sade to let go—and I was through to the other side—the shooter was nowhere in sight.

I stood there, putting my gun back in my holster, feeling little rivulets of blood trickle down into my socks. I hadn't even gotten a fleeting glimpse of the gunman. I couldn't even have said if it was a man or a woman.

I was not in my best mood.

It didn't help my mood any to walk around the shrubs—this time I didn't even *try* to get through them—and come back up the driveway only to find that R.L. and Lizbeth had just gotten back from lunch.

They must've arrived right that minute, because Priss was just starting to tell them what had happened. "Oh, R.L.," she was saying, her voice breathless. "Someone shot at me and Haskell! Really! Somebody actually fired a gun at us!" Priss sounded as if she couldn't believe it.

R.L.'s reaction was something to see. His handsome face went dead white. "What? What are you saying?" He grabbed Priss by the shoulders and looked into her eyes. "What are you SAYING?" he repeated, his voice going off into a crescendo. R.L. was staring wildly around and looking at Priss so oddly, you might've thought she was speaking a language he couldn't understand.

I think R.L.'s reaction surprised even Priss. "It's OK, R.L.," she said, her eyes on his. "I'm all right. Somebody shot at me, but Haskell over there saved my life." By then Priss had seen me walking up the driveway toward them, and the look she gave me was pure gratitude. "Haskell pushed me out of the way."

R.L. and Lizbeth both followed Priss's eyes. Up to that moment, I'd been shambling up the driveway, pulling thorns out of my socks and slacks as I walked. Seeing that everybody was watching me, I decided that from that distance everybody might think I'd was picking off some kind of parasite—like fleas or something. So I straightened myself up and walked straight toward them, trying to look like a hero should. Humble and lovable.

As far as Lizbeth was concerned, I reckon, lovable was out of the question. She seemed to have a problem with humble, too. Apparently, she didn't think I had anything to look humble about. "Maybe Haskell was just trying to save *himself*, and he fell into you while he was doing it," Lizbeth told Priss dryly.

Lizbeth had removed her blue fox coat and apparently left it in her car. She was dressed in a black linen suit with a large red silk scarf draped across one shoulder. It was the sort of outfit that made you wish there was a bull nearby.

R.L., however, didn't seem to share Lizbeth's sentiments. He walked toward me and did something I think was entirely uncalled for. He gave me a bear hug. Before he let me go, I thought I heard a couple of ribs crack. "Haskell," R.L. said gruffly. "What can I say, man?"

I backed away from him, trying to manage a convincing smile. "That's OK," I said. I kept right on smiling and backing away, but I was thinking, if R.L. tries to hug me again, I might have to pull my gun on him.

After that touching display, the entire group moved inside.

I went off to call up Vergil and rub my ribs some, while Priss and R.L. went on into her office. You might've thought it was R.L. who'd been shot at, if you listened to them. "It's all right, R.L., really." Priss kept telling him. "Nobody was hurt. I'm fine."

R.L. kept nodding his head just like he was listening to her. But his feet kept pacing. He literally could not seem to sit down. Priss's office door was still open, and I could see R.L. in there, constantly on the move. It was funny. In my estimation, R.L. seemed about a trillion times more upset over the *possibility* of Priss getting hurt than the *actuality* of his father being murdered.

This was one real strange family.

Speaking of strange, once again, believe it or not, my own near-family was less than delighted to hear from me. "You *still* there?" Vergil said. He sounded every bit as cheerful as he usually does.

I ignored Vergil's tone. "Sure am," I said. "It looks like I'm going to be out here a while, too," I added. "Being as how Priss and I were just shot at."

Truth was, I couldn't be sure whether the gunman had been aiming only at Priss, or whether I had also been a target. But, being as how I'd felt the wind of at least one bullet rush past my right ear, I thought—for Vergil's benefit—I'd just go ahead and include myself as a target whether the gunman meant to include me or not.

I could almost hear Vergil mentally starting up his sirens the second the words were out of my mouth.

While I waited for Vergil to come careening up the driveway, I went out and took another look at the shrubs from hell where the shooter had stood. I stepped around real careful, but there wasn't anything there at all that I could see. No footprints, no spent shells, nothing. It occurred to me, standing there in those sadistic bushes, that the kidnap note Jacob had received had said, "You'll never see Priscilla *alive* again." Maybe it hadn't been a kidnap note after all. Maybe whoever had sent that note had always meant to kill Priss. It was a chilling thought.

I made a move to go inside before the shrubs tore my socks completely to shreds, when I noticed Jolene coming up the sidewalk, evidently returning from lunch. Apparently, I wasn't the only one who saw Jolene returning, because right away, Lizbeth came out the front door and walked down the sidewalk to meet the receptionist. "Jolene, darling," Lizbeth said. "I've been hoping for a chance to talk to you alone."

Darling? Lizbeth was referring to the hired help as "darling"? I held my breath, moved further back behind the killer shrubs, and shamelessly eavesdropped.

"Something's happened, and I need to ask you some questions," Lizbeth said. She actually squeezed Jolene's arm chummily.

Jolene flinched a little when Lizbeth touched her. Looking like she'd just fallen into the clutches of some large predatory animal—which was a pretty accurate description of Lizbeth—Jolene asked, "What—what's all this about?"

Thinking that Lizbeth might be conducting her own little investigation, no doubt to show me up, I half expected Lizbeth to start in telling Jolene all about the shooting. I was wrong, though. Real wrong. Apparently, Lizbeth couldn't care less about a silly little thing like attempted murder. What she was investigating was a lot more serious.

"Well," Lizbeth said, linking her arm through Jolene's, "one of the sheriff's deputies happened to mention to me yesterday evening that R.L. left work at three-thirty. Is that true?" Lizbeth smoothed her windswept hair with a manicured hand.

Jolene's eyes grew about three sizes larger. "I—I believe so."

Lizbeth's eyes grew about three sizes smaller. "Would you believe that man didn't get home last night until well after five? Would you believe that?"

Jolene didn't answer. She just stared at Lizbeth, white-faced.

In the absence of Jolene's answer, Lizbeth decided to help her out. "Well, of course you believe it." Lizbeth gave Jolene a smile so sweet I thought Jolene might need a dose of insulin just to look at it. "That's just the way men are, aren't they? We women have got to watch them every minute. That's why, my dear, I thought maybe *you* might be able to help me out."

"Help?" Jolene said.

Here I believe Jolene was not actually calling for assistance but simply echoing what Lizbeth had just said.

Although I couldn't be sure.

Lizbeth nodded. "That's right," she said, with that insulin-shock smile again. "We women should stick together, don't you think? And all I want to know is one itsy bitsy thing."

The two of them had been moving toward the building, but now they stopped just outside the front door, not three feet from where I stood.

Lizbeth hurried on, but her voice now had lost every bit of its sweetness. Fingernails scraping on a blackboard have sounded more soothing. "Jolene, I want you to tell me the truth now. Has some woman been calling R.L. at the office here lately?"

In my opinion, Jolene answered a little too quickly. "Oh no, Lizbeth," she said, shaking her blond head from side to side. "Oh no, nothing like that."

Lizbeth's eyes narrowed. "Are you sure? Anybody calling him real often, the same voice, all the time?"

Jolene kept on shaking her head from side to side.

"Oh no," she said. "Lizbeth, I'm sure R.L. would never, NEVER, do anything to hurt his marriage." Jolene's voice shook almost as much as her head.

Lizbeth didn't look convinced. "Well, between you and me, R.L. had better not do anything to hurt his marriage, or I'll have both his nuts in a sling."

I stared at Lizbeth. What a delicate flower this woman was.

The two women moved inside, and I got out of the shrubs. None too soon, I might add, since I was just starting to hear Vergil's siren off in the distance.

And the sirens of Vergil's entourage.

Apparently, Vergil had decided this time to bring every car he knew that had a sound-making device. I half expected to see a couple of ice cream trucks heading up the winding driveway toward Vandeventer Poultry.

While Vergil's deputies went out to get their trousers and socks attacked by the Shrubs de Sade, Vergil—to my surprise—did a passing impression of somebody who might've been a little peeved if I'd gotten myself perforated by bullets.

"You OK, Haskell?" Vergil said.

If you didn't count sore ribs, thorn scratches, and a face that has kissed a sidewalk, I'd say I was doing fine. I nodded.

"Your face don't look any too good," Vergil said.

I just looked at him. I was pretty sure Vergil was just talking about the scrape down my right cheek, and not making some kind of general assessment.

I told Vergil in as much detail as I could remember what all had happened. There was a good chance that I dwelt a little too heavily on the part where I shoved Priss out of the way of a hail of bullets, but I reckon that was understandable. After all the grief I'd taken about what had happened to Jacob, I felt as if I needed to get a little of my own back. Still, it probably *was* a tad immodest of me to go on and on the way I did about saving Priss's life single-handedly, the way "any good bodyguard would do."

When I was done, Vergil looked like he was going to

be sick. He swallowed once, stared at me with those mournful eyes of his, and finally said, "Wow."

My face was hurting, and a few of the thorns left in my socks were distracting me some, but I could swear that there was a distinct note of sarcasm in that single word.

Vergil cleared his throat. "Did you happen to get a gander at this gun-toting maniac you saved Priss from?"

I was sure this time. That was sarcasm, all right. "Matter of fact, I didn't," I said, staring right back at him.

Vergil shrugged sadly. "Too bad," he said. His eyes, however, were another story. They said loud and clear that if he himself had been there, he would not only have saved Priss's life but also gotten the name, address, and, no doubt, the social security number of the gunman.

I smiled at him weakly.

We were sitting in R.L.'s office, Vergil having commandeered it this time for doing his questioning, and Vergil started scribbling something in a little notebook he pulled out of his jacket pocket. He didn't look up from the page when he said, "They finished the autopsy on old Jacob, you know."

I didn't know, but I nodded anyway. Then, of course, I realized Vergil wasn't looking at me, so I added, "Really?" So he'd know I was listening.

Vergil's eyes lifted to mine. "You know how they always say that folks who live by the sword die by the sword? That ain't true in Jacob's case."

Vergil pronounced sword by sounding the *w*, but that wasn't why I looked at him the way I did. "What do you mean?" I said. It was unusual for Vergil to get philosophical on me.

"Jacob was kilt by the butcher knife, not the chicken."

I stared at him. Evidently the point Vergil was making, then, was that Jacob—who had lived by the chicken—had not died by the chicken? Lord. Vergil was getting to be a regular poet.

Vergil nodded solemnly. "Yep, whoever killed Jacob knocked him unconscious with that chicken statue first, *then* stabbed him."

I blinked. It sounded as if maybe whoever had killed the old man hadn't wanted him to suffer. So the killer had very considerately administered a quick anesthetic to the side of Jacob's head.

Vergil's sad eyes were still on my face. "Sounds like it could be one of the immediate family, don't it? Or maybe a woman who'd spent a great deal of her life married to the man."

I shrugged noncommittally. But to tell you the truth, I was thinking, Vergil could be right.

Vergil spent the next two hours talking to everybody he could get his hands on. He really did it up big this time. Surpassing even his former questioning excellence of earlier that morning. Vergil talked to Priss, R.L., Jolene—he even talked to Inez, who clearly had nothing to add to the investigation. Inez insisted that she'd been sitting at her desk, in front of Jacob's office, when the shooting incident had occurred. Up until Vergil showed up, she'd been under the impression that the sounds she'd heard were from a car backfiring in the Vandeventer parking lot.

"Three times?" I asked her, when she came out of R.L.'s office.

Inez shrugged. "It could happen."

The day had obviously been a long one for Inez. Her skirt still hung sideways, and she now had a haunted look in her eyes. "You know," she told me, "I told Vergil either he takes down that silly yellow tape or *I'm* going to. I need to get back into that office and clean it up. The place is a mess! They've covered the entire room in that awful fingerprinting powder. That stuff needs to be cleaned up!"

I tried to look sympathetic, but I couldn't help thinking—maybe Inez would like to clean *my* office in her spare time. Spare time being something she seemed to have a lot of these days. Looking at Inez's lopsided skirt, however, I decided against it. The sight of the Bermuda Rectangle might be the final straw for her.

Inez headed back to her desk, muttering to herself again. "If only the phone would ring, or—or *something*. At least then I'd have something to—"

After Vergil finished talking to R.L., R.L. didn't look much better than Inez. He charged into Priss's office, his eyes still wild. "You've got to leave town," he told Priss. "It's too dangerous for you to stay here. It really is!"

At the very moment R.L. walked into her office, Priss was in the act of cleaning the scrape on the side of my face. I, on the other hand, was in the act of trying not to yell while she swabbed it with Merthiolate.

Merthiolate is the orange antiseptic I always make sure I never buy, because it's the one that stings. Mercurochrome is what I always use, if I use anything. I didn't have the heart, however, to refuse Priss after she'd gone to all the trouble of finding the stuff for me in the office first aid kit. I could tell this was Priss's way of saying thanks for getting her out of harm's way, the way she was all of a sudden clucking over me like a mother hen.

Which, now that I think of it, is once again just what you might expect the daughter of a chicken farmer to do.

Priss had started doing her fussing right after she'd gotten done telling her own version of recent events to Vergil. I don't know if going over it with the sheriff had sort of reminded her how she could actually have been hurt or what, but the second Priss walked out of R.L.'s office, Priss started being unbelievably nice to me.

I can't say I minded.

As a matter of fact, I was pretty much enjoying having Priss lean real close to me while she swabbed down the side of my face, and hearing her say stuff like, "Oh, you poor thing," and "My, my, does this hurt?" Of course, the conversation had degenerated some by the time R.L. walked in. By that time Priss had whipped out the Merthiolate, and she was saying stuff like, "Now,

Haskell, don't be a baby," while I gritted my teeth and winced.

If anything, I was kind of glad to see R.L., because Priss stopped applying Merthiolate to my face the minute her brother walked in the door.

R.L. looked real agitated. "Priss, it's not safe for you here," he repeated. "You're going to have to get out of town for a while."

Priss looked at R.L. almost indulgently. "You know I can't leave town," she said. "I've got a business to run, remember?"

R.L. started pacing again. "Priss, you've got to, until all this blows over. YOU'VE GOT TO."

I stood up. Mostly to make a point, but partly to get away from Priss and her Merthiolate. "How about if you stay at my place tonight?"

The second I said it, I was afraid of what Priss might think. Would she think my motives were honorable, or would she decide that this was some half-baked excuse to get her to spend the night with me? To tell you the truth, I wasn't quite sure myself.

Evidently, however, the thought didn't even occur to Priss. Without even blinking an eye, she said, "Why, Haskell, that's a great idea. How sweet of you to offer." She gave me a warm smile. "To tell you the truth, I'm not sure I could get a wink of sleep at my place. I'd be jumping at every sound," she said.

I was just about to say, "Well, then, it's settled," when Priss added, "I want Mama to come along, too. If somebody's after me, Mama's not safe alone in my apartment."

I stared at her. Oh. Right. Sure.

I made myself smile and say, "No problem." Realizing, of course, that it now no longer mattered what kind of motives I had had.

R.L. stopped pacing. "Haskell," he said, "you won't let her out of your sight, will you? You'll, uh, make sure nothing happens to my baby sister here?" His question was clearly directed at me, but R.L.'s eyes were resting anxiously on Priss.

"Don't worry, R.L.," I said. "I'll take care of her."

That seemed to satisfy R.L. He gave me a nod and went on out the door. His eyes, though, still looked real worried. I moved to the door of Priss's office, watching him go. I don't reckon I'd ever seen R.L. so rattled. I guess, up to that moment, I never fully realized how much R.L. cared about his sister.

As R.L. went out of Priss's office, Jolene and Lizbeth were heading down the hall toward the ladies' room. R.L. was going toward his office when he saw them.

He stopped dead in his tracks.

Of course, it probably wasn't just worry over his sister that had R.L. pacing the floor. With Lizbeth nosing around the office, R.L. no doubt had quite a bit on his mind.

I got a full appreciation of just how much was weighing on R.L.'s mind later that afternoon. Vergil had finally left, Priss was back in her office generating paper, and everything had pretty much calmed down again. I was back to sitting in my chair, feeling almost grateful to have nothing to do for a spell, when the buzzer sounded on Jolene's desk.

I was slumped down in my chair, my eyes half closed, but I noticed the quick look Jolene shot my way as soon as she heard the voice on the line. I didn't move. Jolene gave me another long glance and then headed into R.L.'s office.

And closed the door.

I may have been feeling real worn out when Jolene's buzzer sounded, but as soon as she disappeared into R.L.'s office, I was suddenly wide awake. I got up and real easy-like walked over to the receptionist's desk. There I stared for a minute at the intercom. All the buttons were labeled—R.L., Priss, Jacob—and there was a switch marked "Incoming" and "Outgoing."

I swallowed and pushed the switch to "Incoming." Then I pressed the R.L. button and held it down.

What do you know, right away Jolene's voice sounded over the intercom. It was just as clear as if I'd been standing in the room. "—don't have to worry," she was saying. "She doesn't know a damn thing about us, sweetheart. I'm taking care of everything."

I all but gasped. Obviously, it was *Jolene* who was having an affair with R.L. And funniest thing. Over the intercom, Jolene no longer sounded the least bit shy.

CHAPTER
13

I was still feeling stunned that evening at my house. Which was kind of bad, being as how I had Ruby and Priss as houseguests. I sure didn't want to tip Priss off as to what I was thinking about. I wasn't at all inclined to discuss with her what all I'd found out—at least, not until I'd decided what connection, if any, it might have to Jacob's murder.

I didn't rightly see how R.L. playing around with Jolene meant anything significant. Like Priss had said earlier, his being worth more money ought to make it easier for him to divorce, if that's what he wanted.

Still, I couldn't get over it. Truth was, I couldn't have been any more amazed if I'd found out that R.L. had some kind of grape earring fetish—and that he'd fallen head over heels for *Inez*.

Jolene, of all people, just didn't seem like the "other woman" type. Whatever that was. And yet I probably should've suspected something yesterday when she didn't even look up when R.L. walked into the front lobby. I've seen R.L. walk into a classroom, and every one of the girls falls silent. Like maybe he'd taken their collective breath away. For Jolene to actually *ignore* R.L. should've been a tip-off that something was up.

Of course, over the intercom Jolene hadn't exactly sounded like the Jolene I was accustomed to, either. Over the intercom the frightened little mouse had sounded as if it had grown a backbone.

When Ruby, Priss, and I first walked into the front door of my A-frame, Ruby looked every bit as stunned as I felt. Priss had filled her in on the excitement we'd had earlier, so I couldn't tell if Ruby was looking dazed because she was still reeling from the idea of her daughter getting shot at or if it was on account of this being her first look at my living quarters. If I'd known in advance that I was going to be having company, I probably would've picked things up some. At least, I would've gotten the magazines and newspapers off the couch and chairs—and picked up some of the more badly chewed dog toys.

I couldn't help but notice that Ruby's eyes seemed to focus primarily on the toys as she scanned the room. She also focused quite a bit on Rip. As if she were afraid any minute he might mistake her for one of his toys.

Rip, as usual, had been doing his "bark at the guy who lives here" routine when we'd pulled up. Maybe this was Ruby's problem. Maybe she was under the impression me—since from all appearances, he didn't recognize me—that Rip wasn't my dog.

"Don't worry about Rip," I told Ruby. "He always barks like that. He's just practicing. Don't let him bother you."

Apparently, however, Rip was bothering Ruby already. Her perpetual smile looked uncertain. "My goodness, he's certainly a big one, isn't he?" she said. She ran a chubby hand through her cotton candy hair and cautiously took off her coat.

I was a little surprised to see that Ruby was once again wearing her apron with the embroidered pansies. She was wearing it over a pink calico print dress this time. It made you wonder if—like so many other things—she'd simply forgotten to take her apron off, or if the thing was a permanent part of her wardrobe.

Ruby seemed to relax some when Priss walked right over and started petting Rip without batting an eye.

At least, Ruby relaxed right up until we were all sitting around my dining room table, putting away the fried chicken and dumplings that Ruby insisted on making us for dinner. That was when Rip started circling us like a vulture, looking for anything—anything at all—that might slip to the floor.

Rip does this all the time, and it's real annoying. Especially when I have guests. This is, however, a big improvement over what he used to do. Rip used to try to squeeze himself under the table during dinner, scooting in between chair legs and human legs until he found just the right position to catch any falling food. It makes for a real tense meal to have your guests peering under the table all the time, making sure Rip isn't about to fight them for their next bite.

After I introduced Rip to a rolled-up newspaper, though, he saw the error of his ways. These days he settles for just circling—and, on occasion, staring at you pleadingly, whining under his breath.

Ruby, however, didn't seem to realize what a big improvement this was. She kept looking over at Rip, her perpetual smile getting more and more shaky. "Nice doggie," Ruby said.

"Rip's OK," I told her again. "Don't worry, he won't bother you."

I would've put Rip outside on the deck, but I knew that would be even worse. If you put Rip outside when you're eating, he runs around the deck to the dining room window and howls. If that doesn't work, he starts frantically clawing at the window frame, whimpering. It's a real convincing routine. I've had guests start thinking that some kind of beast has crawled out of the woods, and that it's stalking Rip out there.

Ruby's eyes had not budged from Rip's face. "Nice doggie," she repeated.

Priss, however, didn't seem to notice Rip's circling at all. Her eyes were on me. "You OK, Haskell?" Priss said. "You seem kind of distracted tonight, like maybe you're feeling sick—"

Thank goodness, her mother answered before I had a chance. "I bet it's your face, ain't it?" Ruby said.

I stared at her, hardly daring to ask what exactly it was that she was saying. I mean, I know I'm no Tom Selleck or anything, but I'm pretty sure my face doesn't generally cause actual illness. At least, not right off the bat.

"That scrape is hurting you some, isn't it?" Ruby went on.

I didn't say anything, but evidently Ruby needed no confirmation. Her perpetual smile beamed in my direction. "What a wonderful thing you did today, Haskell. Putting your life on the line like that."

It was going to take some doing to remain humble around Ruby. Ever since Priss had given her an account of the day's events, Ruby had been acting as if she was going to put me up for the Medal of Honor.

"I don't know if you'd say I put my life on the line," I said. I could exaggerate a little around Vergil, maybe, but Priss was *there*. She knew very well that all I did was knock her down.

Ruby waved away what I'd just said. "Now, don't be modest," she said. "Here, have some more mashed potatoes. You brave, brave, *brave* man."

I glanced over at Priss. This was getting embarrassing. "I don't know if you'd exactly call me brave. It was more like just a reflex—"

Ruby smiled at me even wider. "Have some more cornbread."

Ruby apparently believed that gratitude is a thing that can be measured in terms of calories. So far, I'd say Ruby was grateful about three thousand calories' worth. And counting.

I shook my head, smiling. "Ruby, I'm full. Really," I said. "I'm stuffed."

Ruby cocked her gray head at me, her blue eyes twinkling away. "You're just saving room for my apple pie, aren't you?"

My smile faded. Lord. I was going to need a forklift to get out of my chair. And yet how was I going to call Ruby off without hurting her feelings? She'd loaded down the table with enough food to feed a football team, and all through the meal she'd kept adding more peas and potatoes and biscuits to my plate. Now she was heading back into the kitchen for *dessert*, for God's sake. I watched her go, and I was pretty sure I was having trouble breathing. If this kept up, I'd be on life support before the evening was over.

It was Rip who saved me.

That fool dog started barking and carrying on just as Ruby came back out of the kitchen. Ruby must've jumped a foot, and very nearly dumped the warm apple pie she was holding right smack dab on my beige plush carpeting. The carpeting that, incidentally, was real inexpensive because it isn't stain-resistant. Fortunately, the pie just wobbled for a second or two in Ruby's hands before she managed to plunk it down on the table, knocking off a few chunks of pie crust when it hit.

"Oh dear," Ruby said, immediately starting to pick up the pieces of crust. She actually looked upset. As if these few pieces of broken crust might spoil the decor.

Rip didn't wait around to get yelled at for barking in the house—he ran for the front door, alternating mumble-barking with real barking. That's, of course, when I realized that Rip wasn't doing this because he had a warped canine sense of humor, but that someone really was at my door.

I was relieved to get up from the table. If nothing else, this interruption would give me a short reprieve before Ruby forced a large slice of pie down my throat.

Even if I hadn't been so full, seeing who it was at my door would've taken an edge off my appetite anyway. Standing there on my deck, shifting his weight uneasily from one foot to another, Vergil—as always—looked grim.

Priss had followed me into the living room to see who it was, and I could tell from the look on her face that

179

she was thinking what I was thinking. Vergil was here, no doubt, to arrest Ruby.

Priss's face went ashen.

That, of course, was before we noticed Belinda Renfrow standing in back of Vergil. The woman was in her usual jeans and moccasin outfit, but evidently she'd dressed up for this occasion. She was wearing the macrame necklace.

"Haskell," Vergil said, nodding his head at me.

"Vergil," I said, nodding mine at him.

The social amenities taken care of, Vergil cleared his throat. "Belinda here called me up." A few more lines seemed to have etched their way into Vergil's tanned face. He blinked sadly and added, "About your dog."

Rip, of course, picked that particular moment to start sniffing Vergil's shoes. Still mumble-barking under his breath. *Barmnf. Barmnf. Barmnf.* It sounded like Rip was trying to bark with his mouth full.

Vergil, as they say, was not amused. He stared first at Rip, then at me.

"Rip, stop," I said.

Rip evidently thought I meant stop sniffing *Vergil's* shoes and start on *Belinda's.* Belinda's shoes must've been a real odor fest, because that silly dog started sniffing a mile a minute and mumble-barking to himself and wriggling all over. All at the same time.

"Hey!" Belinda yelled, and drew back the foot that Rip was in the act of sniffing. Belinda obviously intended to send Rip into orbit.

"Hey, yourself," I said, hauling Rip away by his collar. Rip had flinched when Belinda's foot went up, but evidently his memory span was just about a half-second. When I hauled him away, he whined.

"Why, Vergil, how sweet of you to drop by!"

This, of course, was Ruby. Having cleaned up the pie crust pieces, she came bustling out of my dining room, wiping her hands on her pansy apron. "Lands, you are the sweetest man I ever did see! Did you come by again just to see how we're doing?"

Vergil swallowed guiltily. "Uh, uh, uh—" After that

articulate pronouncement, he then just stood there, his mouth opening and shutting, like maybe it was on some kind of timer.

I've decided that Vergil is even better with women than I am.

He was evidently doing a terrific job with Belinda. "All right, all right," she said, fiddling with her necklace. "Enough of this damn socializing. I mean, what the hell's the hold-up here? I want that damn dog in the county pen."

Vergil blinked sadly, looking over at me. "I reckon you know," he began again, "that Belinda here has filed a complaint."

Belinda decided to elaborate. "Hell, yes, I'm complaining! That damn dog kilt *four* of my ducks. And I saw him."

I stared at her. Four? This morning it had been two. The body count apparently had gone up.

Belinda noticed my eyes. "Oh yeah," she said. "Two more this afternoon. I almost got the varmint, too. Must've missed him by inches. If I'd had my shotgun instead of my .22, we wouldn't have to be here right this minute." She gave Rip a venomous look. "The damn problem would've been solved."

And Belinda called *Rip* a cold-blooded killer?

Vergil's eyes were sad. "You know, Haskell, if your dog is killing poultry—"

I didn't let him finish. "Rip isn't killing anything. Take a look at him, Vergil, does this dog look like he could be a killer?"

I probably picked a bad time to ask that. What I meant, of course, was for Vergil to check Rip out for blood or torn nails or something like that. Something that would corroborate Belinda's story. Vergil, however, made no move toward Rip. Maybe because, even though I still had Rip by the collar, Rip had continued wriggling all over the way he does when he's excited. I couldn't tell if Rip was just getting light-headed from all the attention—every single person in the room *was* looking at him—or if maybe Rip had picked up the scent of

Eau de Dog in Heat off Belinda's shoes. Whatever it was, it appeared to have driven him over the brink. Alternating mumble-barking with snarling, Rip was now lunging forward and back. And wriggling so hard, trying to break my grasp on his collar, that he kept knocking himself off his own feet. That fool dog kept falling down, then getting up, and falling down again.

Vergil stared at Rip, then looked over at me. His eyes were pitying.

I glanced around the room at the others. Judging from the looks on all their faces—Belinda, Ruby, Priss, *and* Vergil—it was pretty obvious that the vote to convict would be three to one. The only vote for acquittal would come from Priss, and staring at Rip's current performance, even she looked a little doubtful.

"Rip never gets off my porch, I'm telling you," I said.

The vote to convict didn't change.

So, of course, I had to show them.

It was real humiliating. I dragged Rip, whining and wriggling, into the dining room, got me a piece of chicken breast meat—boneless, of course—and held it out to him. When I was standing right next to him in my dining room, Rip did a great impression of Neanderthal Dog, jumping and snapping at the meat in my hand.

I had to give him a little piece of it to get him to calm down.

However, when I took Rip and the meat outside, putting the chicken on the fourth step down from the top of the deck, just out of Rip's range, it was an entirely different story. Rip padded to the edge of the deck, sat down, and stared at the chicken. His brown eyes looked almost as mournful as Vergil's. After a second or two, Rip got up, and very carefully leaned over the side every bit as far as he could without losing his balance. Stretching his nose as far as possible toward the chicken. He did not, however, put one paw on the next step.

I looked at him fondly. Good dog, Rip. Good boy, you knucklehead.

Everybody had followed us out to the deck to witness

in person Rip's total lunacy. In back of me, I heard Ruby say, "Well, I'll swan—"

This is something folks in Pigeon Fork say a lot. It means "I'll swear—" How swans got into it is beyond me.

Belinda, who was standing right next to Ruby, looked like she might be ready to swear herself. "So, maybe the damn dog doesn't like chicken?" She looked over at Vergil. "Maybe he just likes *duck*."

I sighed. It looked like yet another demonstration was called for.

Going down to the bottom of the steps—and, incidentally, feeling like a total fool—I whistled and said, "Here, Rip. Here, boy. Come here, Rip."

It went on like this for while. Me calling and whistling and snapping my fingers, and Rip sitting up there at the top of the stairs. Cocking his head first to one side and then the next. Looking at me as if *I* were the one who was nuts.

Belinda snorted. "So, the damn dog doesn't come when you call him. So what?"

I sighed again. This was not going to be pretty. And Rip was definitely going to be pissed. I'd have to remember that it would be for his own good.

Right there, in front of four witnesses, I climbed slowly back up the stairs, took a firm hold on Rip's collar and tried to pull him bodily down the steps.

Rip let out a yelp of shocked surprise. Then he dug in. It looked like every toenail he had was burrowing itself into the boards of my deck. Lowering his head and raising his tail section, Rip braced himself, shutting his eyes. Like maybe if it turned out that he actually lost this one, and I really did manage to pull his sixty outraged pounds down the stairs, Rip didn't want to see it.

Then again, maybe Rip just closed his eyes so he could concentrate better on his howling. From the piteous sound that came out of that dog's mouth, you would've thought I was skinning him alive.

Ruby, I noticed, covered her ears.

Rip howled a couple more times even after I let go of his collar.

It makes a dog owner real proud.

Vergil was now looking at Rip as if he'd just realized the dog needed a straitjacket. Scratching what few hairs he still had on top of his head, Vergil said, "Lordy."

Belinda snorted again. "Lordy, my foot!" she said. "This is just a damn trick Haskell has taught him. I saw that dog with my own eyes. Ripping my poor babies to bits. Why, he tore their throats out and then dragged them around the yard. Dripping blood all over!"

I stared at her. This woman should be writing horror novels.

Belinda was now pointing at Rip dramatically. "THAT DOG IS A KILLER!" she said.

I sighed yet again. The things you have to do to prove your dog is a nut. I went back up on the deck, circled around to Rip's backside, and tried shoving Rip forward from the back. I was aiming to scoot him bodily off the deck, but that didn't work, either. Just when it seemed for certain that I was going to get him to finally budge, Rip would suddenly spring to one side. When he did this, it was all I could do to regain my balance and not end up tumbling head first down the steps myself.

We went through this routine three times. Three humiliating times. The last time, as Rip sprang away, I thought I heard him snicker.

When I finally gave up and we all headed back into the living room, Rip sneezed in my direction, and walked right past me, head down, not looking at me. Evidently, he thought I'd been making fun of his infirmities in public.

I have a maple end table on one side of my blue wraparound couch. Rip went straight over to the end table and crawled underneath it. All you could see of him was his tail sticking out. It was not wagging.

Oh, he was pissed, all right.

Rip had nothing on Belinda, though. "I'm telling you, sheriff, it was *that dog*. I don't care what tricks Haskell can get that dog to do—"

Vergil was staring at Rip—or, rather, his tail—under the table. "You'd think a dog that big would want to run—"

I just looked at Vergil. Obviously, he didn't know Rip, or he'd know you can't make assumptions like that where this particular dog was concerned. How did Vergil think Rip had managed to get that tire around his middle? Rip certainly wasn't running it off every day.

Vergil might have started looking convinced, but Belinda clearly was not. "I'm telling you, I saw that dog kill my ducks! And, sheriff, if you're not going to do a damn thing about it, then I'm getting myself a lawyer." At my front door, she stopped and looked back over at Rip. Or, rather, at Rip's tail. Incidentally, still not wagging. "Haskell, you better keep that damn dog away from me, or it's going to be eating *lead*. Instead of ducks!" Belinda gave her macrame necklace a little flip with the end of her finger and went out the door.

Maybe Robert Frost was right. Good fences do make good neighbors. Real tall, real sturdy fences, with barbed wire on top. And maybe sentries at each corner—with guns.

Unlike Belinda, Vergil didn't leave. At least, not right away. At first I thought it was because the house pretty much smelled to high heaven of Ruby's warm apple pie, and the sheriff had made up his mind that he wasn't leaving until he had himself a slice. I was kind of glad Vergil stayed, too, because for a while there all of Ruby's attention was diverted to seeing that *Vergil* helped himself to as big a piece of pie as she could get him to eat. I got away with eating just a sliver.

As it turned out, though, there was another reason Vergil had hung around. When Ruby disappeared into the kitchen to get Vergil his second cup of coffee, he leaned toward me and Priss and whispered, "I wanted to tell you all something." His mournful eyes at that moment were on what was left of his pie. "Alton Gabbard told me about Jacob's will being changed and all. And about how Jacob was leaving a lot less to Ruby."

Vergil blinked and cleared his throat. "I'm afraid it's

only a matter of time now. Everything is pointing in her direction. I'm going to have to take her in." His sad eyes lifted to mine.

I just stared back at him. What was there to say? I hated to admit it, but I myself couldn't swear Ruby was innocent.

Across the dining room table from me and Vergil, Priss was biting her bottom lip and blinking real hard. Vergil noticed and flushed guiltily. "I don't have a choice. I'm getting pressure from all over to get this thing solved." He swallowed and then pushed his plate away. "I wanted to let you know as a favor to Ruby, OK?"

When Ruby reappeared with his coffee, Vergil stood up. "Uh, I reckon I don't have time to drink another cup, after all. I—I've got to be getting back."

He almost ran out my front door.

Even Ruby noticed Vergil was suddenly acting real funny. As soon as he left, she gave me and Priss a look. "Well, lands' sake, what got into him?"

Priss swallowed once, and then—to my surprise—told her. "Mama," she said, "Vergil thinks he might actually have to arrest you."

Ruby's eyes got very round. "Arrest me? For what?"

I stared at her. Had she forgotten again that her ex-husband had been murdered yesterday? Could something like that have slipped Ruby's mind?

Priss jogged Ruby's memory. "Mama, they think you killed Dad."

Ruby's reaction to this wasn't what I expected. Not by a long shot. She sank into one of my dining room chairs, looking almost as if—any second now—she might actually stop smiling. Then she glanced back over at Priss and me, her blue eyes troubled. "It's on account of them finding my fingerprints on that kidnap note, ain't it?"

For a split second, Priss and I both stared at Ruby as if we weren't quite sure what she'd just said.

So she repeated it.

"They found my fingerprints on them notes, didn't they?"

As my daddy used to say, my flabber was gasted.

Priss's flabber didn't look to be in any better condition than mine. "Mama," she finally said, "*you* sent those notes?"

Ruby's hand went to her mouth. "You didn't know?" Her perpetual smile went crooked. She blinked a couple of times and then said, "Well, shoot! Now I reckon I'll have to tell you all about it." Her voice was resigned. She wiped her plump hands on her apron, as if wiping her hands of the entire thing. "I did it for you, you know," Ruby added, looking at Priss as if she were afraid of being scolded.

Priss opened her mouth, but not a sound came out for a second. "Me?" she finally said.

"Well, sure," Ruby said briskly. "When you told me how Jacob was giving control of the business to R.L. and you were so angry, well, I had to do something. You've got such a temper, Priss, and to tell you the truth, I was real worried about what you might do." Here Ruby glanced over at me. "Priss is a real sweet girl, but I've always thought she ought to have red hair, what with her having such a fiery—"

Priss evidently thought this was a good place to interrupt. "But Mama, why the notes?"

Ruby now actually looked downright pleased with herself. "Well, my thinking was that if everybody thought you were being kidnapped, they'd watch you like a hawk. And you wouldn't have a chance to do something foolish." Ruby nodded her head toward Priss again, her eyes now getting sad. "I also thought that somebody threatening you might make Jacob finally realize just how wonderful you are—and how you cain't never be replaced."

Ruby hung her cotton candy head for a second, her smile now regretful. "None of it worked out like I thought."

Priss reached over and covered Ruby's hand. "Oh, Mama."

Ruby lifted her head. "Of course, when Jacob got himself killed—and then I saw how scared you were—well, I tried to tell you. I wanted you to know that the note was nothing to worry about. But you all weren't listening, I could see that. So I had to send you another note. To ease your mind."

I was sitting there, listening to all this, trying not to look as surprised as I felt. I think it hurts your credibility as a private detective if you always go around looking completely dumbfounded, so I tried to put an "Oh, sure, I suspected this all along" look on my face. Every once in a while when Ruby was talking, I gave a little nod of my head. Like she was reading from a script I'd already taken a peek at.

While I was nodding, though, I was also thinking that those notes had been a great diversion on Ruby's part. If she'd wanted to murder her husband, it would've been a real good idea to create a fictional kidnapper—a sinister outside plot—to divert suspicion from herself.

Right that moment, I was starting to look at Ruby in a whole new light. She was vague and sort of distant, all right, but for her to come up with this kidnapping thing had taken some shrewd thinking. Maybe what this little gray-haired lady had was a dimmer switch in her brain. Sometimes her mind shined bright and clear. Other times her bulb dimmed a little.

Right now, though, it was shining bright as anything. She was looking over at me, her blue eyes sharp. When I saw that look, something else occurred to me. "If you wrote those notes," I said, "then you knew that Jacob was dead before Priss and I did."

Ruby didn't even hesitate. "Oh, sure," she said, with a little shrug of her plump shoulders. "He was dead when I went into his office."

I stared at her. This sure explained why Inez hadn't heard Jacob say anything while Ruby was in there.

"Dead as a mackerel," Ruby went on cheerily. "In fact, that's why I pretended to lose my keys." Here Ruby actually giggled a little, clearly tickled that she'd thought to do such a thing. "I knew Inez never left her desk, and I wanted to make it seem as if, well, as if *anybody* could've walked in and done it.''

I knew, looking at her, exactly what Ruby had been worried about. "You wanted to make sure that it didn't necessarily have to be someone already in the building?'' I tried to make my voice deliberately casual.

Ruby immediately nodded, her glance sharp again. Almost immediately, however, her eyes slid away.

It didn't take a genius to figure out what Ruby had thought. If she was telling the truth, then Ruby had seen Jacob and immediately concluded that Priss had murdered him—that Priss had finally taken her revenge for all the things her father had done. Having come to that conclusion, Ruby had immediately taken steps to protect her daughter.

I didn't want to think of it. But if you eliminated Ruby, the possibility of Priss being guilty was a theory that sure made sense.

It made even more sense when I saw the look that mother and daughter exchanged right after Ruby finished speaking. It was a look both protective and loving. A look that made you wonder if maybe these two hadn't been in cahoots from the very beginning. Lord. Could these two have planned this between them?

I looked over at Priss, feeling real uneasy. Because, let's face it, I knew by then how much I liked her. Was it possible I was growing more and more attracted to a woman who had, only yesterday, murdered her own father?

CHAPTER
14

I may have been getting more and more uncertain about Priss's and Ruby's innocence, but I still had absolutely no doubt about Rip's. The next morning, right after Ruby force-fed me about a million pancakes, a couple hundred eggs, and enough bacon to choke a horse, I got out my Polaroid camera and took a couple of head shots of Rip. I think both pictures showed Rip's best side. It was the side that sits on the edge of my deck, glares at me, and occasionally mumble-barks under its breath.

Rip apparently does not have a real forgiving nature. Of course, I'd suspected this the night before when Rip stayed under my maple end table, sulking, for the better part of an hour. It was only Priss's patient coaxing that finally got him to come out.

As soon as the photography session was over, I put the Polaroids in the right front pocket of my sport coat, and Priss and I headed for the door. Or, at least, we started to. Neither one of us had taken more than two steps in that direction when Ruby planted her plump self right in front of us. She was wearing a pink velour bathrobe over a high-necked pink flannel nightgown, with her pansy apron tied tightly around her middle. I had a feeling that this was not a new look for Ruby.

"This is ridiculous. I don't rightly see why you can't just call in sick for once," Ruby said, folding her arms across her ample chest. Her pink-tinted mouth was still curved in a cheerful smile as usual, so the impact of her words was diluted some. "I mean," she went on, "if getting shot at ain't reason enough to stay home, I don't know what is."

Ruby did have a powerful argument.

Priss, however, wasn't listening to it. "Mama, I can't hide for the rest of my life," she said. Her gray eyes were uneasy, though, even as she said it. "Besides," she added, giving her short brown hair a determined toss, "I'm not about to give whoever it is the satisfaction of knowing he's scared me."

I just looked at her. She was one brave little lady.

I knew very well, however, that there were no doubt quite a few brave little ladies whose courage had led them to take up permanent residence in a cemetery somewhere. I swallowed. "You know, Priss," I said, "maybe your mom's right. Maybe you should—"

That was all I got out.

"Nonsense," Priss said curtly, and headed for the door.

I followed her, feeling real good that, at the very least, I could rest assured knowing that we'd thoroughly discussed all the possible options.

Out on my deck, Priss paused and turned back toward Ruby. Last night after Vergil left, we'd all decided that it would probably be best if Ruby remained at my house while Priss was at work. Just to be on the safe side. With a gunman on the loose, Priss sure didn't want Ruby staying at their apartment. There was too much chance for mistaken identity. Then, too, I thought it might not be the worst idea in the world for Ruby to have herself the services of a guard dog.

Especially if the guard dog in question was currently still in something of a snit.

Which he was. Rip had followed us out on the deck,

and was now standing there, right next to the front door, watching us go. I could've sworn he looked particularly glad *I* was leaving.

"I'll be back at the usual time, OK?" Priss told Ruby. "And if anything happens before then, call me right away."

All three of us knew exactly what the "anything" was that Priss was referring to. It was an "anything" that involved Vergil showing up with an arrest warrant in his hand.

It was funny. As I stood there, watching Priss and Ruby talking to each other on my deck, it was just like their roles had been reversed. With her by-now-familiar apron that tied in the back, Ruby looked more than ever like a little girl. A little girl being left instructions by her mother. Priss was in a dark brown tailored suit that almost exactly matched her hair. The suit made Priss look older than her years. As Priss talked, Ruby blinked her pansy-blue eyes and nodded meekly.

"And Mama?" Priss went on. "If I happen to be out when you call, talk to Inez, OK?"

Ruby nodded again, but you could tell she wasn't real happy about the prospect of having to call up an old friend to tell her that, oh, by the way, she'd just been arrested for murder.

When Priss told Inez about it a little later, Inez didn't look any more happy about it than Ruby.

Inez pulled into Vandeventer Poultry's parking lot not sixty seconds after Priss and I got there. Priss and I arrived a little later than usual, being as how I had to stop twice on the way. Once at Higgins's Stop 'n' Shop and once at the Crayton County Supermarket. At both stores I taped one of Rip's Polaroids in the front window. On the bottom of the photographs, I'd written the words, "LOST, $50 REWARD," and my business and home phone numbers.

I knew very well that for fifty bucks, there were some folks here in Pigeon Fork who would try to pass off their own grandmother as a black half-German shepherd, but it was a chance I would have to take.

Walking in with Inez and Priss, I noticed right off that the aroma was so faint this morning that you had to try to smell it at all. Maybe I really was in a nose coma, after all. I also noticed that Inez was looking a little better today than she had yesterday. Of course, that wasn't saying a whole lot. The green tweed skirt Inez had on today, however, wasn't hanging sideways, and she'd managed to put on *both* earrings. These weren't the infamous grapes, but some kind of crumpled silver metal that looked like a car had run over them. Still, the earrings actually matched each other.

I think one reason for Inez looking more like her old self was that yesterday afternoon Vergil had apparently taken Inez's complaints to heart, and he'd finally taken down the yellow caution tape across the door to Jacob's office. No doubt, before she'd left for the day, Inez had dusted and cleaned in there to her heart's content.

In fact, the only thing about Inez that indicated that she still wasn't quite operating at peak efficiency was the pencil sticking out of her bun. Priss and I followed Inez to her desk as soon as we all three walked through the front door, and you would've had to have been blind not to notice Inez's pencil. Either Inez was now carrying efficiency to new heights—deciding that her bun now doubled as a pencil holder—or sometime recently she'd stuck the pencil in and forgotten it was there.

Inez was getting as bad as Ruby. No wonder the two were such good friends. They understood each other. Which was a lot more than the rest of us could say.

Priss must've spotted the pencil at about the same time as I did, because she immediately glanced over at me and arched an eyebrow. I knew what she was thinking. How could you forget you had a pencil in your hair? I couldn't help staring at Inez myself. Had she absentmindedly stuck the pencil back there after she'd gotten dressed this morning? Or had she put it back there sometime yesterday? Could the woman have actually slept on the thing—and not felt it? This was probably a whole lot more telling than that old "Princess and the Pea" fairy tale.

Once Inez had seated herself behind her desk, Priss wasted no time telling Inez to keep an ear out for a phone call from Ruby. Priss kind of slowed down some, though, when she got to the part about why it was that Ruby would be calling.

Inez, however, looked a lot more than slowed down. She looked stunned. "You don't mean to tell me that they're really going to arrest Ruby," Inez said. Her small hazel eyes looked like they'd just been put through an enlarger. "Why, I can't believe Vergil Minrath actually believes that Ruby could commit murder! I just can't believe it!" As she spoke, Inez reached over and picked up a pencil off the top of her desk.

"The sheriff says he doesn't have a choice." Priss sounded almost as mournful as Vergil himself.

Inez pointed her pencil in my direction. "Mr. Blevins," she said, "can't you do something?"

I blinked. Like what, for instance?

"Surely, you don't think that Ruby is guilty," Inez went on, now aiming the pencil toward her bun.

I watched, amazed. Was she going to start carrying *all* her pencils back there? Wouldn't this make for a real shampooing nightmare?

Sure enough, Inez jabbed the second pencil right next to the first. Her bun was starting to look like a small ball of silver yarn with knitting needles stuck in it.

"I just don't see how anybody could think Ruby could do such a thing. I just never thought for a second that it would go this far." Unbelievably, Inez was now picking up a Bic.

"Matter of fact," I said, my eyes on the Bic, "I find it hard to believe Ruby is guilty, too, but without any more than I've got to go on, I don't see how anything can be done."

You might've thought I was being real clever, pumping Inez for more information by saying this. I wish I could say I'd thought that far ahead, but the truth was, I was so distracted by the possibility of Inez jamming yet another writing utensil into her head that I wasn't thinking much at all. Other than to wonder, in an off-

194

hand kind of way, just how many Bics and pencils could a bun that size hold?

Inez must've taken what I said as some kind of accusation, though, because she immediately looked stricken, dropping the Bic as if it were suddenly hot.

Thank goodness, I might add.

"OK, OK," she said, holding up a scrawny hand. "Maybe I should've told you this earlier, but I—I didn't want to cause anybody any trouble. I—I did hear what all Jacob and R.L. were talking about when R.L. was in there that afternoon."

"You did?" This was Priss. She took a step closer to Inez's desk, and her voice sounded a little less than tolerant. "Then why didn't you say so earlier?"

Inez blinked and reached for the Bic again. "Because I didn't want to cause trouble for R.L. Besides, a good secretary never eavesdrops. NEVER." Here Inez glanced over at her *Secretarial Handbook* with as much reverence as if she were looking at the Bible. "And if a good secretary should happen to overhear something, she never repeats it. NEVER."

Priss looked over at me and rolled her eyes. She opened her mouth to, no doubt, say something real appreciative about Inez's admirable attention to duty, but I jumped in before Priss had a chance. "Well, of course," I told Inez. "No wonder you didn't want to say anything." My voice could've been mixed with vinegar and poured on a salad. "But now, with Ruby being in all this trouble, you've got to tell everything you know, don't you think? Just in case it might be important?"

Inez nodded, tapping the Bic agitatedly on her desk. "I—I guess so. It's just that—well—it's so *embarrassing*." To prove what she was saying, her cheeks actually pinked up. It wasn't enough to offset the general paleness of Inez's long, thin face, but it was a start in the right direction. Inez leaned forward and lowered her voice. Just as if there were scores of possible witnesses standing around. "Mr. Vandeventer," Inez said, "had found out about R.L.'s *infidelity*."

Inez made the word sound like some unmentionable disease.

Having actually said the dreaded word, Inez swallowed a couple of times as if it had left an ugly taste in her mouth. Then, leaning further in my direction, she said in a stage whisper, "Mr. Vandeventer told R.L. if R.L. didn't break it off with *Jolene*"—here she gave the name a little extra emphasis in case I missed it—"that he would tell Lizbeth what all was going on."

Out of the corner of my eye, I saw Priss shoot me a quick look right then. As if she was trying to gauge my reaction to what I'd just heard. I kept my eyes on Inez. "And I heard Mr. Vandeventer say, 'I won't have somebody heading up my company who was engaged in hanky-panky,'" Inez finished.

It was my turn to glance over at Priss then, just in time to catch the strange look that crossed her face. It was a look of irritation and disbelief all rolled into one. I didn't have time to consider what it meant, though, because poor Inez's eyes were tearing up. Apparently, breaking the Secretarial Code of Silence was too much for her.

I brought out my salad voice again. "You did the right thing, Inez, telling us this. I mean it. It's a big help." In reality, I had no idea how in the world this bit of information could help Ruby out. I already knew about Jolene and R.L., and now knowing that Jacob also knew didn't seem all that significant. However, I would've told Inez that she'd just saved Christmas if it would keep her from crying.

I'm not real good around weeping females. In fact, this could be one good reason why I was finding Priss more and more attractive. If ever there was a non-tearful woman, it was Priss.

Like right now, Priss didn't look so much upset as irritated. "Inez, are you sure about this? That this is what R.L. and Dad talked about the *afternoon* Dad died?"

Inez nodded, lifting her pointy chin. "It certainly was." Her voice was at once shaky and defiant. "I remember it very clearly. It was when Mr. Vandeventer called R.L. into his office. Right about two o'clock that afternoon." Inez turned tear-filled eyes to mine. "I wouldn't say it if it weren't so. I'm just trying to help."

"And you're certainly helping a lot," I assured her.

Priss apparently didn't have anywhere near the same regard for Inez's help as I did. She made a scoffing noise and said to me, as if Inez weren't even in the room, "You already knew about Jolene, didn't you?"

This was one of those questions you don't know whether you should answer or not, so I just stared back at her without saying anything for a second. If I went ahead and admitted that I already knew, I might have to tell Priss how. I sure didn't want to have to get into that. Priss would no doubt be delighted to hear that I'd been listening in on the office intercom.

Fortunately, Priss must've decided to let it pass. She gave a quick shrug of her shoulders, and said, "Look, Haskell, Inez has got to be remembering wrong. Dad and R.L. couldn't have had that particular conversation that afternoon."

It was like two doctors discussing the diagnosis of a patient with the patient still in the room. Inez started looking as if she'd just been diagnosed wrong. "Oh, but they did too have that conversation," Inez said, tapping the Bic on the top of her desk. "I heard them. I heard every word." She turned and glared at Priss. Apparently, when a secretary breaks the Code of Silence, she expects to be believed without question.

Priss was unmoved. "Haskell," she said, turning back to me, "R.L. and Dad couldn't have had that conversation, because they'd already had it. *The afternoon before.* Dad jumped on R.L. right in front of me. In fact, Dad seemed to enjoy it. Dragging out all of R.L.'s dirty linen for me to see."

I stood there, looking from Inez's pointy face to Priss's oval one. Priss seemed to be telling the truth. Was it possible that Inez was making all this up? And yet, why would she? Lord. Could Inez be doing this to try to divert suspicion from *herself?* Could Inez herself have killed the old man? Even a good secretary probably had her limits, and maybe Jacob had crossed over them. Maybe Jacob's temper and his being a dirty old man, always on the make, had finally pushed prim and proper Inez over the line.

Inez's voice was shaking even more now. "I am *not* mistaken. It was R.L. and Mr. Vandeventer, and it was the afternoon he died. It couldn't have been the day before, because for a second there, just after R.L. went in, I actually thought I heard Priss's voice in there, and I remember thinking, I must be hearing wrong—it couldn't be. Because Priss wasn't in there. And *that afternoon* was the only time R.L. and Mr. Vandeventer met without Priss this week." Inez gave Priss a look.

Priss gave Inez a look back.

Me, I was just standing there, looking at the both of them. Looking and looking, my mind going about a million miles a minute.

Right that minute, I was pretty sure I'd figured the whole thing out.

To make sure, I had Inez buzz R.L. right after that. It was only a little after nine by then, but surprisingly enough, R.L. was once again already in. I had Inez tell him, "Haskell has found something in Mr. Vandeventer's office that he thinks you should see. And R.L., bring Jolene, too, will you? Haskell thinks you might want her to take notes on this."

You might've thought R.L. would've questioned why I wanted Jolene to take notes when I had Inez right there, but apparently he didn't. I was standing behind Jacob's desk when Jolene and R.L. walked in. R.L. came in first, looking a little uncomfortable in a blue pin-striped suit. His burgundy print silk tie exactly matched the handkerchief poking out of his top right pocket, and I knew—without a shadow of a doubt—that Lizbeth had dressed him.

Behind R.L. came Jolene, wearing yet another pale dress—this time a flowery print with crocheted lace around the collar. She looked real soft, real feminine— and, of course, real shy. She walked in with her head down, her pale blue eyes focused on the floor. She was carrying a stenographer's pad and a ballpoint pen, holding them directly in front of her, as if they were some kind of shield.

I told Jolene to close the door behind her, and I got right to the point. "I'm real sorry to have to tell you this, you guys, but I know what you did. And I know how you did it."

This was something of a bluff, being as how I wasn't absolutely sure. But it paid off. R.L.'s eyes looked like they were going to pop right out of his head. "Why, uh, what do you mean—" He was practically babbling. "What are you saying— Are you trying to, uh—"

The expression on Jolene's face, however, didn't change a bit. She lifted icy eyes to mine. "What exactly are you trying to say?" Once again, her voice didn't sound the least bit shy. In fact, it didn't even quaver. Not once.

Fact is, in that instant, Jolene reminded me of somebody. Somebody strong, somebody completely in charge—somebody cold. Lord. I stared at her as it suddenly came to me.

Lizbeth.

Jolene was Lizbeth all over again. I glanced over at R.L. Hadn't this ever occurred to him? Hadn't he noticed how much the two women in his life were alike? They say that love is blind, but in this case, you'd have had to be walking into walls not to notice the similarity.

Jolene's icy gaze didn't waver. "You can't just walk in here, making wild accusations, Haskell," she said. Her tone was faintly contemptuous. "You don't know a thing—"

Her voice trailed off as I nodded toward the kitchen door. Both R.L.'s and Jolene's eyes followed mine. And we all heard, plain as day, the rumbling voice of Jacob Vandeventer. We couldn't make out every word the old man was saying, but you could tell it was Jacob, all right. That rumbling thunder was unmistakable.

R.L. went ashen. "Oh my Lord," he said, turning to Lizbeth. "Haskell *knows*. He's figured it out." R.L. was almost comical in his movements, turning first one way, then the next, his eyes wild. "Oh my Lord," he said. That pretty much summed up R.L.'s analysis of the situation. *"Oh my Lord."*

In the middle of R.L.'s analysis, Priss walked out of the kitchen, holding in plain sight a small tape recorder. Now we could hear real clear Jacob rumbling on about chicken quotas and poultry prices. The old man sounded as if he were dictating a letter. Which, of course, was exactly what he was doing, being as how Priss was playing one of Inez's dictation tapes.

I reckon I was wrong about Priss not being the crying kind. Her large gray eyes were focused unwaveringly on her brother, and tears were streaking silently down her face.

She didn't even bother to wipe them away.

Jolene, on the other hand, looked real far from crying. She looked like she was about to scream in sheer frustration.

I'd put my gun in the top drawer of Jacob's desk, just in case things got ugly. My eyes were on R.L. for the most part, being as how I wasn't at all inclined to go one-on-one with an ex-football player. R.L., however, didn't look as if he were in any condition to fight with anybody. What he looked was unsteady on his feet. "Priss," he said, his eyes tortured, "you've got to understand. I didn't want to do it, but he—he was going to tell Lizbeth." R.L. said the name with something like horror. I could understand his attitude. "I had to do it. Dad was going to ruin everything!'

I was staring at R.L., actually feeling a little sorry for him, when, from underneath her steno pad, Jolene pulled a small revolver, so quick her hand was a blur. "I hope you realize," she said, pointing the gun at Priss, "that you two have both just signed your death warrants."

For a shy lady, Jolene had suddenly gotten herself a large helping of guts.

This, you see, is the kind of tip they never give you in those assertiveness training courses they're always giving. Just get yourself a gun. Even if you're painfully shy, a revolver will certainly encourage folks to listen to you.

Right that moment, Jolene sure had every bit of my attention. R.L. and Priss seemed to be hanging on her every word, too.

R.L.'s mouth worked for a split second before words started coming out. "Jolene, honey, this is no good," he said, moving toward her.

Jolene shook her head, her gun still pointed at Priss. "It's the only way," she told him. "We can't let them tell everything they know."

R.L. was still moving, edging between Jolene and Priss. "No, Jolene, can't you see?" he said. "It's over—"

I tried to jump in here and back up R.L.'s way of thinking. "It *is* over," I said, my eyes never leaving the gun in Jolene's hand. "I've already—" If I'd been given the chance, I would've gone on to say how I'd already told Inez to give Vergil a call the minute the office door closed, and that—no doubt—Vergil and his entire legion of law enforcers were going to be arriving, sirens screaming, real soon now.

Unfortunately, I didn't have time to get all that out. By the time I'd finished with the word *already*, Jolene had already taken a step closer to Priss, lining up the barrel of her gun with Priss's chest. After that, things started happening real quick.

I stopped talking and started moving, opening the desk drawer in front of me and reaching for my gun. At the same time, R.L. was also moving, jumping in front of Priss, yelling, "NO-O-O!" at the top of his lungs.

In the movies the hero can always manage to draw his gun and shoot before the bad guy gets off a single shot. I've always wondered how they do that. I was moving as fast as I could, but I wasn't anywhere near fast enough. I'd only just barely gotten my gun out of the drawer when Jolene's gun went off.

And R.L. went down with a yelp of pain.

CHAPTER

15

I wish I could say that it was my quick action, jumping in and taking charge of the situation, that kept Jolene from shooting again, but the truth was, once Jolene realized that it was R.L. she'd shot—and not Priss—all the fight seemed to go right out of her.

This wasn't, of course, immediately apparent, being as how she was still standing there with that weapon in her hand. So I went on and pulled out my gun. I pointed it at Jolene and yelled, "All right, FREEZE!" just the way I used to when I was a cop.

Jolene didn't even look in my direction.

Her eyes, instead, were riveted on R.L. Still holding the gun, she dropped to her knees beside him. "Oh my God, what have I done?" Her voice was a wail. "What in hell have I done?"

R.L., lying on the floor, had a real quick reply. "You shot me!" He was holding his shoulder real tight, and blood was trickling through his fingers. "You really *shot* me!"

While Jolene's attention was diverted, I went over and took the gun from her hand. She didn't even seem to notice that I was taking it.

"Oh, R.L., I'm so sorry," she said. "Oh, my sweet, sweet darling, I'm so, so sorry."

R.L. didn't look particularly moved at Jolene's repentance. "You *shot* me!" he repeated. "And you tried to kill Priss!"

Jolene didn't try to argue. "Well, yes, I did," she said, "but I was just trying to get us out of this, R.L. That's all. I was just trying to do what had to be done."

Priss had run off into the kitchen to get a towel, and she was just returning when Jolene said this last part. Her face hardened like it had been set in concrete. Priss settled herself on the floor beside R.L., wadded up the towel, and started to press it against R.L.'s shoulder.

Before the towel even made contact, though, Jolene reached for it. "Let me do that," she said.

Priss glared at her. "Haven't you done enough?" she said. Her eyes were on Jolene when she pressed the towel against the dark red circle on R.L.'s shoulder.

R.L. responded with a moan of pain.

Listening to him made me cringe inside. I wasn't sure if Priss was holding the towel that tight just to stop the bleeding, or if maybe she was paying R.L. back a little.

I decided not to ask.

After that, there wasn't a whole lot to do, except hold my gun on Jolene and R.L., and wait for Vergil and the others to show up. Inez, of course, came banging on the door right after Jolene's gun went off, but being as how I wasn't all that inclined to have Inez's civil defense siren start up, I wouldn't let Inez come into Jacob's office at all. I had her call us an ambulance, and then I insisted that she wait out front for everybody to show up.

Jolene got real talkative while we waited. Maybe shooting somebody does that to a bashful person. It sure seemed to loosen up Jolene's tongue. That and having R.L. real mad at her. Right after Priss started applying pressure to R.L.'s wound with the towel, Jolene tried to take R.L.'s hand in hers. R.L. pulled away.

In case Jolene had forgotten what he was mad about,

R.L. apparently decided he ought to remind her. "You *shot* me," he said. "And you tried to kill *my sister*."

Apparently, Jolene could actually murder his father, but R.L. drew the line at trying to kill any of the rest of his family.

Jolene looked as if R.L. had slapped her. She blinked back tears, and sat there on the floor beside R.L., looking like she'd shrunk a little right into her clothes. She actually started looking older, believe it or not. Waiting those few minutes for Vergil, I think Jolene aged ten years.

"I know you've got to take us in," she told me brokenly, "but I want you to know one thing. It wasn't R.L. who killed Jacob Vandeventer. It was me. R.L. couldn't bring himself to do it—" Jolene blinked here and shrugged. As if she were talking about having to change a tire on her car or something. "—so I had to. All R.L. did was knock him out for me. That was all."

I stared at her. That may not sound like a lot to Jolene, but it sure sounded like accessory to first degree murder to me.

"I'm the one that killed him. *Just me,*" Jolene went on. "And I'm the one who planned it. Not R.L."

Now, this wasn't exactly a surprise. As you recall, I was already pretty well convinced that R.L. wasn't capable of planning a birthday party, let alone a murder.

According to Jolene, she'd told R.L. to conceal a small tape recorder in his pocket and record a conversation with Jacob. The conversation R.L. had chosen had also included Priss at the beginning. It had taken place the afternoon before the murder, just as Priss had said. After hitting Jacob with the bronze chicken, R.L. had played the tape for Inez's benefit, to give Inez the impression that Jacob was still up and talking. R.L. had left the recorder on Jacob's desk for Jolene to also play when she came in with the daily status report. When Jolene left Jacob's office, she'd taken the incriminating recorder with her.

"It should've worked perfectly," Jolene finished. "It really should've." I had to agree with her. In fact, if it hadn't been for R.L., who'd rewound the tape a little too far back, it probably would've worked. Inez, of course, had been right when she told me that she'd thought she'd heard Priss's voice in Jacob's office the afternoon he died. She'd been listening to Priss's voice on tape.

I glanced over at R.L. I'd bet R.L. had not gotten around to telling Jolene about his little error. No doubt she'd be tickled pink when she found out about it.

"It really should've worked." Jolene repeated. She now actually sounded injured. As if it were she and R.L. who'd been wronged. Call me insensitive, but I found it real hard to sympathize with her. I mean, she'd actually stuck a *knife* into an old man, and now she was talking about it, sounded almost proud of herself for doing such a thing.

If I'd had any doubt about that, her next words removed it. "You know, I'd do it again, if I had to." Jolene's pale blue eyes looked defiant. "That slimy old creep deserved what he got."

I guess I looked a little doubtful—how many folks really *deserve* to be hit over the head with a chicken, let alone being stabbed?—because Jolene lifted her chin and hurried on. "You don't understand. That old man was after me—and after me—and after me. Every time I walked into his office, there he was. With his creepy old hands, trying to touch me." Jolene shivered. She looked over at me, her pale eyes huge. "And after he found out about R.L. and me, he was even worse. The old coot thought I was some kind of a—a—a—"

Tramp, I believe, was the word she was looking for. I decided I'd better not help her out.

It was a good thing. "—a *loose* person!" Jolene finished. "All I wanted was a life with R.L. For us to be together. Was that so much to ask?"

I stared back at her. Actually, that part wasn't so bad. It was the part where she murdered another human being to get that life—that was a bit much.

"I—I did it all for him," Jolene said, her eyes now on R.L.

R.L. hadn't said a word the whole time Jolene was talking, but now, evidently, he decided he ought to add his two cents' worth. He twisted a little, trying to get to a sitting position, but apparently the effort was too much for him. He sank right back down again. "It was him leaving me the company that did it," he said, looking over at Priss sitting on the floor opposite Jolene. "You know I can't head up no company! And yet, he wouldn't take no for an answer. I tried to tell him, too, but he wouldn't listen." R.L. reached out with a shaky hand and grabbed Priss's arm. "He was going to *own* me, Priss. And—and so was Lizbeth," R.L.'s voice was getting weaker, but he seemed determined to get all of this out. "If I was worth a lot more money, you know Lizbeth would *never* let me go. I was going to be tied to her forever."

I could sympathize with R.L. there. That did seem to be a horrible fate.

I stared at R.L., and I remembered right then what I'd forgotten all along in this case. You know, what I mentioned at the beginning, the thing you're supposed to learn right away as a detective?

Never assume.

I reckon you can't make assumptions about human beings any more than you can about dogs. Just because most men might want success, power, and more money doesn't mean all men do.

"We were going to run away together," Jolene said, her eyes tortured. "We were going to have this wonderful life."

In theory, it did sound pretty good. Jolene and R.L. off together somewhere, basking in the sun, and Priss still here in Pigeon Fork, continuing to be in charge of Vandeventer Poultry just like always. Quietly sending R.L. his share of the profits.

And yet, was life with Jolene really going to be all that hot? Instead of living with Lizbeth—who could no doubt make you wish you were dead—R.L. was going to be living with Jolene, who could not only make you wish you were dead, but could actually help you along in that direction. Maybe I was being picky, but neither option looked real appealing from where I stood.

R.L. now seemed to be leaning toward that opinion himself. He looked over at Jolene, and there was something cold in his eyes that hadn't been there before. "You lied to me before, didn't you? You weren't just trying to scare them. You really did try to kill them both. Didn't you?"

What he was talking about was pretty easy to figure out. It had obviously been Jolene who'd shot at Priss and me from the shrubbery as we returned from lunch yesterday. No wonder R.L. had acted so panicked when he'd heard about it. The second Priss had told him what had happened, R.L. had known exactly who it was that had done it. Jolene must've soothed him by saying it had just been a scare tactic, and since R.L. had not been there to see just how close those bullets had actually come, he'd believed her.

Up to now.

Jolene paled. "I heard the two of them talking." Her voice was getting to be a wail again. "They were putting it all together. And Priss was going to tell Haskell about us. They were figuring it all out. Somebody had to do something—"

R.L.'s mouth tightened, and he shut his eyes. As if he could no longer bear to look at her.

Jolene grabbed his arm. "R.L., it was the only way! Haskell was getting too close—"

R.L. wrenched his arm away. Unfortunately, it was the arm connected to the shoulder with the bullet in it. R.L.'s face twisted in pain, and the look he gave Jolene was clearly unforgiving.

It wasn't much later that Vergil finally showed up. Sirens going full blast. Again. You could tell Vergil wasn't exactly delighted that I'd solved his case for him, but he was a gentleman about it. He even mumbled, "Good work," as they were carrying R.L. out on a stretcher. Vergil said the words in exactly the same way as the coach on the opposite team always says, "Good

207

game," after their team has stomped your team into the ground, but he said it. Which counted for something.

I had a moment with Priss just before she climbed into the back of the ambulance with R.L. "I think they'll go easy on him," I told her, "being as how he saved your life the way he did. And particularly since he didn't actually strike the fatal blow."

I was trying to be comforting, but Priss didn't look particularly soothed. She just nodded at me. Real quick. That was all. She didn't look my way again.

I reckon this was one instance in which I should've ignored the rule and gone ahead and assumed. But I didn't.

Even when I went on home and drove Ruby to the hospital, sitting with her a spell until the doctor came out and got her, I still didn't question why it was that Priss didn't come out and say anything more to me. I just thought that Priss was probably staying real close by her brother's side, and besides, what did I expect her to say? "Good work"? Like Vergil?

Like an idiot, the next week I called Priss up at work, under the pretense of checking on R.L. and seeing how she and Ruby were doing. I hadn't seen either one of them since the day R.L. was shot.

It was Inez who answered Priss's phone. This, of course, I expected. I'd heard around town that Inez had moved into the job that Jolene had vacated, being as how Jolene wasn't going to be performing any secretarial duties from a jail cell. I felt kind of glad for Inez. A secretary as efficient as she was didn't deserve to be out of work.

Inez got Priss on the line right away, and Priss told me what I already knew, having heard it from Vergil this time—that R.L. was recovering fine. While Priss was talking, though, I couldn't help but notice that her voice sounded real odd. Stilted-like. Unfortunately, it kind of reminded me of conversations I'd had toward the last with Claudzilla. Conversations during which you could tell that, no matter what is being said, something else is being thought. "Are you upset with me about something?'' I asked. This was a familiar question, too. You'd think a detective would know better than to ask something that obvious.

"No, not really,'' Priss said.

If Priss had been hooked up to a lie detector, the thing would've gone crazy right about then. I knew this, but did I hang up right then and call it a day? Of course not. I went right ahead and said, "I'm real sorry about your brother and all.'' I meant it. I was sorry he got hurt. Sorry about what he'd done. Sorry he'd gotten himself into this mess.

"So,'' I went on, my mouth getting dry, "do you reckon you and I could go out sometime? Maybe get a bite to eat?''

I could hear Priss do a quick intake of breath. Like maybe she'd just laid her hand on something hot. "I don't think so, Haskell,'' Priss said. Real quick. No hesitation at all.

This is the part where I decided that I must be a masochist where women are concerned. Because, sure enough, I went on and asked, "Why not?'' I don't know what I expected Priss to say. I don't find the Howdy Doody type all that appealing?

Priss sighed. "Look, Haskell, I wouldn't feel right about it. Dating the guy who put my brother in jail. I just couldn't.''

It was my turn to sigh then. Apparently, it had slipped Priss's mind that I was also the guy who had kept her *mother* out of jail. I decided this probably wasn't the right time to bring it up. Particularly since I didn't think Priss was going to give me extra credit for a little thing like that.

"Well, it's been nice talking to you,'' I said, and then I did what I should've done right at the first. I hung up.

Oh well.

Priss evidently was somebody who held grudges even worse than Rip.

Unlike Priss, Rip got over *his* grudge. In fact, he was pretty much over it by the time I came back to pick up Ruby and take her to the hospital right after R.L. was shot. I think it had taken Rip that long to make the connection between me and his food supply. That sort of thing can turn a dog's head.

Speaking of which, Rip's head shots did the trick. Three days after I stuck the Polaroids in the front windows of the two groceries, a farmer by the name of Orson Wells brought a dog into my office. That's right. Orson Wells. The second he walked into my office, Orson explained that the "other" Orson Welles spelled his name with an *e*. Otherwise, he seemed to be hinting you might get the two of them mixed up. This from a man who was so thin, his overalls looked like they were still hanging on a hanger. Orson (the farmer) also appeared not to have a tooth left in his head. In spite of all this, believe it or not, it was not Orson (the farmer) that I found myself staring at, when he walked into my office.

It was the dog he had on a ragged leash.

They say everybody has a twin somewhere in this world, and I reckon that must go for dogs, too. This dog was Rip's double.

In looks, anyway.

In personality, there were some distinct differences. For example, Orson's dog climbed all the way up the stairs to my office, and shortly after that, he did an even more amazing thing. He climbed down.

Orson's dog did his amazing climb down my stairs just before Orson and I headed out to Belinda Renfrow's. Once there, Orson's dog did yet another un-Rip-like thing. He lunged straight for Belinda's ducks, barking and drooling—and generally doing a pretty good rendition of a duck connoisseur.

Belinda didn't seem at all chagrined at having picked out the wrong dog from her mental lineup. "Well, do tell," she said airily. "That damn dog sure does look like your'n, don't it?" She turned to Orson, who was giving us both a wide, toothless grin. Incidentally, not a pretty sight.

"Anybody could've made a mistake like that, couldn't they?" Belinda said.

Orson nodded his grizzled head. I had the feeling Orson would've agreed that the dog he had on a leash was a person in black dog's clothing if it meant that he was about to collect fifty dollars.

Which, of course, he was. The fifty dollars I paid Orson, I might add, didn't include taking Rip's impostor to the county pound. I had to do that myself.

I've been waiting ever since Orson and Rip's double showed up for Lizbeth or Alton Gabbard to give me a call about her trampled garden, but neither one of them has. I reckon Lizbeth has too much on her mind here lately to bother about her tulips.

These days I can't help but wonder if Rip appreciates at all that I've just spent quite a bit of money keeping him out of the slammer for crimes he didn't commit.

Rip sure doesn't seem to appreciate it. He still barks at me whenever I pull up into my own driveway. And he still, of course, expects me to carry him up and down stairs. He even whines at me if I'm a little slow getting to it. Like maybe I'm this dull-witted servant he's hired.

Rip also doesn't seem to appreciate something else. So far, I've had fourteen different people—count them, *fourteen*—show up at my office with black dogs in tow. Most of these animals don't even come close to Rip's photograph, but the folks that bring them in actually *argue* with me. Their chief contention appears to be that my dog has been lost so long, I've forgotten what he looks like.

Nowadays Melba no longer answers my office phone with "Yeah?" She has taken to answering it with "Is this about a black dog?" If the caller says yes, what Melba has to tell them could probably get her arrested.

I can't understand why these folks keep showing up. I took Rip's Polaroids down the day after Orson showed up—which has been a couple weeks ago—and yesterday, number fourteen climbed up my stairs with yet another black dog. This one was a toy poodle.

I just stared at the guy. Wearing snakeskin cowboy boots and a Stetson, he acted as if I were lying to him. "Are you sure?" he said, rubbing the stubble on his

211

chin. "It shore does look like the picture I seen. In the face, anyways."

I then stared at the dog. Was it possible that Cowboy Bob here thought that Rip had run off and gotten himself a permanent? And then maybe *shrunk?*

"It's not my dog," I said.

Cowboy Bob blinked a couple of times, rubbed his chin some more, and then actually tried to get me to pay him *mileage*. "Well golly," he said. "Being as how I just drove nigh onto twenty-five mile"—this I didn't believe for an instant—"just to bring you this here dog to take a gander at, why, I just assumed—"

I reckon you can guess what I told him.